the **ORIGINALS**

The Rise

www.HQNBooks.com

ISBN-13: 978-0-373-78889-7

THE ORIGINALS: THE RISE

An HQN Books novel/February 2015

Dear Reader:

If you're reading this letter, then there's a good chance you love the Mikaelson family as much as I do. For Klaus, Elijah, and Rebekah, our beloved vampires at the heart of the hit CW drama The Originals, an hour a week barely scratches the surface of their story. That's why Harlequin HQN, in association with Alloy Entertainment, will be publishing a new trilogy of books that offers never-before-told stories of the Original vampires.

We've seen this family's epic struggle to live and love in New Orleans while mired in conflict between the human and supernatural factions. But was it any easier for them back then than it is now? Klaus often isolates himself from the idea of romantic love, but what would happen if he actually opened his heart to it? Elijah prides himself on being the constant pillar of self-control, but when a mysterious witch captures his heart, will his noble restraint remain unbroken? Rebekah, never a stranger to love, meets a handsome army captain, but will she be able to keep her emotions in check when she discovers he might be a vampire hunter?

In *The Originals: The Rise, The Loss,* and *The Resurrection,* you'll get to know all three Mikaelson vampires as you've never seen them before. Read on for all the passion, drama, and bloodthirsty adventure of the TV show, and get ready for a book with a lot of bite.

With best wishes,
Julie Plec
Creator and Executive Producer of *The Originals*

CREATED BY JULIE PLEC
based on the Vampire Diaries

the ORIGINALS

The Rise

HQN™

www.HQNBooks.com

PROLOGUE

1713

Vivianne Lescheres was not afraid of the dark. The night felt like a warm cloak around her shoulders. The nearly full moon bathed the bayou in black and gray, hiding and shifting its truths, but Vivianne's feet were sure and her heartbeat steady, even as a girl of ten. In the darkness, she was free.

Vivianne, born of both a witch and a werewolf, had both clans as her protectors, her family. No danger could come to her, even from New Orleans's roughest residents. There had never been any part of the city where she feared to tread.

Yet on this night, as she got closer to the wide, lazy river, all she could smell was death. She slowed, scanning around her for what was amiss. The night couldn't keep secrets from her eyes for long, and she watched as a ghost ship crept along the edge of the swamp. She set one boot down in front of the other, wading closer to the open water of the Saint Louis River.

The ship looked small, but sturdy enough for an ocean crossing, if not big enough to journey in any comfort. Yet even Vivianne's sharp eyes couldn't spot a single soul on board. It just slid through the water, timbers creaking slightly with the gentle roll of the midnight current.

She reached the edge of the bayou and heard a shout go up from one of the watchmen. Finally, they had noticed the ghostly vessel. Slipping behind a stand of cattails, Vivianne felt a powerful impulse to set the ship on fire and let the water sweep it back down to the ocean. Whatever it was and whatever it carried, she didn't want it in her city.

The ship stalled at the banks, inviting the watchmen to come to it. They wasted no time, clambering up the ladder built into the side of the ghost ship's hull. She thought about calling to them, but she could not imagine what warning a child might give that could turn the men away from what they believed was abandoned treasure.

The moonlight glinted off the pale skin and golden

hair of a man sneaking across the deck as he followed the guards below. He moved with inhuman speed and strength as he pulled a man up into the ship's rigging. Screams began to rise from the deck. The warm night air turned clammy and clung to Vivianne's skin, making her shiver. The coppery smell of blood drifted across the river to her, and she'd seen enough: She ran.

The darkness closed in on her, roots and hillocks reaching up to catch at her feet as she flew across the swamp. Something new had come to New Orleans, and the night would never be safe again.

ONE

1722

"Crashing a party" had a beautifully destructive ring to it, but Klaus found the reality a disappointment. It had been too easy to get invited, and Elijah's constant reminders that violence was prohibited turned out to be entirely unnecessary. All that awaited them inside the villa was an ordinary party. Witches and werewolves drank and danced with their own kind, each casting occasional disdainful looks at members of the other clan. The ballroom was stuffy, and the human servers moved numbly through the crowd, controlled by some sort of spell that made them just as dull as everything else. Klaus couldn't figure out why his brother had been so eager to attend this event, but Elijah's reasoning was often unsound.

A doe-eyed young woman handed him a glass of champagne, and Klaus tasted it gamely. It was probably of very high quality, but it made no real impression on him. He was, after all, hardly the best judge of beverages served in polite company. "Wait," he called, and the young woman turned obediently, a tray of glasses still balanced on one hand. Klaus stepped closer to her, taking in the honey glint of her hair and the gentle throb of the pulse in her throat. "I need some air." He improvised. "Can you show me to the garden?"

The human girl hesitated for a moment, her lips parted as if she knew she was supposed to refuse, yet couldn't. She put down her tray, and Klaus followed her to the edge of the glittering ballroom. He caught her before the door had fully closed behind them, his eyes adjusting immediately to the darkness of the garden. His right hand curled around her mouth, muffling any sound that might escape, while his left hand brushed her hair away from the skin of her throat. He felt his teeth extend and sharpen as he stared at her smooth neck. His fangs reached for her pulse, tore into her throat, and locked it in place while her hot blood flowed into his mouth.

Klaus's mind had already begun to wander by the time her heartbeat grew faint. His eyes roved the moonlit garden, looking for hiding places. The minute the serving girl was dead he carried her to a honeysuckle-covered wall and concealed her among the clinging vines. Klaus didn't bother to inspect his work too carefully. Leaving the boring party for a boring kill had unexpectedly made him feel even more out of sorts.

He slipped back through the carved double doors, struck for a moment by the light and music inside. His return went almost entirely unnoticed, but not quite. The glow of a dozen chandeliers glinted off a pile of perfect blonde curls, and a pair of serious blue eyes was fixed on his face.

Rebekah must have been spying for Elijah and catering to his tiresome obsession with "fitting in." Making sure the wayward half brother didn't do anything to endanger their brilliant plans.

Together, the three Original vampires could have taken ownership of this fledgling city in a heartbeat, making it a fortress against the enemy that hunted them. Instead, they had spent nine long years cowering in dark corners, feeding only when necessary and ingratiating themselves with the locals. Klaus had agreed to it all for the time being, but he couldn't be expected to forego all entertainment while bending to Elijah's schemes.

He turned away from his sister in disgust, only to see that he was being watched by someone else. The girl staring his way was one of the witches, he thought, although he was almost sure he had noticed her dancing with a lanky werewolf earlier. A lovely young witch who wasn't afraid to stray from her own kind? *That* might be enjoyable and could even redeem this dreadful party. With her raven hair, porcelain skin, and intensely black eyes she could *almost* have been a vampire, but Klaus knew that the spells that filled her pretty head were nothing compared to his power.

Klaus imagined splitting the white skin of her throat; he could hear her begging him to. He could be the last man to soak up the light that seemed to radiate from her before putting it out forever.

He watched the young witch move through the room, pausing to speak here and dance there. Now and then her shining black eyes found his before darting away. Klaus moved closer, stalking her through the ball gowns and frock coats like a tiger slipping through tall grass.

The music changed, and the dancers obediently separated into groups of eight, one couple at each corner. Klaus ended up one group over from his new prey—was it his imagination, or had she begun to move away as she saw him come closer?—but that was easily remedied. The dancers stepped and turned to the music, and Klaus let them carry him and the girl toward each other. He watched until she was just behind him, and then he spun.

"May I cut in?" he asked flatly, not waiting for an answer as he pulled her into his arms. Her partner stammered something and then backed away. Klaus didn't bother to watch him go.

The girl's red lips quirked up in a rueful smile. "Poor Gerald," she sighed, her black eyes glittering in the candlelight. "I don't think he saw you coming."

"I think you did, Mademoiselle," Klaus countered, spinning her away from his body and then back in, closer this time.

"Vivianne," she replied, holding up her gloved fingers expectantly. He turned her hand over to kiss the underside of her wrist, letting his lips linger on her skin a bit longer than the usual. She didn't blush the way most girls her age would have; instead she raised a skeptical eyebrow.

"Niklaus Mikaelson," he returned. "It's an honor."

"I'm sure," Vivianne murmured. She glanced away, distracted. Then she looked back up at him and smiled, and it was as if the sun had come out: dazzling, powerful, and dangerous. "Who dragged you to this tedious affair, anyway? Or did you just wander in and lose sight of the exit?"

From across the room, Klaus noticed Elijah lurking at the outer edges of the ballroom. His brother's brown eyes were searching, boring into his. Elijah jerked his head, trying to catch Klaus's attention without anyone else noticing. Klaus stared at him curiously, intrigued by the vehemence of his silent protest. "My siblings assured me this party would be the social event of the season," he answered. "I wasn't convinced, but it certainly has improved dramatically in the last few minutes."

Vivianne's eyebrow ticked up again; he couldn't quite tell if she was flattered or just amused. "I wouldn't have thought you were the sort of man who enjoyed pattern dancing."

"Neither would I." The music signaled a change of partners, but Klaus glared at the young man who held his hand out to Vivianne. "I don't quite have the hang of it," he admitted, "but you dance beautifully. I wasn't aware this city could turn out such polished young women; have you traveled?"

Her onyx eyes glittered with mischief. "I think you want me to know that *you* have," she interpreted dryly. "You must have seen extraordinary things."

"Oh, I have." Sights that would have made her hair stand on end, but Klaus could save those topics for another, more intimate time. "But you didn't answer, Mademoiselle Vivianne." In fact, he noticed, she hadn't even given him her last name.

She leaned closer to his chest than the dance strictly required. "How terribly upsetting for you." Sarcasm dripped from her voice like honey mingled with blood. "I'm sure you're accustomed to getting your own way."

A short, surprised laugh burst from his throat. "Oh, mysterious Vivianne, I think I would rather have you deny me than get my way with anyone else tonight."

"You shouldn't insult the guest list," she chided playfully. "For all you know, *I* invited all of these people. They may be five hundred of my closest friends."

"Half of them may be, at any rate." The division between the two clans was still evident; there were no werewolves on their side of the ballroom.

"Peace is a wonderful thing," Vivianne replied, so blandly that he suspected she was thinking something quite different. The long war between the witches and werewolves of New Orleans had finally drawn to a close, and Klaus had seemed alone in not choosing to celebrate. Was it possible that this witch had doubts of her own about the truce? Elijah was adamant that it must go forward with no interference from the vampires, but if some of the witches themselves were dissatisfied . . . this charming young woman could be much more than just a meal.

Klaus realized that he was smiling genuinely for the first time that night. Maybe he ought to let the pretty witch live; New Orleans seemed less dreary for having her in it. "I will have to stay close to you and borrow some of your popularity," he teased. "I don't think I have many friends here tonight."

"How lucky that I'm here to protect you from all these horrible people." She rolled her eyes dismissively, looking for a brief moment like the girl she was.

He smirked. "Protecting the innocent is what *I* do, Mademoiselle. I'm surprised my reputation hasn't preceded me."

The song ended, and the dancers stopped with it. Vivianne stretched onto her tiptoes, bringing her face so close to his that Klaus could have bitten her lip.

"Oh, but it has," she whispered, her wicked smile blocking out everything else in the decadent ballroom. She reached up to touch him, caressing the corner of his mouth with one long finger. He turned to kiss it, to devour it, but she pulled back out of his arms, and he saw that her fingertip had come away red. A forgotten bit of the serving girl's blood; it must have been there all along.

Vivianne was halfway across the ballroom by the time he thought to follow her, and before he could move, horns gave a celebratory flourish. Frustrated, Klaus waited, impatient but confident there would be a better, more private opportunity to catch her soon.

"Ladies, gentlemen, distinguished guests," a voice cried, silencing the chatter around them. "It is my great pleasure to welcome you to this happiest of occasions. I have the honor to present to you, for the first time as a betrothed couple, Armand Navarro and Vivianne Lescheres." Vivianne reached the side of the werewolf Klaus had seen her with earlier, sliding her arm through his as if they had never been apart. Her smile was absolutely brilliant as she raised one white arm and waved to the crowd.

The ballroom exploded in a frenzy of applause and cheering, but Klaus was utterly still. Suddenly, the party made perfect sense. They weren't just celebrating the end of the war; they were sealing it with blood. The Navarros were the premier werewolf family in New Orleans, so a Navarro was marrying a witch—and for them to agree, Vivianne must be an extraordinary witch.

Klaus narrowed his eyes. Extraordinary, indeed. She must be the one he had heard about: the daughter of both a witch and werewolf. He'd always dismissed the rumors as foolish, and yet the daughter of both clans stood before him with a beating pulse. When Elijah had mentioned this party, he had certainly failed to include some key details—and the only reason Klaus could think of was that his brother didn't trust him to stay out of the deal that was being struck under their noses.

But someone *should* intervene. Klaus felt safest when

his rivals hated one another at least as much as they hated him.

Besides, Vivianne was far too good to waste on a werewolf.

"She's not for you, Niklaus," Rebekah snapped, appearing beside his elbow. "This alliance has been a generation in the making. Interfering with it is absolutely out of the question, so just forget she exists."

Klaus watched Vivianne dance with her fiancé. Her lithe body moved gracefully across the floor, her skirt following a moment later like a white echo. He didn't answer Rebekah; there was no need. They both knew her warning had come too late.

TWO

*T*he ballroom around Elijah hummed and spun with happy chatter and lively dancing, but underneath it all he couldn't stop looking for trouble. What would be the first sign that would allow him to be faster, smarter, and more prepared than everyone else? From the relative peace of the darkened corner, he watched the wallflowers, the whisperers, the outsiders. But of course, as he turned his gaze to the dance floor, he realized he was looking in the wrong place. The trouble was right in the thick of the party, dancing with the bride-to-be. His fair head bent close to her dark one, listening, his expressive mouth smiling and murmuring in a way that conveyed instant intimacy. Why did Elijah ever bother looking anywhere but at Klaus?

Had it been a mistake to keep his impetuous younger brother in the dark about the werewolves' terms for peace with the witches? Like all worthy feuds, this one was ending with a wedding between the two families, and Elijah had promised that the vampires wouldn't disrupt their arrangement. He'd thought the key to keeping Klaus in line would be to divert his attention away from Vivianne and her betrothal, as his brother seemed to have an unnatural penchant for wanting what wasn't his. But that plan had failed miserably.

Vivianne Lescheres, the rare child of both a witch and a werewolf, was a woman with a destiny. The fragile new peace of the city's supernatural denizens depended entirely on her impending marriage, and the Mikaelson siblings depended on that peace. Rebekah had argued passionately and convincingly that telling Klaus a beautiful young woman was off-limits to him would only guarantee that he would seduce her, but apparently *not* telling him hadn't helped a bit.

"Do you see that?" Rebekah sighed, rounding a column to join her brother in the dark. "Trust him to find a way to get in the middle of everything, without even knowing what it is."

"We have to tell him now," Elijah growled, sure of their mistake. "He'll be even worse if he finds out on his own."

"Has he ever been better, in order to become worse?" Apparently content with that parting shot, Rebekah returned to the dance floor, her gown sweeping across the polished floor. She frequently made it clear that she believed there *wasn't* a way to handle Klaus, but Elijah refused to stop trying. The three of them had managed to stay together and survive this long—for almost a thousand years. There was no future for them without one another.

He tried to signal to Klaus, but only managed to catch his attention for a short second before Klaus returned his eyes to the half witch. Elijah wondered what the girl was saying to him; somehow he doubted that they were discussing her fiancé.

It would be too insolent to interrupt now. He could only watch as the trumpets sang and Vivianne left his brother's side to join her future husband's. From the reckless flush on her cheeks, Elijah felt sure that she had been toying with Klaus. Considering that Klaus had probably intended to eat her, it was hard for Elijah to hold a grudge, but it looked like Klaus wasn't the only one who would require some careful watching.

"I understand the witches struck a deal to let you stay in New Orleans," a voice rumbled in his ear. "If it had been up to me, I would have thrown you right back into the Saint Louis." Solomon Navarro was the sort of man who wore his true nature on his sleeve. Huge, burly, and sporting a wicked scar down the right side of his face, he looked more like a wolf masquerading as a human than the other way around. Not even his impeccable coat could give the illusion of civilization winning out over savagery.

"Congratulations on your son's engagement," Elijah replied politely, struggling with all of his will not to show his fangs to the massive, glowering man. "You must be very proud."

Elijah had felt that it was more important to be seen there, paying their respects to the powerful local clans, than to get hung up on the fact that they'd snuck in. Perhaps he had underestimated the tension of such a happy occasion.

"She thinks and acts like a witch," Sol growled, nodding contemptuously at Vivianne. "Her father died too early to have any hand in raising her, which was an opportunity lost. But as a symbol, her parentage will be useful. Unless that *thing* you brought in with you gets his teeth in her, obviously. Have you ever considered curing your brother of his wretched immortality?"

"Niklaus will not be a problem," Elijah assured the giant man, with a quick glance at his brother. Klaus was well out of earshot, but he still always seemed to know when his siblings weren't entirely on his side. Klaus's belief that he didn't belong in their family—being only a half brother—was the poison that divided and endangered the Originals. Yet, despite his best intentions, Elijah could never quite convince his brother otherwise.

Still, Sol's anger was somewhat justified, and not just because of the ill-advised dance in progress. Klaus had begun his time in New Orleans hunting werewolves. The witches had turned a blind eye, requiring only that the Mikaelsons make no new vampires. But with the wedding, the balance of the supernatural landscape had shifted. A massacre—even a small one, even one that had been over for years—could be held against them now by the witches and the werewolves both. In retrospect, the Mikaelsons really should have skipped the party after all.

"He's *been* a problem since the three of you washed up on shore," Sol spat, and Elijah could hear that he was still nursing his grudge. "I've been informed that there's a dead body in the east garden. One of the humans."

Klaus.

"I don't know what you're angry about, then," Elijah replied with a tight shrug. He found his own patience for diplomacy wearing dangerously thin. "If he's busy with humans, he's not threatening your kind. Still, it wouldn't hurt to remind your pack to stay inside after dark. It's just common sense for anyone who can't take on a single vampire alone."

The blow caught Elijah entirely off guard, crunching into his jawbone and spinning him all the way around before he could even react. He heard a snarl, and a pair of wild eyes glowed yellow somewhere in the shadows. Elijah felt his teeth grow sharp and deadly, but then the growls multiplied, and he froze.

"That's the thing about being a pack," Sol said jovially, his broad face creasing into a vicious smile. "We're never really alone."

Elijah guessed there were at least five werewolves that had joined them.

"Your brother hasn't paid for any of the blood he's spilled," a voice beside him sneered. It sounded familiar—Sol's younger son perhaps. "And yet you just walk in here thinking all will be forgiven?" The group echoed him with dark murmurs of agreement.

Elijah bared his fangs, and smirked as the werewolf took an uncertain step back. His name was Louis, Elijah remembered, and unlike his slim brother, he had inherited both their father's height *and* his heavy frame.

This is why the Mikaelsons need to stay together, Elijah thought angrily. For *his* "pack," six werewolves would be nothing. Caught on his own, he would have to improvise. "Sol," he began, as strong hands grabbed the collar of his white shirt.

"Take him outside," Sol ordered quietly, and Elijah was pulled nearly off his feet.

He had just enough balance to push off the floor and flip behind the circle of werewolves. He lashed out with his fists, not caring who he hit as long as he made contact. A swarthy werewolf with startling green eyes got close enough to jab Elijah in the ribs, and Elijah repaid him by breaking his arm. It cracked with a sickening splintering sound. Louis pushed his injured packmate out of his way in a bid to reach Elijah, and Elijah kept one wary eye on his progress. Louis was substantially bigger than the rest of the werewolves, and only one of Sol's lackeys was effectively out of the fight.

Another blow caught Elijah in the kidney: He was surrounded again. He turned faster than a human eye could see to meet the new attacker, realizing too late that he had turned his back on the most formidable of his enemies. Before Elijah could think of a way to defend himself against Louis, he heard the big werewolf yelp in pain and fall to the floor.

Klaus stood behind him, his eyes and mouth standing out vividly against the pale fury of his face. Elijah waited for the next attack, but by then Rebekah had arrived as well. Her slim white hand rested on Sol's sleeve, her grip deadly. Although his broad face was still hot with anger, Elijah knew Solomon was smart enough to recalculate the odds. Together, the three Original vampires were no one's idea of easy prey.

"That's enough now," Rebekah warned, her voice low with her implied threat.

Louis struggled to his feet, brushing off his wrinkled coat and looking absolutely murderous. But obedience won over fury and he looked to his father for his cue.

"We're here to celebrate Armand and his fiancée," Sol agreed after a long moment. "This is not the night to address the city's vermin problem." The werewolves around them began to slink back into the crowd, Louis leaving last of all. When only the three vampires remained, Sol straightened his cravat. "Think hard about how you three fit in here," he advised coldly. "Thanks to this alliance, both we and the witches can now devote more attention to cleaning up this city. You might find that you're more comfortable elsewhere." Solomon turned on his heel, and was gone.

Elijah drew closer to his siblings. Rebekah still glanced warily around the room, but Klaus only had eyes for Sol's back. "So," Klaus began lightly, "I think I heard something about an 'alliance'?"

"Don't start," Rebekah snapped. Even as she spoke to Klaus, her blue eyes scanned Elijah up and down, probing for any sign of serious injury. "You understand perfectly well why we didn't tell you about the marriage pact." Elijah knew that Klaus understood, but that was the problem. "And *you*," she raged, pushing Elijah hard in the chest. "What were you thinking, starting a fight tonight, of all nights? Isn't one Niklaus enough?"

"We might have been better off staying home," Elijah admitted, rubbing at his chest ruefully, "but I could have used a few more Niklauses once they started in on me." He turned to smile appreciatively at his brother, but to his alarm he realized that Klaus was now covertly watching Vivianne.

Rebekah must have seen it, too, because she moved between them, cutting off their brother's line of sight to the half witch. "This is serious," she argued urgently. "Our place here was precarious already, but the were-wolves will have more influence now. With Sol in their ears, the witches might decide to stop ignoring us."

"You know what *I'll* suggest." Klaus leaned back a little, trying to catch another glimpse of the bride-to-be. "Army, slaughter, safety."

"No army," Elijah disagreed vehemently. "We can't break the deal first. Just one new vampire will be all the excuse they need. They won't just drive us out; they'll band together to destroy us."

Rebekah looked from Klaus to Vivianne and back again, her expression thoughtful. "But there's already an army here," she mused. "The French have a permanent camp just a few miles away. They're human, obviously, but turning them can't be the only way to get them on our side. We have other methods of persuasion. Isn't that right, Niklaus?"

Klaus frowned in surprise, but Elijah realized what Rebekah was getting at. "People *will* do foolish things for love," Elijah agreed thoughtfully, "and a little compulsion wouldn't hurt our cause, either."

Elijah could tell that, at least for the moment, Klaus was back in the fold. "My sister the general," Klaus teased, almost warmly. "Seducing the entire French army should be an interesting new challenge for you."

Rebekah laughed, and for a moment Elijah remembered them all as children—as humans—again. "I think seducing just the captain will suffice," she said primly. "*Soldiers* obey orders."

"How dull," Klaus responded with an exaggerated smile, hooking Rebekah's arm in his. "Speaking of which, this party has gone terribly stale. Let's go find something to eat."

"Leave it breathing," Elijah warned under his breath, but he couldn't keep a grin entirely off his lips.

THREE

*T*hey never saw her coming.

The cart horse shrieked as Rebekah launched herself at the humans, who had mistakenly believed the twilit forest north of the city a perfectly safe place to be. But the warning came too late for the couple, who didn't even manage to look up before Rebekah was upon them. Climbing up onto the wagon, she snapped the woman's neck with her left hand, and with her right she pulled the man's head back to expose his weathered throat. His life ended in a burst of thick, hot blood before he could even wonder why.

Rebekah normally would have preferred to take a little more time with her meals, but she had too much to do. The army patrol passed by these woods every hour, and she had no intention of greeting them as a murderess.

She ripped apart the straps of the harness that yoked the horse to the wagon. She raised a hand to shoo it away, and the beast bolted as soon as it was free. The broken harness dangled uselessly in the dirt, and Rebekah kicked in one of the wheels for added effect. Spokes shattered and the hoop cracked, emphasizing how helpless and stranded she was supposed to be.

The woman, of course, must not be found. Rebekah dragged her from her seat, carrying her into the trees until the broken wagon was no longer in sight. Roots and thick undergrowth made digging even a shallow grave a risky waste of time, so she shoved the body under the densest bush she could see, and then examined her work. It had been wise not to drain the woman, even though she wouldn't have minded a second course to her meal. The ground was barely disturbed, and this way there would be no telltale trail of blood to lead anyone to the corpse.

Rebekah ran back to the clearing, turning her full attention to the dead man. The bite marks were small, but a more obvious cause of death would be an improvement. Eyeing his neck critically, she found a knife in the cart and slashed it across his throat, severing an artery and hiding the marks from her teeth. It wasn't perfect—and he didn't have nearly enough blood left to make it as dramatic as she would have liked—so she added a few extra cuts to his hands and arms to tell a more detailed story.

Finally, she lifted him from the cart and propped him against an oak tree in what she cheerfully imagined looked like a valiant—if hopeless—last stand. Her rescuers might notice how quickly she healed if she injured herself, but she carefully ripped at her own clothing, creating a few artistic tears in the powder-blue fabric. She rubbed her hands in the dirt. Wrinkling her nose a little, she smeared some on the apples of her cheeks, then streaked her delicate collarbone and the skin where her torn dress revealed a creamy slice of abdomen. She could hear hoofbeats now, so she tousled her hair roughly while glancing around one final time at the scene she had set. Then she collapsed against the oak tree next to the dead body.

From the sound of the horses, she guessed there were six men. They stopped, and she heard startled murmuring. It was all she could do to keep her eyes closed and her body still while they took in the disaster in the clearing. They approached carefully, and she could picture them examining each of her clues. Even though the sun had already slid below the tops of the trees and the light was poor, she was glad she had been so thorough.

"She breathes," one of the soldiers announced

suddenly, and Rebekah let her long eyelashes flutter open. She stared around in apparent confusion, pressing one hand to her head as if it ached. Six soldiers stood in long blue coats that cut away to show flashes of red. The French army had arrived to save the day.

Rebekah's head rolled to the side so that she could see the dead man propped against the tree trunk. "My husband!" she shrieked, clutching her hands to her chest. One of the rips in her dress gaped strategically, and out of the corner of her eye she noticed several of the men watching it keenly. "Those horrible men killed my husband." She threw herself melodramatically across the wagoner's lifeless chest, hiding her smirk against his shirt.

"There have been reports of bandits on this road, but nothing like this," one of the soldiers told the others quietly. "Do you think it's the villains that the captain has mentioned?"

"It may be." She heard some of them shift uncomfortably, and wished she could stop playing her role long enough to look up and read their expressions. The soldier's voice dropped so low that a human wouldn't have been able to hear it, although of course a vampire could. "She called them men, but we can't be sure that it's not one of those other crimes." His volume returned to normal. "The bandits must be getting bolder. The new captain will surely want to increase patrols."

"You won't be able to spend so much time in the city brothels anymore," another one chuckled, and Rebekah heard sounds of scuffling.

Really? A murdered man and a damsel in obvious distress, and they still acted like children? Humans could be so predictable, so undisciplined. She could barely remember how it felt to be their kind of alive—the kind that was temporary. She cleared her throat a little and straightened up again, tossing her loose blonde hair as if it were the accidental result of her movement. Once again, she had the patrol's undivided attention.

"Madame," the nearest soldier began, diplomatically placing a hand on her shoulder, "I am a lieutenant in the garrison here, but please just address me as Felix. I am terribly sorry this has happened. We will escort you back to the city." He was reasonably attractive, Rebekah decided, with thick black stubble and a hooked Gallic nose. She still intended to aim for the captain, but a lieutenant could be useful as well. More important, this Felix could be enjoyable enough company while he escorted her to her real target.

"I can't go back," she disagreed, taking hold of the wide cuff of Felix's sleeve. "My husband had debts; the Navarros were looking for us. My husband hoped to join his cousin in Shreveport, but he hadn't answered our letters yet when we were forced to leave. I don't even know if the cousin is still there." She softened her grip on the lieutenant's arm and made her eyes wide blue pools of shock and sorrow. "I warned him his gambling would ruin us."

"We can't send her back," a short blond soldier said worriedly. "The Navarros are criminals; she won't be safe if she can't pay them."

"We can't very well escort her all the way up to Shreveport," another countered. "And who even knows if she has people there?"

Felix nodded his head decisively, as if agreeing with his own thoughts. "We will bring her back to camp for now," he ordered. "She will have military protection until the captain can determine a safe place for her to go."

"Thank you," Rebekah whispered. "Thank you all so much." Fainting seemed like overkill, so instead she let the hook-nosed lieutenant help her onto his waiting horse.

"Bring the husband. The captain will want to inspect him," Felix called over his shoulder as he mounted his horse and situated himself behind her. "And of course we must give him a proper burial," he added more softly for, Rebekah assumed, her benefit. She shifted forward in the saddle as much as she could. *Oh, dear.* She had hoped to leave the body behind entirely to avoid further inspection, but that had probably been unrealistic.

The patrol arranged the wagoner on a roll of canvas secured with rope, and Rebekah hoped that her late "husband" was fat enough that the ropes would break from his weight.

Even with the extra burden of the dead man, the encampment was only about a half hour's ride. Rebekah was relieved, as it quickly became apparent that she had drastically overestimated her lieutenant's charms. No matter how many hints she dropped about her new status as widow, he had little to say aside from clumsy attempts to console her. She hoped that his captain would demonstrate a little more imagination; she preferred to save compulsion for emergencies rather than relying on it for every little thing.

There was no doubt which tent was his: It stood proudly in the center of the camp and fleur-de-lis decorated every available surface. Rebekah had to remind herself not to dismount too fluidly, instead falling into her gallant soldier's waiting arms with deliberate clumsiness. The horse helped by shifting and shying away as she moved; it was better trained than the cart horse had been, but it was no more fond of her. "Please be brave, Madame," Felix whispered as he released her hand, and Rebekah stifled a laugh.

The short blond man must have run on ahead to alert the captain, because Rebekah noticed him hurrying back toward them on foot, and he was not alone. The new arrival crossed the camp in long, easy strides that indicated effortless authority. Although there was no doubt in her mind that he was in charge here, he was younger than she had expected; maybe not even over thirty.

The French had a sizable army stationed outside of New Orleans, so either he was an unusually adept commander or extremely well-connected. Or, most likely, both. His hair was thick and brown with just a hint of gray at the temples, which Rebekah immediately decided was attractive. His eyes were a warm hazel shade, and surprisingly kind—with an alluring hint of mischief. When he looked up at her and smiled, she felt so protected and reassured that she forgot she wasn't in any real danger. Rebekah knew that a man this handsome could only lead to trouble, and she felt herself already starting to travel down that dangerous path. A striking Frenchman in a position of authority was exactly her type—and she'd been long starved of it.

"Madame," he said, his voice rumbling and powerful. "I am sorry to learn of your circumstances. You will be safe here until we can arrange for your passage home."

"Home," she repeated softly. Her brothers were the only home she had. Their parents had made them immortal and then turned on them, believing that their own children had become monsters—that saving their lives had been a terrible mistake. What kind of home could she build with that shadow constantly hovering over her? In truth, she was even more adrift than the character she was playing for the captain.

"We will search for your family and your late husband's," he clarified. "Or we will find something else. Please don't worry about all that now—you have already been through so much this evening."

"Thank you," Rebekah said.

He smiled again, as if weapons and death didn't surround them, but his eyes flickered to her hands as if he was looking for something—and then she realized that she had forgotten to take that damned woman's wedding ring, and her daylight ring sat on her right index finger. The ring allowed her to be in sunlight, and she dared not take it off even though the sun was already beginning to dip below the horizon. She chided herself for being so careless, and hoped that no one would wonder that bandits had left such a striking gem on her hand. "My name is Captain Moquet," he told her. "But call me Eric. Do you mind if I ask you a few questions about your attackers? I think that they have stolen your ring?"

"*Yes,*" Rebekah replied with deliberate eagerness. "I feel so strange to suddenly be without it."

"I understand, Madame," Eric assured her with such conviction that she wondered if she had inadvertently compelled him without realizing it. Then his hazel eyes turned to the dead wagoner, and every trace of softness—everything human—disappeared from his face.

He approached the corpse, and the soldiers stepped back. He leaned down, his long fingers tracing the wounds Rebekah had inflicted without quite touching them. "Bandits, you said?" he asked, pointing toward the short blond soldier without looking away from the dead body.

A few of the men glanced nervously at Rebekah and then away again. Some shifted uncomfortably. She had heard one of the men refer to him as "the new captain." How well did he know his new post? She decided it was best for her to say nothing and wait.

"No," Eric said at last, bringing one fingertip down on the edge of the long slash across the dead man's throat. "The marks are almost hidden, but they are here. This is not the work of any man." He looked up finally, his eyes burning into Rebekah's so deeply that she couldn't possibly look away. When he spoke again, it was as if the words were meant only for her. "There are unnatural and cursed things in those woods. You were lucky to escape with your life."

FOUR

$\mathcal{K}$laus moved across the cobblestones, grimac-ing at the chattering roar of hooves and carts passing by. When the Mikaelsons had arrived in New Orleans, there had been nothing except dirt tracks, but civilization had not left their grimy little French outpost alone. In addition to the elegant manor houses and villas that seemed to spring up like weeds, there was now a bona fide town center, with cobblers, jewelers, a sur-prisingly up-to-date milliner, and a few taverns.

Progress marched onward, Klaus supposed philo-sophically, but not everything was an improvement . . . especially not after the dizzying, skull-shattering night he had just spent on the town. New Orleans may have grown more sophisticated, but its whores were just as raunchy and wild as they had ever been. And the brand of whiskey served at Klaus's favorite brothel, the Southern Spot, was almost enough to drive the residue of discontent from Klaus's tongue. *Almost.*

There had come a point when he could no longer see her glittering black eyes, when her mocking smile no longer broke in on his every thought. But, to his intoxicated vision, every neck he had tenderly bitten had looked like her slender and marble-white throat; every drop of blood had tasted of her. Niklaus drank because oblivion could not come too soon and, given his headache this morning, it had probably come far too late.

The sun was high and the locals were bustling. He kept reflexively touching the daylight ring on his finger, willing it to somehow work *more*. Everything was too bright and too loud—until suddenly it was perfect. He didn't need to glimpse more than the merest sliver of her profile to know who it was. With the way she fit into her white muslin dress, she might as well have been created with Klaus alone in mind.

Her. She glowed; she pulled the light in. It was as if he'd made her appear. No matter what people whispered about the cursed fate of vampires, at that moment, he felt positively blessed.

Luckiest of all, she was unchaperoned. Vivianne stood alone at the side of the high street, gazing into the window of a couturier, who boasted of having just arrived from Paris. There was no one to interfere in their conversation, unlike at that miserable engagement party.

Klaus took a moment to brush off his coat and smooth the collar of his loose white shirt. She didn't need to know how he'd spent the night. As he approached her, he could feel the whiskey mixing treacherously with the blood in his stomach, but he would have bet his never-ending life that she would not be able to tell how deeply their first meeting had shaken him.

"Mademoiselle Lescheres," he purred, trying to keep his voice from rasping. His throat felt sore and hoarse, which was hard to understand given how many hours he'd spent lubricating it with food and drink. "You are even more radiant in the sunlight than by chandelier."

She did not bother to conceal her shock at the sight of him, but it was unclear how happy the surprise was. "Niklaus Mikaelson," she said formally, as if demonstrating a true society girl's gift for memory. As if he'd made no real impression on her at all. "I would not have thought to encounter you here so early in the day."

Because sunlight was poison to his kind? Or because she could see the previous night's excesses written on his face? Knowing that she had bluffed her way politely through several dances without mentioning the blood on his mouth, it was difficult to guess what else she might choose to leave unspoken.

He felt an almost overpowering need to check his coat for telltale stains or tearing.

"My lady Vivianne," he replied instead, with what he knew was a winning smile, "had I known that you would be here, I would have arrived even earlier so as not to miss a moment of your company."

Her answering smile was perfunctory, but she seemed distracted. A cart piled high with crates of produce rattled by, and she watched it go as if even carrots were more interesting than Klaus Mikaelson. "That would have been unnecessary," she explained in a clipped tone, "as recently I can't seem to turn around without meeting you."

Impossibly, she didn't sound pleased by this coincidence. Had his first impression on her really been so unremarkable? It was understandable that the sight of blood might upset a young woman. But in Klaus's considerable experience with women, upsetting them did not tend to make them any less intrigued. Yet Vivianne's face showed no fear, no disgust, no curiosity. Could it be that he was drawn to her *because* of her disinterest?

He ached to gently brush back a tendril of black hair that had snaked free from under her cap and coiled along her collarbone. Then, perhaps, to throw an arm around her narrow waist, pull her to him, and kiss her. And maybe bite her, just a little, as well. Surely she would have to feel some real emotion toward him then.

"Speaking of unexpected pleasures," he recalled, "I have not yet had the opportunity to congratulate you on your engagement. You must be deliriously happy."

"Deliriously," she confirmed, ignoring the sarcastic edge in his tone completely. "Thank you for your well-wishes."

"I would have offered them more promptly, had you mentioned your situation when we met," he said. Not that he actually cared, but he trusted her to understand his real meaning—that she had deliberately kept the news from him as long as she could. A woman who avoided mentioning her betrothal usually had a motive, and it was typically one that her fiancé would disapprove of. Vivianne might not show any overt signs of interest, but she had some kind of game on her mind. He felt sure of it. She was far too aware of him to care as little as she was acting.

"I thought you knew!" she said smoothly, raising an eyebrow. "You were attending the *engagement* party after all."

"I *gate-crashed* the engagement party," he corrected. "I was simply in search of decent champagne."

It bothered Klaus that the entire city seemed to know of her engagement before he did. Once he started listening, there was nowhere he could go without hearing about the beautiful girl who had ended the war between the witches and the werewolves of New Orleans. Under the circumstances, getting so *very* drunk for the past few days had definitely been the best course of action.

Vivianne shrugged and ran a gloved hand along the filmy fabric of her skirt. "I assumed you were simply desperate to be among the first to congratulate me. Us."

It was a very minor slip of the tongue, but it gave him hope. "You know," he offered impulsively, "I could escort you on your errands today, and save you all that trouble of trying to run into me again by chance. These streets are not always the safest for a lady alone anyway."

A real smile touched her red lips, and he felt his pulse quicken in triumph. But she wasn't looking at him. "Armand," she answered, a little more loudly than he had expected.

She lifted one gloved arm to wave to someone farther along the cobblestoned street behind him.

Armand, most likely.

Klaus resigned himself and turned around. Indeed, the lanky werewolf was making his way toward them with amusing haste. His foot slipped on the cobblestones and slid into a muddy puddle, but he was so eager to interrupt them that he did not even appear to notice his wet shoe.

"Vivianne," Armand called out a tad too cheerfully as he approached, and Klaus smirked. He may not have made much progress with the young half witch, but it seemed her fiancé had his own doubts about his ability to hold her attention. It wasn't much, but it was yet another of the tiniest of encouragements that could add up over time. And Klaus had plenty of time.

"Armand," Klaus repeated heartily, holding out his hand so that the werewolf could not reach Vivianne without either shaking it or mortally insulting a vampire in broad daylight. Armand glowered, but opted to shake; his hand was disgustingly hot in Klaus's cool palm.

"I'm sorry to leave you alone for so long, Viv," Armand continued, as if Klaus's greeting had never interrupted him at all. "But I saw this and simply had to have it for you." He sidestepped his rival and held out a lavishly wrapped box, and Klaus rolled his eyes without the slightest attempt at discretion. There was a distinction, after all, between thoughtful and pathetic.

Vivianne's eyes widened for a moment in surprise, although whether at her fiancé's rudeness or his gift Klaus could not be sure. However, she accepted the box gracefully, rising onto her tiptoes to kiss Armand's cheek in thanks.

Armand smiled down at her, and Klaus fantasized about splintering his neck into dozens of tiny shards of bone. If he struck now, the tall werewolf would never even see the blow coming.

"We should really be going," Armand said smugly to no one in particular. "Lingering where you've no business does nothing but invite trouble."

Vivianne's lips pressed together, concealing either disapproval or a smile. Klaus still could not read her any better than when they had first met, and he was starting to wonder when—not *if*—he would ever have the opportunity to learn. The werewolves would be keeping a close eye on her, and he couldn't count on her cooperation if he tried to spirit her away. She couldn't possibly love the priggish, correct Armand, but if she never got the full experience of Klaus's charms she might faithfully marry Armand anyway. And live a dull, proper life. It would be too terrible a waste to contemplate.

"Of course," Vivianne purred, turning to go without so much as a meaningful glance over her shoulder.

For a moment, Klaus played out what would happen if he broke Armand's arrogant, undefended spine. Vivianne would be angry—Elijah would be livid—but eventually everyone would agree that the world had not come to an end because of one dead werewolf. Time would prove Klaus right; it always did.

Then he noticed the way Vivianne held her head high as she walked along the bustling cobblestones. Klaus sighed and let the idea go. Killing the competition had its advantages, but for a woman like Vivianne, it might not suffice. To win her, he would have to pull out all the stops: Klaus would need to prove himself to be the better man.

FIVE

$\mathcal{E}$lijah Mikaelson was a survivor. It didn't hurt that he was invincible, of course, but on top of that he had a real gift for adaptation, for getting along.

Since he and his siblings had arrived on the muddy shores of the crime-ridden outpost known as Nouvelle-Orléans, those talents had served him well. After Klaus's initial rampage, they'd eventually made peace with the local witches and werewolves. They'd had to swear not to sire any new vampires, but the cost of making a home was worth it. The balance was fragile, but the truce had held for nearly a decade. After years of being chased by their murderous father across Europe, they'd finally landed on their feet.

But times were changing, and it was time for the Originals to change with them.

As Elijah headed out of the city, the close-packed buildings began to grow sparse, and the noise of the city center faded as his horse plodded forward. Humans rode and so he did, too, to maintain his facade, but mortal creatures moved at an achingly slow pace.

His path would be shortest if he cut through the private cemetery on the outskirts of town, and after the slightest of hesitations, he urged the horse beneath the high iron gate.

It was deserted, as any graveyard was likely to be with night falling, but Elijah did not feel alone. Unlike the public burial grounds, this small one teemed with the magic of its deceased inhabitants. No one but witches was buried here, and the concentration of their remains was potent. Incense burned beside many of the curiously inscribed stones, and the light from dripping candles distorted the shadows into fantastical shapes. There was no doubt that the place was thoroughly haunted.

Elijah's horse shied and pranced, liking this place no better than he did. But the curve of the bayou would take him miles out of his way if he didn't cut through the cemetery. It could be considered a test of resolve for Ysabelle's potential visitors: Would they brave the unholy ground? Or take the longer path and lose an hour to their cowardice? Or, as she probably preferred, would the mortals stay away entirely, whispering tales about the witch who lived on the far side of the cemetery?

This place of magic reminded Elijah briefly, powerfully, of another witch who'd surrounded herself with this sort of beautiful ritual: his mother, Esther. A thousand years ago, he had considered her the strongest, most perfect and elegant woman in the world. Then she had cursed him in a desperate bid to save her family from rampaging werewolves, never admitting that she'd had more to do with those wolves than any of them would have guessed.

Her spell had made her husband, Mikael, and her children immortal, invulnerable, and murderers a thousand times over. She had done what she thought was best, but had come to regret it. She had died believing that all her children—those fathered by Mikael: Rebekah, Finn, Kol, and Elijah himself, as well as her bastard son, the half werewolf Niklaus—were abominations. She had died believing that it would have been best to let the werewolves kill them all.

Their father, the first vampire hunter, had made it his mission to eradicate the scourge of Esther's children. Elijah and his siblings had run for centuries and crossed oceans to escape their father's wrath. Whenever the thought of his mother crept up on Elijah, it hurt him to his core—the belief that his parents would never love him and wanted him dead.

There was nothing to be done except to focus on the witch at hand. Ysabelle Dalliencourt wasn't half the witch that Esther had been, of course, but that could work to his advantage now. She was known to be ambitious: Her desire for power far outstripped her natural talents for magic or leadership. She might be inclined to do favors for other powerful beings in exchange for alliances and gratitude, and Elijah found himself in need of a rather simple favor.

The pact with the witches had not only cost the Mikaelsons the ability to make new vampires; the Originals had soon found that their attempts to buy or barter for land within the city limits, no matter how enticing—or menacing—were refused. The message was clear: They could stay, but they shouldn't get too comfortable.

As a result, Elijah and his siblings had spent the last nine years living in inns, boardinghouses, and eventually hotels. Their accommodations had admittedly grown more comfortable as the city's population swelled and prospered, but even the most lavish hotel room wasn't a home. It couldn't be owned; it couldn't be defended. It certainly was no place for Kol and Finn, his two brothers who slept in their coffins after Klaus had daggered them in anger. Elijah could see the winds of change blowing into their city, and he had no intention of being swept away by them. It was time for the Mikaelsons to own a slice of New Orleans, and all he needed was one amenable witch to allow him to claim it.

The smell of incense faded as he left the graveyard, and the forest rose up ahead of him. His horse pranced sideways a little, objecting to the gloom. Elijah patted its neck reassuringly and kicked it forward, his sharp eyes scanning the edge of the trees for a shadow that was different from the others.

Just as he spotted the little house, a flickering light appeared in its window, and the horse shied again. Elijah sighed and dismounted; it had been overly optimistic to attempt to travel on the beast. Animals had never been as naturally suspicious of him as they tended to be of his siblings, but it was clear that a vampire was not the sort of companion this creature preferred.

Elijah couldn't really blame it for that.

He tied the reins to a hardy sapling and covered the remaining distance to the house on foot. There was no one around to notice him being more than human, but by force of habit he walked, trying to look unremarkable. By the time he reached the house, more candles had been lit, and through a window he spied the shadow of the witch. Yet, when he knocked firmly on the door, there was not even the slightest rustle from inside.

He knocked again and waited: nothing. "Madame Ysabelle," he called, trying to sound as polite as possible while shouting through a closed door, "I have come on business that I believe might interest you."

"Every stranger comes on business," a voice warned from behind him, "but it's rarely any business of mine."

She spoke in a singsong, otherworldly lilt, so when Elijah spun around he was surprised. The woman who stood behind him on the whitewashed veranda was tall and slim, dressed smartly in a striped pink dress that might have come directly from Paris. Her auburn hair was piled neatly on her head, and gleamed softly in the moonlight.

He realized with a start that he had seen her before: She had been at the ill-fated engagement party. Somehow he had never connected the murmurs about the odd and reclusive Ysabelle Dalliencourt with the stylish, even elegant woman before him. Youthful, as well: Vivianne Lescheres was her niece, but Vivianne's mother must be a considerably older woman.

"Madame," Elijah said formally, recovering himself enough to bow politely. "Thank you for speaking with a stranger."

Ysabelle's full lips twitched. "Vampire," she said, "I'm sure you can understand why I do not intend to invite you into my house."

"Of course," Elijah said. "And your reasonable concern highlights the intention of my visit—even though I mean no harm."

She smiled. "You'll do me no harm," she promised him, reaching out to take his arm and steering him away from the door. Together they strolled around the perimeter of the tiny house, toward the looming forest. Ysabelle's sure feet found a path that Elijah had not noticed before, and she led him beneath the sweeping oak trees that dripped with Spanish moss.

"My family has lived here a long time, Madame," he began as the clearing faded behind them. "Nine years. And yet we are not truly a part of this city; we do not belong the way that you and your kin do."

"Whose fault is that?" Ysabelle asked tartly, gathering her skirt to step across some sprawling roots. "Your family hunted the werewolves on your arrival, and even after the truce was struck, you are still a threat to my kind. I can't trust you, but that's not your fault," she went on thoughtfully. "You live by killing. You can't help it if that's your nature."

Elijah gritted his teeth, but with the discipline of experience he kept his voice mild. "My family is very close, and we've learned to keep to ourselves"—he paused—"as I'm sure the other citizens prefer. But, Madame, by the decree of *your* family we have nowhere to keep ourselves, and so we remain homeless in this city nearly ten years after making it our residence."

He felt her hold on his arm tighten. "That is not my decision," she replied after the briefest of hesitations. Did that mean she agreed with him?

"We would like to own land here," he pressed, not daring to look at her. "We think that, perhaps, if you could influence your brethren—"

"I have no influence," Ysabelle interrupted, her tone sharp. "Certainly not to do what you mean."

"Madame, I have heard nothing but praise for your wisdom and judgment." It was a lie, but not an egregious one—he hadn't heard the opposite. "And consider as well that you would have our undying gratitude. Gratitude that might be worth its weight in influence someday. It would not be the first time the Mikaelsons had taken an interest in local politics."

Ysabelle gave a small laugh. "You think the favor of the vampires will give me a real voice in the affairs of this city?" she asked. "And all you require is some of our ancestral land?"

Elijah didn't reply as Ysabelle steered him along the uneven path.

"For what it's worth," she continued, "I agree with my people in this. I don't think it was wise to tolerate such an abomination as your family in the first place, and we certainly should not broaden the invitation. Especially now—"

"Because of the werewolves," he finished for her. Elijah bristled at yet another witch calling him unnatural and denying him sanctuary. He was tired of being rejected by those who revered the magic that created the "abomination" in the first place.

"Oh, so you *are* aware that we are in the process of allying with your enemies? I thought you must have forgotten in order to ask such a thing. If I went before the witches and argued that we should play both sides, when the wolves are a legion and you are three, they would laugh at me."

They emerged into the same clearing they had left, just to the other side of Ysabelle's house. Elijah hadn't even noticed the path curve. Perhaps she had enchanted it. "They would be wrong," he told her, although he knew that it wouldn't make a difference. "I have no more wish to quarrel with the werewolves than I do with the witches, but if it comes to that, we three will not need numbers, allies, or even the small parcel of land I hoped for in order to meet them on equal terms."

"If that were true," Ysabelle retorted, releasing his arm and moving gracefully to her front step, "you would not have come here tonight."

In spite of his disappointment, Elijah found himself

smiling. He rather liked the reclusive witch, and he suspected that she was not nearly as unwilling to negotiate with him as she wanted to seem. "I'll return," he said impulsively. "I will find a way to show you that you helping us serves your interests, and I'll be back."

With her hand resting lightly on the doorknob, Ysabelle turned and smiled so broadly that he knew he had guessed correctly. "You know where to find me," she replied, "but I doubt I will see you here again anytime soon."

You will, he vowed, but did not speak the words aloud. They both knew the challenge that he had thrown down, and they both knew that she had accepted it.

SIX

"**I**t all happened so fast."

Rebekah had been repeating this mantra for *days*, and yet Captain Eric Moquet never seemed fully satisfied. That kind of restless curiosity might be appealing in a lover, but it was downright annoying in an investigator. She enjoyed the attention lavished on her by the captain, but he was becoming difficult, and Rebekah wasn't sure how much more patience she had for these soldiers she had so confidently offered to win over to the Mikaelsons' cause.

"But we must know, and only you can provide the truth." Eric held Rebekah's arm as he led her across the treacherous campgrounds. The soldiers had done their best to tame the terrain by the river, filling in marshy holes and cutting back undergrowth, but the wild bayou was barely contained by the orderly sprawl.

She sighed in frustration. Eric had decided that it was terribly important to help her, find the bad men, and punish them. He still wanted to root out her imaginary attacker and bring him to justice, and he was increasingly baffled by Rebekah's reluctance to cooperate. Eric believed that the rule of law would win out over chaos, and she could not convince him otherwise. It was actually an endearing, if idiotic, belief.

Still, the more Eric questioned her about the supposed attack in the forest, the more Rebekah worried that she might have made a terrible mistake in staging the murder. He did not want to let the crime go unpunished, which she supposed was natural enough. But the problem went far deeper than that.

Until she had met Eric Moquet, Rebekah had allowed herself to forget that humans could be intelligent, insightful, or intuitive. She had expected a single-minded and military pursuit of the wrongdoers, which would run into the dead end she had created. Instead, Eric's mind had shown flexibility that was, frankly, alarming. He attacked the problem with creativity and inventiveness, so that sooner or later he was bound to notice that she was lying.

As if to make her predicament worse, Eric had also

proved himself to be extremely chivalrous over the last few days, not to mention even more handsome than she had realized at first. His hazel eyes were warm and sincere, while his dark hair with its scattering of silver strands made him look dignified and thoughtful. Combined with his deep rumble of a voice that was worth listening to at least as much as his carefully measured words, she found herself fascinated every time they spoke. He walked a gentleman's fine line flawlessly, managing to provide attentive, charming company without intruding on her privacy. In spite of the worries that never left the back of her mind, they had spent many hours together in perfect companionship. The captain had even shared a wonderful amount of news and gossip with her from his home city of Paris, reminding her fondly of the time she had spent there and the people she had come to know.

But he had rarely spoken about himself, not even to hint at whether a wife and family were waiting for him back in France. Nor would he confide in her much about his obvious interest in the occult, which frustrated her greatly. That ridiculous fixation was *almost* certainly harmless—she had once caught him reading what looked to be a book of fairy tales with rapt interest— and she saw no sign that he knew anything specific or dangerous to her. But it would have been better if he knew nothing at all, and Rebekah was determined to steer his attention in a more productive direction.

Unfortunately, at the moment, his preferred direction seemed to be tracking down her imaginary bandits. He wanted her to look at the assorted criminals he'd caught in the last few days to see if any of them were her attackers, and wouldn't take no for an answer.

In a burst of inspiration, it occurred to Rebekah that one of her problems might be the solution to the other. If she connected the mystery of her attacker with Eric's interest in the supernatural, then he would solve one investigation while explaining the other. After all, what was one human's life—a troublemaker anyway—compared to the safety of her and her brothers? If Eric didn't know exactly what he was looking for, then Rebekah could convince him that any one of the suspects was the "supernatural" terror.

"Captain, I know you believe that we were set upon by . . . by some unnatural fiend," she reminded him. "Could you not eliminate any suspect that's a mortal man?"

"You saw these creatures in action and still believed them to be mortal men," he pointed out, his eyes searching hers. "Perhaps we have caught one such fiend without even knowing it."

"Well, then," she agreed thoughtfully, "let me get a look at them."

It took them only a minute more to reach the newly constructed prison. The building was more solid than the surrounding tents, but still rough and unfinished, cobbled together from whatever the soldiers had scrounged from the forest. It looked no better on the inside. The dozen or so men who had been unlucky enough to get caught were crammed into one small cell. Rebekah could only imagine how uncomfortable it must be to sleep. The straw beneath them was dank, and barely any air came from the one high, barred window.

Eric's second-in-command, the black-stubbled, unimaginative Felix, stood guard by the door. He watched her intently as she passed, and Rebekah felt an inexplicable chill as his eyes raked across her face.

"You are perfectly safe," Eric murmured in her ear, mistaking her disgust for fear. "Do you know any of them?"

"Perhaps." She had to force the words out past her teeth, and she wished she could take them back as soon as she did. "These are your suspects?"

"They are, Madame," Eric confirmed, his sun-weathered face looking satisfied.

Rebekah frowned as she scanned the group. There were more men than she had thought there would be . . . surely they were not all new arrivals. "Which of these were caught after I came here?"

To her surprise and mild alarm, Eric hesitated. In

what light filtered in through the small window, his expression was unreadable. "I am a fair man." Pride rang in his low voice, but there was an apology in the words as well. "Madame, if you know one of these criminals, then I am sure you will be able to distinguish him without us separating the new from the old."

In other words, he would not narrow down her choices, testing her as much as the men in the jail cell. That made things considerably more difficult. If she pointed to the wrong thug, Eric would know it, and worse, he might even direct his inquiry toward *her*.

If she wanted to keep suspicion off herself, she'd have to pick the *right* wrong man. She could compel Eric to believe her, but she knew from experience that lies acquired lives of their own, and one lie always led to more.

She glanced at the caged men. Perhaps she could make some kind of guess based on which were the least filthy? It was not an easy distinction to make. Then, to her delight, she realized that she actually did know one of the faces . . . and had seen it the night before she'd killed the wagoner and his wife. Green eyes glittered brilliantly out of his swarthy face, and his left arm was bound in a grimy sling. Elijah had broken it, she remembered, when Solomon and his pack had surrounded her brother and ambushed him, six to one.

"That one," she said confidently, raising her hand and

pointing. "That's the man who attacked me. I would know his face anywhere."

Eric looked pleased, but the caged werewolf looked murderous. "The bitch lies," he snarled, throwing himself forward to grab the bars between them, and she thought she detected some yellow starting to blossom in the green of his eyes.

She clutched Eric's arm and pressed the side of her body against his, for good measure. "It's him," she whispered, and her apparent fear snapped him into action.

He spun her outside before slamming the door decisively behind them, then gestured for Felix to approach. The wind caught at Rebekah's gray gown, twisting its skirt around her legs. "Bring the one with the broken arm to my tent," Eric ordered. "I need to question him, and then I will carry out the execution myself."

Felix saluted sharply, then cast one more lingering glance at Rebekah before he moved to obey. She wondered if he was jealous of the time she had spent with his captain, if he worried that he might be replaced as Eric's confidant. If so, though, surely the wisest course of action would be for him to perform his duties more smartly and expediently than ever before. As if he had reached the same conclusion, Felix pulled a ring of keys from his red coat and marched stiffly back into the jail.

So that the captain can question and then kill the prisoner.

Rebekah could only imagine how confused the werewolf would be by Eric's questions. But he wouldn't say anything that might incriminate her—of that she was sure. No lowly pack member would take it upon himself to reveal the existence of his kind to humans, and in protecting his secret he would have to protect hers as well. How fortunate that any werewolf would rather die than betray his kin, because die he would. And it would serve him right.

As they escorted the struggling werewolf out of the jail, Eric bent to pick something up off the ground. It was a fallen tree branch, and as she gasped he snapped it across his knee. Eric held one splintered half up to the light, and she knew exactly what it was: a stake.

Rebekah felt a sudden tightness in her throat. What would Eric want with a stake? The only reason he'd need one would be to kill *her* kind. All of a sudden the good Captain Moquet was looking less like an eccentric scholar of the occult and more like a fledgling vampire hunter. She raced back to the warmth of her tent to remove herself from any further involvement.

It was hours before she heard enough of a disturbance to peer outside. Four soldiers were carrying the werewolf's lifeless body toward the edge of the camp. Even from a distance, with night having fallen across the bayou, she was sure she could see the broken tree branch still protruding from the left side of the man's chest.

SEVEN

The stately three-story white house that rose before him belonged to the Lescheres family—Klaus was sure of it. It had taken him half the night to find, but it wasn't as if he'd been capable of doing anything else. Vivianne was the only thing on his mind. He balled his fists tightly, feeling rough patches of stray paint smears all over them. He had tried to lose himself in the art that usually soothed and consumed him, but every canvas his brush touched turned out dull and lifeless. The whole world had been dull and lifeless, without the sight and smell of Vivianne to breathe new energy into his endless nights.

In spite of his very confident hopes, he hadn't run into her again, and his siblings were an insufficient distraction. Elijah's quest for a homestead had made him moodier and more withdrawn than usual, and Rebekah had apparently decided to just enlist in the French army; she had been gone nearly a week without bothering to send word of her progress. There was nothing to take Klaus's mind off of the absence of Vivianne, and so he had decided to take the initiative and find her himself.

He had circled the witches' quarter for hours, skulking, eavesdropping, and tailing, and finally had narrowed it down to a single street, and then a single mansion. Now he hesitated, though, trying to decide what to do with his discovery. Somehow he had imagined that Viv would be sitting in a lighted window, gazing longingly out into the street when he arrived, but of course she was not. It was unreasonable to knock on the door, but it would be irrational to stand outside of a young woman's house with the hope that she might leave it.

If she was home at all. She might be out somewhere, just as he would be, normally. She was probably out with her depressingly serious fiancé, in fact. His hands clenched, his nails biting viciously into his paint-streaked palms. Armand Navarro might be pretty useless, but even he would have the sense to steal a kiss from Vivianne on a hot summer night in New Orleans. She would probably feel obligated to allow it, and let him put his stupid paws all over her.

Klaus caught sight of a flash of white movement in the courtyard, and he scaled the latticed fence and dropped down on the other side before his heart could even skip its next beat. It was her, stealing carefully toward the house. She seemed to have just snuck in through the back gate. Out without her parents' knowledge, he guessed—Viv was definitely his kind of girl. The nickname suited her, as vivid as she was.

She was watching the ground, placing her feet carefully on the damp grass to avoid stumbling in the dark, and the soft smile on her face made him wish that it were for him. Then she looked up and froze, her whole demeanor changing. Instead of joy at the sight of him, she looked afraid. The thought of her fearing him gave him a strange, secret thrill, but in the next moment she glanced nervously at the house, then quickly back to Klaus. She gestured at him and then at the gate, urging him silently to leave.

She wasn't afraid of him at all, only afraid to be caught by people who would have expected her to be in her bed, sleeping. He couldn't remember the last time a woman had prioritized her reputation above *him*. It was maddening, and it was indescribably attractive.

Of course, leaving was not an option. Instead he crossed the distance between them faster than her eyes could follow, positioning his body between hers and the elegant manor house. "I came only to talk." He offered her his most dazzling smile to apologize for the lie, but she didn't look in a mood to be charmed.

"I have nothing to say to you," she whispered urgently. "Go now, before you're seen out here."

"I ask only a few minutes of your time, Mademoiselle," he persisted. He would not let her pass, but he noticed that she did not especially try. Perhaps curiosity was finally winning out over her well-bred stubbornness. "If you'd prefer, we can go inside, away from prying eyes and gossiping tongues."

She was silent for longer than he would have liked, considering the options he'd left open to her. "Five minutes," she agreed at last, her tone terse and business-like in spite of the concession. "We can use the drawing room. No one will notice us in there. I left that door there unlocked." He stepped aside, and she ran lightly across the grass. It crossed his mind that she might attempt to trick him and escape into the house, but when she reached the door she turned, and he could see the outline of an irrepressible smile on her lips. "Come into my home, Niklaus," she said, as formally as a person could sound while whispering.

He had already reached the interior hallway while her hand was still reaching for the doorknob, and he held the door open for her with a courtly flourish. Her smile widened, and she dipped her head to conceal it as she joined him inside the house.

It had been smart to visit—Klaus was very nearly irresistible in person.

Vivianne lit a candelabra, and then turned to him expectantly. Klaus flashed her his most charming smile, then stepped forward and reached for her hand to kiss it. "I said five minutes," she reminded him, stepping back out of his reach, "but I would certainly appreciate it if you took less."

"I don't believe that you truly would, Vivianne," Klaus disagreed. "I don't believe that a woman of your spirit and intelligence could possibly be happy in the life that has been laid out for you here, and I think that you understand on some level that meeting me is an opportunity for much, much more."

An emotion flashed through her black eyes, and Klaus felt sure it was recognition. "It may have been laid out for me since birth, but that does not make it an unworthy life," she countered. The words were persuasive, but her voice was not, and Klaus studied her face carefully. How could someone as clever and high-spirited as she was become so placid and docile at the thought of being used as a pawn? "It's an honor to help bring the fighting and death in this city to an end."

Someone had told her that, he knew, and probably

had repeated it often. Klaus stepped closer to her, feeling drawn toward her in a way he could not quite describe. If she was torn she would not show it. "It is your life, my lady," he told her, "not some abstract honor."

"My life," she repeated, a shadow falling across her pale face. He lifted a hand to her cheek almost without realizing it, but she stepped away from him again, her shoes making no sound on the thick blue rug of the drawing room. He let his hand drop back to his side, tingling with the false hope of contact. "It must seem so insignificant to you. We live and die in no time at all, compared to your kind."

"That's not true." His voice was heavy with honesty. If that was the reason she'd kept herself so aloof from him, then he needed to make her understand that wasn't the case. "A year is still a year to me; a lifetime is a lifetime. Having had more than a few of my own makes them no less vivid or important to me."

"And yet you end them, left and right, in order to sustain those lives of yours." Her mouth turned downward in disapproval. "I have no wish to get involved with your kind, however well-meaning you might be tonight. I want to end bloodshed, not befriend a creature who must survive by it."

It took him a moment to even understand what she meant, and when he did he struggled to remain composed. The comparison between the nameless people he drained for food and her shining, crackling bonfire of a life was so ludicrous that it was all he could do not to laugh. But her moral qualms about his existence were apparently a real concern for her, and so he tried to remain serious.

"My kind are not what you think. I'm not what you think—yes, I must kill to live, but you make me want to be different. After decades of emptiness, you make me feel complete. I feel I have known you my whole life, Vivianne, and I can understand you as no one else can," he said. He lifted her chin with one hand until her endless, unfathomable eyes met his, and she did not recoil from his touch. He could feel the delicate line of her jawbone through the warm, supple flesh that stretched across it. "I know you have a kind and willing heart, and I also know you long to be free."

Her eyes closed for a long moment, and Klaus held his breath. "I remember when you first came to this city," she said finally, and he frowned in surprise. He released her, the heat of her skin lingering on his own. Whatever he had expected to hear, it wasn't that. Her eyes opened, but she looked everywhere but him. "You destroyed whatever peace was left in the city. Until now."

She must have been a child, he calculated frantically.

Surely she had been afraid of the rumors that had spread on his arrival. And it was true that he had taken it upon himself to control the werewolf population for the first couple of years—her father's family. That had perhaps been rash, although there was certainly no shortage of the beasts in New Orleans. It was past time for his little massacre to be forgiven and forgotten. "Vivianne, do you know *why* Elijah and Rebekah and I came here?"

"No one else would have you?" she guessed tartly, reminding him without quite saying so that he'd not exactly been welcome in her house, either.

"Our father hunts us," he explained, and the edges of her teeth bit down on her full bottom lip. "He will not rest until we are dead. We fled here, and were met with suspicion and open hostility. The witches were generous enough to accept our presence, but the werewolves made no such allowances. They saw us as their natural enemies, so that's how I treated them. I couldn't let them drive us out, Vivianne, that was all."

Her face had softened, just a little. "But then nothing has changed," she argued, although it sounded halfhearted. "You—we—are still natural enemies, are we not?"

He saw his opening and pulled her close to him, feeling the race of her heartbeat against his chest. "Are we?" he murmured, bending down so that his breath stirred her hair. "If you and I can find common ground, I'm sure that the rest of our kinds can be persuaded to do the same. We could lead them by example into cooperation and coexistence. We could create a legacy of peace that will be a beacon to the world."

He almost had her, he could see it. If he kissed her now, she would respond. Her lips were parted, wet, waiting. But she'd come to regret changing her mind so quickly, he knew: She would distrust this kiss and doubt her judgment if he pressed too hard. Making her wait would be smarter. Let her think about him, miss him, want him . . . and compare him to that fool Armand every time the stupid werewolf opened his mouth.

When Klaus won her, he would win her completely.

He reached down and lifted her unresisting hand to his mouth, completing the more formal kiss she had denied him earlier. He could feel a faint trembling in her skin, and he smiled to himself as he released it. "I think my five minutes have passed," he murmured. "I will not trouble you any more tonight. Just know, Vivianne Lescheres, that if you allow me, I will give you the world."

He turned and left before she could answer. He felt suddenly inspired to take up his painting again—he knew exactly what the last canvas was missing.

EIGHT

$\mathcal{E}$ lijah suspected that the edges of the city would be the most likely spots. Witches and werewolves had eyes everywhere in the center of town, and the new residential neighborhoods were too orderly and visible for a purchase to go through unnoticed. But the outskirts, where the city faded into the bayou and the untamed forest, were still a half-wild paradise and the perfect place for a vampire to call home.

He rode out at night, while Klaus sank ever further into his lovesick misery and Rebekah gallivanted around with the French army. One of the Mikaelsons had to keep an eye on their true purpose and, as usual, the task had fallen on him.

Where the houses and shops gave way to patchy fields and makeshift farms, Elijah rode, surveyed, and occasionally made the most discreet of inquiries about land for sale. He had not yet met with any success, and in fact had been chased away by several suspicious residents. But he only needed to be lucky once, and he had a lot of ground left to cover.

There were still traces of the setting sun in the sky, but candlelight glowed in several spots, dotting the stretch of land he intended to ride over that night. One man, stooped and white-haired, was still outside, struggling to lash a wide piece of canvas over some barrels stacked at what Elijah judged to be the very edge of his land. There were full, heavy clouds on the horizon, and after watching him for a moment, Elijah rode toward him.

"Can I help?" he called when he was close enough, and the man spun around.

"You can stay where you are," the man suggested sharply, and Elijah saw that, while his face was lined and tired-looking, his blue eyes were sharp and focused with intelligence. The house behind him was modest but in good shape, and he had kept his land clear of the forest that encroached on three sides. This was not a man who would drift into his old age in a featherbed, surrounded by fat great-grandchildren.

Elijah dismounted to put them on somewhat more

even footing, and held up his empty hands meaningfully. "I am sorry to startle you," he said softly. "I have been searching for a place near here to settle with my family and saw you working so late, that's all. It seemed as though you could use an extra pair of hands."

"An extra everything is more like it," the man admitted, sizing up Elijah's broad shoulders. "I should have made moving these into the cellar a condition of the trade in the first place, but I thought it would be just as easy to throw on a rain cover if I needed it." He smirked wryly. "I was mistaken."

"I can move them for you, if that would be better," Elijah offered—in for a penny, in for a pound. It couldn't hurt to have a friend among the homesteaders out here, and the man's uncomplaining attitude toward a task that was most certainly beyond him was charming.

"It's a two-man job." The man looked at the barrels. Elijah realized that he meant he wasn't one of those men, as he wouldn't be able to lift his side of a barrel. It didn't matter, since Elijah was much stronger than an ordinary man, but he hurt for the old man's wounded pride all the same.

He walked to the barrels, tipping the nearest one into his hands and lifting it easily. "It is," he agreed. "So please show me the way and open the cellar door for me. I'd rather not hold this any longer than I need to."

The man looked incredulous, then delighted. There was a noticeable spring in his step as he crossed his little patch of land, making for the stump of what had once been an impressively massive oak tree. He pulled at an iron ring in the ground beside it, and a section of turf swung upward, revealing a gaping hole below. The cellar had been hollowed out beneath the spreading roots of the tree, and Elijah felt carefully with each foot for the next uneven dirt stair while balancing the large barrel against his chest. The next four trips went just as smoothly, and then the man closed the trapdoor behind them and wiped his hands on his trousers.

"The name's Hugo Rey," he grunted, his voice thick with emotion, holding out his right hand. Elijah tried to remember the last time a human had offered to shake his hand and couldn't.

He accepted the gesture warmly, and gave his name—his real name, to his own surprise—in return. "Can I do anything else for you while I'm here?" he asked courteously, rather hoping that Hugo would take him up on the offer.

"You can join me inside for a drink, son," the old man told him firmly. "That was hard work you've just saved me, and the least I can do is provide hospitality in return. You must be thirsty after all that lifting."

Normally, the inadvertent invitation to feed would

have whetted Elijah's appetite, but the thought of hurting Hugo didn't even cross his mind. "It would be my pleasure," he agreed sincerely, and together they made for the house in the center of the field.

It had grown dark and rain was nearly at the doorstep. Hugo set about lighting candles and clearing odds and ends from the rough-hewn kitchen table. Bits of hardware along with paper covered in lists of figures and painstakingly precise drawings were swept away before Elijah could put his finger on what they were, and he refocused his attention on the stocky earthenware cups that Hugo set out in their place.

They were filled with a rough but serviceable liquor—a few steps down from rye, but a few crucial notches up from moonshine. Elijah sipped cautiously, while Hugo drained half his mug in a single swallow. In the candlelight, he looked even older than Elijah had assumed at first. It was astonishing that he still lived out here, all alone, keeping his house and land in decent order and even attempting manual labor at his advanced age.

"That stuff keeps you young," Hugo said, lifting his half-empty mug by way of explanation. It was as if he had followed the line of Elijah's thoughts perfectly, as if Elijah didn't *need* to speak to be understood.

Had it ever been so easy with his own father? This man was centuries younger than Mikael, but much older than Mikael had been when Elijah was still his cherished human son. And yet there was something about him that reminded Elijah of a father, of the way a father should behave toward a child who had grown up and chosen a path for himself in the world. Moving the barrels had not been a tremendous challenge for an Original vampire, but nonetheless, Hugo didn't seem merely grateful: Elijah had the sense that the old man was *proud* of him.

"Have you lived out here long?" he asked politely, sipping again at his liquor.

"Twenty years at least," Hugo replied vaguely. "The city's closer to my doorstep now than it was." He sounded as if he disapproved of that development.

"I'm a rather private person, myself," Elijah offered. "I've been looking for land out here, actually. My sister and my brother like the nightlife in town, but I think we'd all be more comfortable with a quieter place to come home to."

Hugo's smile was distant. "I always thought I would have children," he said suddenly, and Elijah blinked in surprise. "My life was never the type that gives much room for a family," the man went on, "but I think there's a part of you that never stops planning for the future as if there is one."

Elijah wondered how Mikael would have responded

to that. His own children obviously had no place in the future he wanted to build. Did Mikael have some other sort of legacy in mind, or did immortals eventually cease to think about such things? Elijah always thought of the future, although perhaps not in the way Hugo meant. When Elijah looked to the future, he was always still in it. "Family is a blessing," he mused noncommittally, "but blessings can come in many forms."

Hugo nodded and refilled his cup. He held out the bottle meaningfully, offering more to his guest. Elijah, whose cup was still nearly full, took the bottle from him politely and poured in just a few drops more. It was always proper to accept hospitality, in his experience, or at least to make a reasonable show of it.

"I suspect I've been blessed enough," Hugo answered thoughtfully, swirling the liquid in his mug and staring into it for a moment before taking another long drink. "I've used my talents in my work, made and kept a good reputation my whole life, and owned this square of land outright since probably before you were born."

Elijah was not inclined to correct him on that last point; instead he simply nodded. It was clear to him that the wheels of the old man's mind were turning, and he suspected that, if he waited, Hugo would say more. A silent moment proved him right.

"A man should have a home he can call his own."

His voice was low and forceful, almost a growl. "It's not natural to be adrift, family or no."

Unnatural once again. *Abomination.*

"I'll drink to that," Elijah replied, and matched action to words. "And to that note, do you know if any of your neighbors are thinking of selling? We have had some trouble with going through official channels in this matter, so we would be open to offering a nice price for someone willing to sign over the deed quickly, with no formalities."

Hugo's lined face crinkled into a knowing smile. "Not so popular with the higher-ups, are you, my boy? Local politics have no winners, at least not for long. Why do you think I'm all the way out here? I don't have to deal with anyone who doesn't value my time and work, and I prefer it that way."

"I think I could learn much from your example," Elijah admitted.

Hugo pushed his chair back from the table abruptly, and when he rose Elijah noticed that he was unsteady on his feet. That was a surprise. Although Hugo had partaken quite liberally of the liquor in his cup, Elijah had been under the impression that he did not normally drink less. He should have been accustomed to his generous nightcap, and yet he swayed as he crossed the room as if he were on the deck of a ship.

He returned with an intricately mosaicked wooden box, which he set down wordlessly in the center of the table, halfway between the two cups. With a long exhale, Hugo opened the box to reveal some worn, yellowed papers. Elijah stared at them, unsure whether he was meant to pick them up and examine them himself.

"I have a house, and not much more need of one. You need a house and do not have one." Hugo's gruff voice was blunt, but his blue eyes avoided Elijah's as if he felt suddenly shy. "Keep searching among my neighbors if you like, but if you want it, this home will be yours upon my death." He produced a fountain pen from one of his pockets, and Elijah stared keenly at it. Such pens, with a reservoir of ink hidden neatly inside of a metal casing, were rare—yet another unexpectedly interesting item in this modest little house. Hugo scribbled on the papers before him, then signed his name at the bottom of each page with a flourish. "I have not met a man in a long time that I would wish to consider my heir," he mumbled when he had finished. "But I cannot stop thinking of the future, even now. And here you are. . . ."

He trailed off, his eyes still fixed on the papers before him. Elijah understood that they were two of a kind. "I would be honored," he told the old man gently, "and grateful. Eternally grateful," he added, a little ruefully. If Hugo wanted his home—and his memory—to live on, he could hardly have chosen a better beneficiary. "But I hope that it will be a long time before we have the use of this remarkable gift. I would rather come to visit you here again, and often, if you will allow it."

Hugo smiled and sat down heavily in his chair, although he was not a large man. "I would like that, too," he said serenely, his gaze fixed on something in the distance that Elijah could not see. His lined face looked flushed in the candlelight. "But I think that the time for visiting is largely past. It has been very enjoyable, though. Very satisfactory."

Elijah frowned and glanced down at his cup again. Was Hugo ill? Did he know something about his death that he had chosen not to share? His eyes moved forward to the signed pages between them on the table. He had made it his goal to own land, but now he felt deeply troubled about accepting it. As hard as it had been for the Mikaelsons to carve out a foothold in New Orleans, to find a friend had always proved even more difficult.

"I will use whatever time is left, then," he promised, and a smile creased Hugo's face. He poured them another glass from his bottle of liquor, which already more than half gone, and Elijah raised his mug in a silent toast.

They talked well into the night. Their silences grew and lengthened as the hours wore on, and several times

Elijah thought that Hugo might have dozed off. During these lapses, Elijah's eyes roamed the room, taking in each small detail. He imagined how it would feel to have a home of their own again, a place as personal and lived-in as this one. Then the old man would rouse himself, and their conversation would resume. Hugo's cheeks were still unnaturally flushed, and at times his mind appeared to wander, but he seemed to want their evening to continue, and Elijah was perfectly content to oblige him.

Finally, silence fell again, and to Elijah's keen ears this one was deeper and more perfect than all the rest had been. The rainstorm had come and gone, and he could hear cicadas and bullfrogs outside. In the distance, the lazy spill of the Saint Louis River swept along. But inside the house, there was no sound at all.

Hugo Rey sat in his chair, one hand wrapped around his mug, but his eyes were empty and lifeless. The rise and fall of his chest had stopped, while Elijah's attention had been diverted. He had passed, silently and peacefully, in his home and attended by a friend. Elijah knew that few humans were so lucky, but still, as he collected the papers from the table and returned to his horse he felt a painful twisting of regret in his chest.

NINE

*T*he attack came at sundown. Cries went up from the sentries near the river first, and then Rebekah heard a second set of shouts rise from the woods to the west. The setting sun had turned the Saint Louis River into a long line of glittering fire, blinding the soldiers and confusing their line of defense. The attackers had chosen their approach well.

They looked human, but Rebekah knew better: A dead werewolf had been carried out of the camp the night before, and now his pack had come for vengeance. Soldiers called to her to stay in her tent as they ran past, and Eric shouted to Felix and pointed her way. His hook-nosed lieutenant immediately separated four men out from the ones running toward the battle to form a ring around Rebekah's tent, keeping her safe within.

She wanted to tell them it wasn't necessary, that she was better equipped to protect them than they her, but there was no point. Men would die who didn't have to, but that was the nature of the world. She could hardly look out for their interests and her own at the same time, and so she waited patiently in her tent, listening to the brutal sounds of death all around it.

By the time it was fully dark outside, it was clear that the worst of the battle was pitched along the western edge of camp, and all of her guardians but Felix himself had left to join it. He had refused, sending the others to glory or death while he stayed behind, under orders.

Rebekah was restless. There were other things she could do than stay put, if only Felix would leave her alone. While the attention of the soldiers was elsewhere, this would be the perfect time to explore the forbidden reaches of the camp. The gruesome fate of the were-wolf she had condemned weighed on her mind, and she needed to find out how much Eric knew. And, even more important, what his intentions were.

Rebekah had been inside the public chamber of Eric's tent many times, but she doubted that he'd conduct an interrogation and an execution across his polished rosewood desk. Did he have a secret room that he was hiding from her? She'd previously assumed that his private chamber was a sleeping space, but now she wasn't so sure. It was time to find out, and to see what else Eric kept secreted away.

The werewolf would not have revealed anything intentionally, but Eric was too clever by half. He was an impressive man all around, really: intelligent and generous and obviously well respected by his men, even after such a short time in command. It frustrated Rebekah that the same qualities that made him so agreeable to spend time with also made him more of a danger to her kind. If things had been different, Rebekah could see herself falling in love with a man like him.

Eric knew what he wanted from life and how to take it without resorting to cruelty, setting him apart from the men she'd been surrounded by for most of her interminable life. If she was honest with herself, Rebekah knew she was having trouble combating her attraction to Eric, even in spite of her very reasonable suspicions about his activities. In her heart she hoped that his tent would reveal nothing nefarious, and she'd be able to let her feelings of affection grow without fear . . . as if she had ever been so lucky.

She peeked through her tent flap's opening, ready to make her move across the barracks to Eric's headquarters. Felix was prowling the perimeter and saw her immediately. He was obnoxiously devoted to his job, but as long as she was stuck with him as her "protector" she decided she might as well use him.

She beckoned Felix close with one finger, and then let the power of compulsion fill her. "Escort me to the captain's tent," she ordered, her voice quiet but throbbing with magic. "I have business there, but no one else must know."

His face clouded, and then, inexplicably, cleared. "You must stay here, Madame," he disagreed. "I have been given my orders."

Rebekah rocked back on her heels, stunned that he would—that he *could*—defy her. She could not think of another human who had resisted an Original vampire's compulsion. That shouldn't be possible. Maybe it was her own nerves, she decided, and tried again, leveling her powerful gaze into his eyes and repeating her demand.

"We will go at once," he agreed thickly. It was as if he had never argued in the first place. Felix looked around to make sure no one was watching, then took her arm and led the way.

Together they crossed the camp, crouching low and staying near the walls of other tents. There wasn't anyone around, but Felix took her command of secrecy very seriously, sometimes shielding her body with his own when he seemed to notice a movement nearby.

Felix stopped at the entrance of Eric's tent, looking sadly purposeless. "Stand guard," she ordered, compelling him anew. He shifted as if he wanted to object, but she took no chances, layering her power over and over itself until whatever restless will he had of his own was buried beneath the weight of hers. "Let no one enter until I have returned." It was unlikely that anyone would attempt to come in while she was there, but in the very worst case she would hear the scuffle if they did. Felix, unable to reveal what he was really doing there, would seem to have gone mad, but such things were common enough even among seasoned officers. His fellow soldiers would be surprised, but hardly suspicious.

Apprehensively, Rebekah lifted the fleur-de-lis–covered flap of Eric's tent. It was empty, and yet she felt like something was waiting for her.

The outer office looked just as she remembered it. The room was dark, but she could see perfectly well with her heightened vision. Nothing looked amiss, and she wished she could leave it at that. She liked Eric, she had to admit to herself, and she was reluctant to find out his secrets. Exposed secrets usually led to someone dying. And that wasn't going to be Rebekah.

With a deep breath and a muttered curse, she shoved aside the curtains to the inner chamber with defiant force.

And then she froze.

It wasn't a bedroom at all. It wasn't a sanctuary or a place of repose . . . it was a shrine to *death*. The fabric walls were covered with crosses and mirrors, and around three sides of the room sat carved wooden chests. They were piled high with stakes, objects wrought in silver, crossbows with wooden bolts, and even strings of garlic cloves. One chest held piles of dusty books stacked among instruments she didn't recognize with purposes she could not guess. Rebekah approached them carefully, studying each one. This was a room designed for catching and killing vampires.

It was all wrong, she realized with a sigh of relief. Some of the books looked ominously authoritative at first, but most were nothing but fairy tales. She nearly laughed aloud at one pretentiously titled *The Mythes and Truthes of the Monstyrrs Known Throughout the Known Worlde as "Vampyrre."* She didn't see anything in the tent that would especially hurt her. The thing that stung, actually, was that a man she'd begun to like had built a room dedicated to discovering the weaknesses of her kind.

She felt as though a heavy weight sat in her chest when she forced herself to admit just how wrong she'd been to trust Captain Moquet. She could no longer entertain her attraction to his relentless curiosity, not when it was such a clear threat to her. What if she'd been completely blinded by their chemistry, and he was using her much as she had intended to manipulate him?

She had to admit it was possible that Eric had never been interested in the human widow at all, and might have suspected Rebekah's true nature all along. What if he was keeping her close in order to learn her weaknesses? Her hands shook as she picked up one cruel-looking artifact after the other, inspecting them for anything that might cause irreparable harm.

So far, the Mikaelsons had been both lucky and careful—rumors of vampires hadn't spread from the Old World to the New. But Eric had recently arrived from France, and the truth was that he had never said much about why. What had really brought him to this distant swampland? Had he come to bring order to a lawless land for the greater glory of King Louis, or had he been sent to follow the trail of vampires?

Her eye fell on something she recognized, and she bent forward to pick it up. A small gold ring set with lapis lazuli hung on a chain that dangled from the corner of a silver mirror. The jewelry was twin to the one on her own finger. There were only six daylight rings in the world, to the best of her knowledge, and they were treasured family heirlooms. *Her* family's heirlooms. What was one doing here? Had it been enchanted, like the ones Esther had made, or was it just a copy?

One thing was certain: Eric's interest in the occult was much less haphazard than he had let her believe. He wasn't just after "unnatural fiends"; he knew exactly what he was searching for. And in spite of all the things he seemed to have gotten wrong so far, he was also getting some things dangerously right. The lapis ring might look like nothing but a pretty trinket, but it would not have been created—and it certainly would not have been *here*—unless it had been meant for the finger of a vampire.

She could imagine him turning it over in his calloused hands, studying it. She could picture him prowling around this room, trying to connect all of its pieces into a coherent picture. The way his eyebrows furrowed when he concentrated, the strong line of his shoulders beneath a thin white shirt . . . Rebekah clenched the ring in her fist, furious with herself.

It was obvious now that she didn't really know him at all. That brooding strength, that concentrated power . . . she could not afford to be attracted to the very qualities that would make him an effective killer of her kind.

Of course this was Eric's secret. *Naturally* Rebekah had gotten involved with the one man who was the most dangerous to her. It was the same mistake she had made over and over, and every time that she thought she'd learned to choose more wisely, she was proven wrong. It was as if her heart had some instinctual longing for misery and pain.

Gingerly, she put the ring back exactly as she found it and moved on, continuing her investigation.

On the far side of the chest she nearly tripped over something thicker than the piled carpets, and she looked down in surprise at what must be Eric's bedroll. She had almost forgotten that this was also the place he slept. She would never have thought him to be the type of man who would find rest among such chaos and darkness. He was serious, yes, but she had never imagined him as morbid.

For a moment she could see his dark hair with its sprinkling of gray at the temples on the crisp white pillow below her, his thoughtful hazel eyes gazing into hers. Maybe there was some kind of misunderstanding; maybe Eric's fascination with vampires wasn't what it seemed. Maybe there was another explanation entirely, and they could make a fresh start with none of her lies and none of his. . . .

She lowered herself down onto his blankets, wanting to see how it was that he woke up every morning. The mirrors and some of the crosses that ringed the walls glittered in the light that flickered through the tent, and the nearest chest was so close she could have reached up and touched some of the strange instruments within. Vampires were his first waking thought and the last thing on his mind as he fell asleep. Despite lying amongst sheets that smelled of him, and feeling the spot where his body lay every night, Rebekah had to admit that there was no question that Eric's job was to hunt vampires, and everything else—the army, the city, the king's law—was nothing but a smokescreen.

Rebekah rose onto her knees, preparing to leave and steal back to her own tent, when something incongruous caught her eye. There was something resting on the ground beside Eric's bed. Picking it up, she saw that it was an intricate gold locket, left open to reveal a miniature portrait within.

The flaxen-haired woman it depicted was lovely, and Rebekah was surprised to feel hot jealousy rising in her throat. *It might be Eric's mother or his sister,* she reminded herself. And it didn't matter anyway, because Eric had been sent across an ocean to find and destroy *her*. If the woman in the portrait was his wife, then as far as Rebekah was concerned, she could keep him.

She realized she had stayed too long. There was no sound from Felix or the battle. Her expedition had given her a great deal to think about, and probably enough evidence to leave this place and report back to her brothers. She was, after all, surrounded by the army of a vampire hunter and shouldn't risk any more spying when she was almost certainly being watched.

But she needed to know more. The evidence of Eric's obsession was troubling, but there could be ugly consequences to assuming she knew what it meant. If she let her brothers get hurt because she did not want to believe . . . if she let Eric get hurt because she believed too easily . . . She could not accept either risk. She wouldn't tell Elijah or Klaus what she'd found yet, but she owed it to them to investigate fully.

Rebekah smoothed the blankets and plumped the pillow, trying to angle the locket exactly as it had been—although perhaps a little farther away from the bedroll than she had found it. She slipped through the outer chamber and poked her head out of the tent to find Felix still waiting. At least that one thing had gone as expected.

"Felix," she whispered, and he turned attentively. "We must return to my tent now," she told him, ensnaring him again with the power of her voice. "Once I have gone inside, you will forget that we ever left. You will know only that you followed your captain's orders and guarded me throughout the battle."

"I always follow my orders," Felix told her amiably, and she had no doubt that he meant it.

TEN

*K*laus kept to the walls, watching the garden for the first sign of movement. Any stirring might be Vivianne . . . or it might be a pack of werewolves emerging from the mansion to tear him limb from limb. There was no shortage of lights and voices within the house, but outside nearly an hour had passed with nothing shifting except for the wind.

Klaus reread the note clutched in his left hand for the thousandth time. He was in the right place, and while he had arrived early, she was now late. Vivianne had asked to meet him here, in the garden behind the ballroom where they had first danced together, tonight. Now. Where was she?

Without his meaning to, his gaze drifted to the vine-covered walls where he had tried to conceal the body of the unfortunate serving girl he'd fed on that same night. Solomon Navarro had learned of that little incident all too quickly, and Vivianne had seen evidence of it herself. If she was setting him up for revenge, she could hardly have chosen a better spot . . . but he didn't believe that. He was sure he'd reached her the other night—he had felt the softening of her cool, skeptical exterior. She had wanted to believe him.

Surely she would come.

He heard the sound of soft footfalls on the grass, and he knew it was not an ambush. Vivianne hurried across the lawn, her cheeks flushed and her eyes shining with some emotion he could not name. For a moment, it was enough. "I'm glad you came," she whispered when she reached him, and in spite of his own promise to wait out her hesitations, Klaus could not repress a smile.

He couldn't remember the last time he had felt this way about a woman—a century? More? She'd asked to see him, and now she was here . . . If Mikael had been standing behind him with a white oak stake at that exact moment, Klaus might have died a happy man. Better than that, though, was to live—to live in the astonishing glow of this remarkable young woman, and to know that it was within his reach to win her over.

"I could not have stayed away," he murmured, speaking the absolute truth. He had never seen her handwriting before that evening, but he had recognized it on sight. Nothing could have kept him from this meeting, not even the very real possibility that it might have been a trap.

He had never truly believed *that*, though, not really. This was not Klaus's first midnight rendezvous with a woman, and they usually all had the same purpose. Crickets sang nearby, and the scent of honeysuckle wafted toward them from the vines that climbed the garden wall. It was perfect.

"I needed to see you again," she breathed, so softly that at first he thought he had misheard her. Then she lifted her face to gaze at him earnestly, and he knew there had been no mistake. "I thought I knew who you were before I even met you, Niklaus Mikaelson," she told him, "but every time we speak I seem to learn something new. There is depth to you, and passion of course, and a kind of honor I didn't expect to find. I am more drawn you to every time I see you, but we could never be together. Now that I've come to know you a bit more fully, I feel it's only right to tell you so myself, face-to-face. I have asked you here tonight to make you understand that you must let me go."

Klaus found himself at a rare loss for words. So he

kissed her instead, his lips pressing firmly against her warm ones and his hand gently holding the back of her head in place. She kissed him back, tentative but curious. When she pulled back she rested her dark head against his chest, and he could feel her heart racing. He could have stood there just that way for the rest of the night, if she would agree to it.

"Niklaus, I'm engaged," she reminded him. Her voice was a bit muffled against the collar of his shirt, but to his keen ear she sounded confused and indecisive. Then she straightened, running her hands over her face as if to brush away any lingering traces of him. "I wish that the things you said the other night could become our reality, but my engagement is too far gone already. I have made promises, and I made them of my own free will. I have an opportunity to seal the peace for good, and if I back out now there will be a slaughter. Hundreds dead on both sides, and it will all be because of me. Because I was weak, and because I put my own selfish desires above the lives of everyone else I love."

It was unsettling that she chose the past tense when speaking of him, but he did not feel that hope was lost. "Nothing needs to be decided tonight," he urged gently. "You are not yet married—there is time to consider."

"It's not just that." Vivianne would not meet his eyes, and Klaus felt a stab of fear. Why had she said that she could "seal the peace for good"? What did that mean exactly? It could not be the simple act of her marriage. There was something more, and it was something that he needed to know.

"Tell me," he insisted, and he saw her shiver.

"They want me to change," she whispered. "The Navarros. They say I was raised as a witch, and so I need to become equally werewolf."

Of course they did. Klaus understood it all immediately. If Vivianne were to activate the wolf within her, then the alliance would be undeniably skewed in favor of the werewolves. She would be truly stuck between both worlds, and married to a man who belonged to only one of them. "And they do not want you to speak to anyone else about this," he guessed.

Her answering nod was small, and she glanced over her shoulder at the villa behind her. She knew something was wrong with this request, no matter how much she wanted to believe that neither family would let her come to harm. She was young, and for all of her steely intelligence, she was also naive. She did not yet understand how vulnerable her sweetness made her, and so it would fall to Klaus to rip the throats out of anyone who attempted to use it against her.

"It was part of the pact," she admitted haltingly, "that they wouldn't ask me—that I wouldn't have to—"

The witches had been wise, but it may have been all for nothing. The werewolves weren't as interested in the pact itself as they were in using it to gain the upper hand. "That you wouldn't need to kill a human and become a full werewolf," he finished sternly, wanting to make her hear the full measure of what she was considering. In order to activate her werewolf side, she'd have to commit murder, and then she'd change on the full moon . . . and every moon after that. "I can't imagine anyone who loves you wanting that for you."

Not to mention that there were those who believed it was bad enough to be one type of supernatural being, and the thought of two active powers living in the same body sounded hellish. Klaus himself had killed thousands of times, and yet he could not become a werewolf, because his mother had prevented it. She had cast a spell to cut off that part of him, locked it away forever and called it "balance." Her magic honored nature, except when her pride or infidelity perverted it. Because of Esther's hypocrisy, this was a path down which he could not follow Vivianne, should she choose to go.

"*I* don't want it for myself," Viv retorted, her lovely face betraying her agony. "But I want it for them. For us. For New Orleans and my parents and the werewolves and the witches and the humans who won't be caught in the crossfire anymore. Becoming a true werewolf is the only way I can ever really be a part of their pack, so that they will listen to me and accept my marriage."

Why would they bargain for it if they didn't intend to accept it, Klaus wanted to ask her, *unless it was to spring this on you when the moment grew near?* But she wasn't ready to hear that truth, he knew, and it would only drive her away from him. "If they do not want you as you are, they do not deserve to have you," he growled instead, and then wrapped an arm around her waist and pulled her near to kiss her again, despite her halfhearted resistance. "Come with me tonight, and leave this trap before it can close around you."

She rested her forehead against his collarbone, closing her eyes, struggling with herself. "This has to end, you and me," she argued, and her voice was rough with tears. "I felt like I had to tell you in person, but I am sorry if that only caused you pain. It hurts me more than you know."

"Then undo it," Klaus said. "I will forget that you ever said these things, and you can do the same. Nothing is done yet. No one is married; no one is dead."

"It *is* done," she argued, pulling back and staring up at him earnestly. "It was done as soon as I was born. I can't know what is required of me and walk away. How can I? You don't understand what it's like, to live between two warring worlds like this. I never asked for the responsibility, but there is no one else who can accomplish what I can. If I refuse now, it will ruin everything."

She was as right as she was wrong: Klaus's dual heritage had *started* a war, just as Vivianne hoped that hers would end one. "I am already ruined, Viv," he told her. "Meeting you has ruined me. What do I care if the rest of the world burns as well? Having you with me would be worth any price."

Light and laughter spilled out into the garden from an opened door, and Klaus shrank back against the wall, pulling her with him. "Vivianne!" a merry voice called. "Darling, where have you gone? You're needed at cards—my mother has made a fortune off us in your absence."

She gave a panicked start and pulled violently out of his arms. "Klaus, please, don't make this harder than it has to be," she pleaded, but if leaving him was difficult for her then he was certainly not going to make it any easier.

"Vivianne Lescheres," he began, then paused long enough that she stilled to listen, her curiosity getting the better of her. "I have never had the pleasure of meeting a woman like you, and I've lived long enough that I would know if there were any. For you I'm even willing to beg: Please don't break my heart *quite* yet."

She gave him a hesitant little smile despite herself, and when she looked up at him again her eyes held a gleam that had nothing to do with tears. "Be careful what you wish for, Klaus," she began, and then gave a small sigh. "Perhaps we could meet again, if only so I can tell you no once more."

"My dear, I promise you that the only thing you'll be saying with me is yes, and you'll say it more than once. I'd be more than happy to prove it to you, if you'll meet me again tomorrow night. Here?" Klaus felt reckless, ready to risk anything to keep from losing her.

"Vivianne, where are you?" the voice called again, and Klaus would have been happy to gut its owner with his fingernails.

Vivianne bit her lip, her entire body tense with worry, but she leaned up to give Klaus one more kiss. It lasted a second longer than a polite good-bye, and Klaus took that as the only answer he needed. He'd be here tomorrow night, and every evening after, until Vivianne made good on the promise of that kiss by meeting him again.

She struggled out of his arms and he watched her silhouette run across the grass, toward the light and the tall, thin figure waiting for her in the doorway.

Klaus didn't have to see his face to know who it was. If he could kill every living being who was unworthy to speak her name, he would have started right then with Armand. It would end up as a massacre . . . which, now that Klaus thought of it, actually seemed rather appealing. He wondered how many werewolves were in the festively lit mansion before him—Armand and his mother, apparently, but from the voices and sounds of clinking glasses, probably quite a few more. It would not be worth facing Elijah's wrath unless he succeeded in killing every one in the house—in the city, actually—this same night.

A worthy goal, but an unlikely one, and so he vented his rage on the high wall of the garden instead. His fist was unharmed, but the wall cracked and crumbled, leaving a satisfying hole in the mortared stones. It was a physical reminder that he would not give up Vivianne without a fight, even if it could not be the bloody battle he'd have preferred.

ELEVEN

*T*he cemetery was darker than Elijah remembered. Clouds concealed the moon and stars, and it seemed there were fewer lit candles than during his previous visit. A cool wind blew in from the sea, picking up the murky scent of the bayou as it came.

Elijah weaved his way through the tombs on foot, careful not to disturb any of the stones. A mournful howl drifted toward him on the wind. The covered moon wouldn't be full for a few more weeks, but the skin on his arms and neck still prickled at the sound. There was something happening in the cemetery, some kind of magic, and it was clear that outsiders would not be welcomed.

He'd rather be anywhere else, but he'd made a vow to Ysabelle Dalliencourt to prove her wrong. With Hugo's will and the deed to his house, Elijah intended to show the witch that she had underestimated him. Hopefully, she would be impressed enough by his resourcefulness to reconsider her position on granting favors to his family. The service he needed now was much smaller than a gift of land.

Ysabelle wasn't home when he'd gone to look for her, so Elijah had guessed that the only other place she'd be was the witches' graveyard. After searching through the enchanted maze for the better part of an hour, Elijah's sharp eyes finally found Ysabelle in the center of a ring of candles. She was dressed in a lilac shift with her reddish hair loose around her shoulders. Her eyes were closed, but she did not look at peace. If anything, she looked angry.

Elijah hung back and watched as she muttered to herself then opened her eyes and began to furiously mix some substance in the copper bowl that lay at her feet. She straightened again, closing her eyes and looking as though every part of her body strained against some invisible force. He wasn't sure what she was trying to do, but he could see the moment when she failed. Based on the slump of her shoulders, it looked like she'd been attempting the spell for a while without much success.

Her frustration was just another asset to him.

"Good evening, Ysabelle," he called, rather more cheerfully than was appropriate for a cemetery, especially in the middle of the night.

From the way she turned and glared at him, he was lucky that her magic wasn't cooperating at the moment. Yet another point in his favor, he thought, approaching confidently. She knew he was not intimidated by her power, and she hated it.

"And a good evening to you, sir. Can I ask why you've come to bother me in this sacred place?"

"I've come to ask a favor," he said, reaching the ring of candles that surrounded her. Their flames were so steady in the still night air that they didn't quite seem real.

"I see, Monsieur Mikaelson. But I feel like we've had this conversation before," she said, sounding interested in spite of herself.

"Elijah, please," he countered. "That other night, I wanted your help in securing a home. Now I have one." He pulled the folded papers from his breast pocket, holding them at a careful distance from the flames.

Ysabelle stood, and her deep-set brown eyes widened. "And which of my neighbors did you murder for *that*?" she demanded.

Elijah started to explain how the house had come

to be his, but even before he spoke he realized that the story would only confirm her suspicions. A complete stranger had promised his land to a vampire who wanted a home, and then had died that same night. Even if Elijah were to repeat every single word the two of them had exchanged, the tale would still sound exactly like a self-serving lie.

"None," he replied shortly, rather than making things worse by trying to defend himself. "It was left to me in a proper will by a man who died of old age and nothing else."

"Strange that you seemed to know nothing of this will when you came to me the other night begging for aid." Was her tone thick with just suspicion, or could he also detect pride? It seemed like she was *offended* that he had resolved this problem so quickly and without her help.

"I believe I told you, Madame Ysabelle," he chided, "that I would prove to you that mine is not the losing side."

She considered this, glancing at one of the gravestones so briefly that he almost missed it. "You did," she agreed, "but doing so by murder was no way to secure my allegiance."

Elijah stared through the haze of light to read the names on the stones within her circle of candles. He saw at least three marked DALLIENCOURT—Ysabelle was trying to contact her ancestors. He didn't know why, but if he could help her communicate with them, he was sure he could leverage that to gain her trust. He did, after all, know a thing or two about witches.

"There was no murder," he reminded her firmly. The idea continued to take shape in his mind as he spoke. "If you want, we can speak with the shade of the man himself, and he will confirm that he died naturally. Assuming, of course, that such a spell is not beyond your abilities."

Ysabelle's eyebrows drew together, and her mouth tightened. She obviously didn't want to admit that Elijah was right.

"I see that you are interested in ancestry, Madame Ysabelle," he went on before she could invent a reason to refuse and save her pride. "How much do you know of mine?"

The question seemed to catch her off guard, and she hesitated again before choosing an answer. "I have heard of your family," she admitted cautiously. "Your mother is a legend."

We are legends, too, he wanted to retort. Esther's reputation was the one that mattered for his purposes, but the existence of vampires was her most impressive achievement. "She worked the immortality spell on me, and here I stand before you, as alive as I was that day."

Ysabelle's lip curled in disgust. "It is not usual for a witch to fear death so," she said.

To his surprise, the criticism stung. Ysabelle was still fairly young, and didn't have a husband or children of her own yet. How could she know what a mother would do to protect her family? Esther had fled a plague only to find her family surrounded by werewolves. She had done what she believed necessary to keep the Mikaelsons together.

"Yes, but her answer to her fears provides us with a rather neat solution to both of our problems," he compromised.

"I doubt that a vampire has much to offer when it comes to my particular concerns," Ysabelle said. "If it's your tainted blood you're offering, go peddle that nonsense elsewhere. It is clean, pure magic I wish to do here, nothing mingled with the stuff that keeps *you* in this world."

"My blood is not available for purchase or trade," Elijah answered stiffly. *And you couldn't afford it if it were.* "The legacy of which I speak is a set of books containing all of the spells my mother ever worked or learned. 'Clean, pure magic,' as you say . . . for the most part, at least. Have you heard of a grimoire? I never knew if they were common among witches, or just a habit of my mother's own."

Ysabelle's mouth hung open in speechless surprise. "A grimoire—*Esther's* grimoire? It was lost centuries ago; it's nothing but a myth."

"It's a family heirloom," Elijah corrected. "It has remained with her family. Although I'm sure you can imagine why we thought it better to let the world believe it was gone."

"If we had known . . . the things she could have taught us . . ." Ysabelle twined a long lock of auburn hair around her fingers pensively. Elijah could almost see the calculation taking place in her mind. "I understand you did not want to be hunted for them, but the books are no use to you."

"They are family heirlooms," he repeated, his voice dropping to a stern rumble. She shook her hair back behind her shoulders and folded her hands together, an oddly girlish demonstration that she was listening. "What I offer you now is the use of them only, not possession. They could help you with whatever you are trying to accomplish here tonight. There is a spell that will allow you to speak with the dead; it will reach both your ancestors and Hugo Rey, who gave his house to me last night. You will speak with him to confirm the story I have told you, and then, in exchange for the gift of this spell, you will cast another one for me."

Ysabelle's face was rapt as she listened to his terms, but

at the final condition he saw doubt creep into the set of her jaw. "Which spell?" she breathed, as if she were afraid to hear the answer. "The bargain you offer seems tempting, but I *must* know what you want in return. I cannot betray my people or my principles, no matter what gifts you promise in exchange." In spite of her decisive words, she licked her lips, and Elijah smiled confidently.

"It is a simple matter," he assured her. "There is another spell in the grimoire—a protection spell. It is meant for a dwelling, to defend a home and those within it from surprise or attack."

"And you have a home now," Ysabelle finished, looking somewhat relieved. Elijah could tell that she had feared he would name some terrible price. In her eagerness, she had already conceded that the house was rightfully his.

The candles between them suddenly, inexplicably extinguished themselves. Ysabelle stepped forward and held out her hand to shake his, confidently as any man would have. "Come at dawn with the spell book. I'll be waiting for you." For a moment she reminded Elijah of her bold, lovely niece, Vivianne. But he hoped, for Klaus's sake, that Vivianne was not so eager to compromise her values.

TWELVE

O nce the French soldiers recovered from the initial surprise of the attack, it hadn't taken them long to gain the upper hand. Rebekah could tell that the werewolves were cunning, using their knowledge of the wild environs to their advantage, and laying one ambush after another. Their plan was clever, but it hadn't been enough to overcome the larger, well-organized, and better-armed French soldiers. By the time the sun rose red as blood, the wolves had melted back into the countryside.

When the sounds of ringing metal and bursting gunpowder were finally silent, Felix was called away from his guard of Rebekah. He was needed, he explained tersely through the door of her tent, to command the men in the aftermath of the battle, and to supervise the care of the wounded. Still mulling over the discoveries from Eric's room, it took some time for Rebekah to realize the full implications of Felix's new responsibilities. What he described was the role of a commander, not a second-in-command. And if Felix was in charge of the army this morning, it meant Eric was not.

She knew her brothers would say it was for the best. Eric's knowledge of vampires was dangerous, and normally Rebekah would have agreed without a second thought. There was even a possibility that he specifically knew about the Originals, and had been sent from Europe to find them. It was feasible that their father had sent spies to the New World to locate them—even if he'd probably want to save the honor of slaughtering them for himself.

If Eric had met some glorious end in a battle with "rebels," she should be grateful that he had saved her the effort of killing him herself. And yet, every time Rebekah considered the possibility that Eric Moquet was dead, her throat felt tight.

She kept picturing his strong hands and his smiling eyes. She could not believe that he wished her harm. If only she could ask him about the room, her heart insisted that he would be able to explain. She could see all of the might-have-beens so clearly that it would be too cruel for the universe to simply take them away from her.

Besides . . . she had to learn if he truly had a wife back in Paris.

She ventured out of her tent in search of information. It was a ghastly scene outside, and the enticing smell of blood was almost overwhelming. The damage was mostly contained to the outskirts of the army encampment, but the battle had been devastating. Structures had been knocked down, trampled, and burned. The prison hut was nothing but ashes. By Rebekah's count, not many soldiers had been lost, but dozens were wounded, and some might yet die—the thought whetting her appetite. It had been days since she had fed—almost a week. She *knew* she should have drained the wagoner's wife as well, and she regretted that oversight now. It was almost impossible to prevent her fangs from extending.

It would be worse in the makeshift infirmary, she knew, but there was nowhere else she could go to get answers. If Eric was alive he would be there, and if he was close to death she might not get another chance.

The infirmary tent was hot, airless, and absolutely rancid inside. Blood was everywhere, so mingled with the scent of every other bodily fluid imaginable that Rebekah didn't know whether to feel hunger or nausea.

When she caught sight of all the fresh and bleeding wounds, hunger won out.

Rebekah held a scented handkerchief to her mouth and searched for Eric. It was surprisingly difficult to recognize any individual man: They blurred together into a squirming mass of flesh and pain. They complained and screamed and prayed and laughed, and none of them looked like anyone she had ever met before, in spite of the fact that she'd seen them all at one point or another.

She did recognize the chief medic, a burly, short-haired man who looked more like a butcher. He looked careworn and harried, and his jaw was set in grim determination. She called out to ask for his help, but he couldn't hear her or pretended not to. She watched him for a moment as he moved from one patient to the next, barking orders to his assistants and keeping his weary gaze on wounds rather than faces.

Rebekah guessed that Eric would probably be somewhere apart from the enlisted men, even in a section of his own. Some parts of the long, low tent were curtained off, but anxious-looking men with bloodshot eyes and bloodstained hands shooed her away whenever she approached. No one seemed to have time to reassure or even answer her, but at least no one cared why she was there.

Finally, she found Eric in his own private corner. The

breath rushed out of her lungs and for a moment she felt almost weak with unexpected relief. She hadn't let herself think about how very much she had wanted to find him alive.

Eric's warm hazel eyes were unfocused, and his forehead was wrapped with a dingy-looking bandage. "Marion," he whispered as she approached his cot. *"Enfin, mon ange."*

Rebekah jerked back at his words. So the woman in the locket had been his wife after all. A contented smile played on his lips, and that he thought she was another woman was a stake to her heart. *"Je ne suis pas ta femme,"* she told him coldly, taking a step back from his bed.

Eric's pupils swam, then focused. "No," he agreed, his voice rasping hoarsely. "Not my Marion. You are a different kind of angel entirely. I'm glad it's you who is here with me now." The intelligent part of her wanted to be skeptical, but he seemed too weak and confused to lie deliberately.

Besides, he had thought she was an angel. It was ironic, certainly, but it was also the sort of compliment that could go to a woman's head. It also meant he had been so badly wounded that he thought he might die, and that brought the taste of her fear right back into her mouth. "Were you badly hurt?" she asked, almost afraid to know the answer.

"A scratch," he claimed with as much dignity as he could muster. "Maybe a few scratches, actually, and some bumps and a nasty kick from a panicking horse." He smiled with charming self-deprecation. "I will heal, is what I mean to say. The doctors have given me laudanum, but I think your presence for just these few minutes has done more to improve my condition than all of their arts."

After a moment's indecision, Rebekah found a nearby stool and pulled it to his bedside. "Tell me about this angel, then—about Marion," she urged, taking his hand and pressing it between hers. If her company was a balm to him, then he would have it. Besides, asking about his wife could turn out to be the best way to learn his other secrets, such as why he'd collected such a frightening mass of occult objects.

Eric winced as he turned his head so that his gaze could find her again. "Your hair is a little darker, but you looked like her, standing there," he explained with painstaking slowness. "I thought she had come to take me away."

"Back to France?" Rebekah asked, uncertain of what he was trying to tell her. Humans were so breakable, so fragile. A few angry werewolves later, and this formidable leader of men could barely form a coherent sentence. She had never given much thought to Eric's vulnerability before, and she found the whole idea quite upsetting. She tried to push it from her mind, to converse as if he were not lying in a hospital bed. "Is she waiting for you there?"

Eric's lips twisted in a bitter smile. "I don't think she waits for me anywhere," he said quietly. "I have studied and searched, and all I can believe by now is that death was the end for her. A cart horse bolted and struck her in the road, a pointless, random accident that need never have happened. And yet in that one trivial moment she went from existing to not. It seemed impossible that someone so full of life could be extinguished so utterly. I never would have believed before then that the world might simply take her from me in the blink of an eye."

"Death," Rebekah sighed, relieved. The woman in the portrait was *dead*—that was so much better than what she had thought. Then another word he had uttered caught her attention. "Studied? You've studied . . . death?"

He coughed, and she half jumped from her seat, ready to demand the doctor come at once. But the cough subsided quickly, and she sat back down. "I've studied the dark arts," he grunted. "Death and those who claim to have conquered it. Whether it's true that some people walk the earth forever, untouched by mortality." He paused to catch his breath, then went on,

"There are wealthy, powerful men in Europe who have devoted their lives and fortunes to learning the truth of such stories, and they saw promise in me. One such man sent me here to chase these tales. He thinks that the end of death itself has come to the New World, and I am someone who wants to believe that death can be ended."

The end of death. Was that what she was? How many thousands had died to sustain her eternal life? But she was glad that one thing was clear: The clutter of destruction in his tent wasn't an obsession after all. It was only an assignment. "Did he tell you more than that?" she asked, trying to keep her tone conversational, hoping it wasn't her father who had sent Eric. "I would not know where to begin to look for 'the end of death,'" she prompted.

He smiled again, the corners of his mouth crinkling in that way that always made her want to smile as well. "You are too modest," he disagreed. "I think you could find anything you set your mind to. I am only a curious widower. . . . I can hardly believe my luck that my employer invested such faith in me. He would have done better to choose someone as spirited and tenacious as you are."

She smiled automatically at his flattery, but behind it her mind worked in steady, relentless turns. That was it, then. Eric had taken an interest in eternal life, and it had led him almost innocently to a position as her nemesis. The whole thing was, just as she had hoped, a misunderstanding. In a way.

Still, Elijah would want to know about this immediately, and she had a duty to her family that went far deeper than any feelings she might have developed for Eric. The way he smiled up at her, the pressure of his strong hand beneath hers, the admiring light in his eyes . . . none of that could matter more than their safety. If Mikael was involved with the local military, she had to warn her brothers, no matter what unwelcome decisions they might make based on that information. Even if Eric was blameless.

"Your ring is beautiful," he said suddenly, and she startled to see him gazing intently at the hand that still pressed his own. "That sort of stone is rare in the colonies, is it not?"

Rarer than he knew, but one of the few in existence was in his tent and she could not possibly explain the presence of its twin on her finger.

She shifted her hand so that just a sliver of the stone was visible and half of the metalwork around it was hidden. Perhaps he only thought it looked faintly familiar, or perhaps he hadn't even connected it with the one he possessed. After all, he'd sustained some sort of head wound, and obviously had been given generous amounts of laudanum. He wasn't thinking clearly.

She pulled her hand gently from his and folded it in her lap. "A trinket," she answered airily. "A gift from my mother when I was a girl. I think it's a piece of glass—she never said."

Eric paused with the tip of his tongue resting on his lower lip, as if he was trying to think of how to keep her by his side. She found herself longing to be drawn out, to be seen and touched. She imagined the feel and taste of his mouth against hers. But the pain or the drugs had dulled his usually sharp mind, and the silence stretched out between them. The groans and whimpers of the injured men around them filled her ears, seeming to grow louder until she could no longer stand it.

"You must be tired." She realized it abruptly, jumping to her feet and smoothing the sheet that covered Eric's strong, lean torso. "I came to see that you were well, but I should not have strained you by talking so long."

"It is no strain to speak with you," he disagreed, and his hands clutched at the sheet, as if they were searching for hers. "You must visit me again. Your company will improve my health faster than any doctor."

Rebekah's answering smile was immediate and genuine, in spite of her endless questions and misgivings.

The one thing that she *knew* to be true was that she felt at home with Eric, and that he felt the same. The happy, loving, normal life she had always longed for lay before her on a folding cot in a stinking infirmary, surrounded by men who might die. And yet, he might have been sent by her father to murder her. Rebekah expected nothing less from cruel fate.

She always chose the wrong man at the wrong time. She would fall in love, making it too late to undo her mistake. "I will return," she agreed, not knowing if she spoke the truth. She stood and shook out her skirt, trying not to notice the way he watched the motion of her hands. "Rest now."

Then she strode from the tent, ignoring the groans of the wounded men as she went. She was no visiting angel who would sit by their bedsides as they lay dying. She was death herself, and she had business of her own to attend to.

THIRTEEN

*K*laus stumbled against the doorframe, cursing the long flight of stairs that led to his hotel room. Loudly. He had not been drinking, and yet he felt drunk. Over the last couple of days, he'd managed to steal a few hours with Vivianne, and the time they spent together was more potent than any liquor.

She'd not yet agreed to call off her farce of an engagement, nor would she promise to forgo the ceremony that would make her a full werewolf. But since their first clandestine meeting in the Navarros' garden, it'd become clear that she was not willing to give up Klaus, either. Every time he came to her, she lit up as if from within. Even blood could not bring him the same satisfaction, the same fullness, as the planes of her perfect face when she angled it up toward his.

But it was a different face that waited in the dim shadows of his hotel room—soft sweeps of peaches and cream rather than Vivianne's sharp, contrasting angles. Klaus felt his lip curl into a snarl. "Sister," he greeted her as politely as he could, under the circumstances. "I would have sworn this was *my* room."

"I would have sworn you were too drunk to know the difference," Rebekah retorted casually. She lounged comfortably on his tasseled bedding, her eyes on some scrap of paper in her hand.

"I am surprised you even remembered which hotel we live in," he sniped back, stepping forward to get a better look at the paper. It seemed familiar, although it was hard to be sure. Pointedly, he didn't close the door behind him. He wanted her to understand that she was free to leave just as soon as she liked. Sooner, even. "Haven't you enlisted in the French army by now?"

Rebekah looked up at him, the rage in her eyes visible even in the gloom. "And whom have *you* joined forces with?" she snarled contemptuously, shaking the page in her hand as if it should have made the answer obvious. "You certainly aren't working with *our* family anymore."

Klaus lit a candle, holding his hand around the tiny

flame to shield it until it could catch. The room warmed into shades of gold and green, with heavy walnut furniture scattered across an intricately patterned rug. The extra light also showed Rebekah's temper, but he still couldn't see what was written on the other side of the paper. Klaus felt a twinge of frustration, but was not about to admit any weakness.

"I hardly think you're in a position to say what I'm doing or whom with," he told her coldly after he had set the candle down on a table, "considering how long it's been since you've bothered to check in. Where is this human army you were supposed to be securing for us, Rebekah? Have you won their allegiance to our cause or just wasted your time whoring around with a few of the prettier officers?"

Rebekah leaped from the bed and slapped him hard across the cheek. "Have you lost your mind?" she shouted, and Klaus could hear agitated voices complaining from nearby rooms. Rebekah didn't seem to care as she shoved the bit of paper closer to his face. "Explain this," she demanded, at an absolutely unreasonable volume, considering the hour. The sun was not yet up, and neither were most of the hotel's guests. At least when Elijah secured them a home they could fight in peace.

Klaus's eyes focused on the paper, and he felt a rage rising within him that would drown out his sister's like the ocean swallowing a single drop of rain. The long, sloping handwriting on the page was immediately, intimately familiar to him, and his mind raced with all of the private, practically *sacred* things Rebekah might have read. She had no right. "That belongs to me," he reminded her, his voice a low, warning growl. "Show some sense for once in your interminable life. Set it down, and go."

"Sense!" she snorted, tossing the letter on the bed as if Vivianne's thoughts and words were trash. The note in which she'd invited Klaus to their first meeting was the most important treasure he had in his possession, and Rebekah simply threw it aside. "Tell me all about sense, brother. Tell me all about how your torrid affair with that child is really just a plot, and not a total betrayal of our kind. Tell me what sweet nothings you whispered in her ear to seduce her into *marrying that goddamned wolf* like she was supposed to do all along!"

"My affairs are none of your business," Klaus argued. "That cursed alliance between the witches and the werewolves was never what you and Elijah thought. You should thank me for interfering, and you would if you weren't so blinded by your own stupid optimism."

"My 'optimism' doesn't apply to anything done or said by *you*," Rebekah spat viciously. "You've been a walking disaster for one century after another. I've given up on expecting you to ever stop and think before you bring the walls down around our ears, but surely even you can see how incredibly predictable your behavior is by now. Life gets too easy, and you get bored. Things go smoothly, and you do everything in your power to ruin them."

"Enough!" Klaus shouted, losing his self-control. "Of all people, Rebekah—of everyone in the world—I would expect you to remember that passion does not ask our permission before it strikes."

Rebekah hesitated briefly, but then her jaw set in anger. She thought he was manipulating her, he realized, and it was best to let her believe that. He'd rather she think him a bastard than a fool. He was suddenly shattered by his feelings; he felt possessed by them.

"All you desire is *trouble*," Rebekah scoffed. "Seeing the rest of us struggle to clean up after you when we could have just followed our perfectly good plan from the start."

"Speaking of that good plan," he said, his voice a low rumble, "I *still* haven't heard your report on our army. But I *did* hear about something else interesting: a werewolf attack, right on the spot where my own dear sister was supposed to be pressing our agenda. So I asked around a bit. Imagine my surprise to hear that my same sister had been dining with the handsome captain every night, and then she visited him in the infirmary like a good little camp follower. So tell me, Rebekah, where has your plan failed? You are in position. You have his trust. Why have you not moved to take command of his men?"

Rebekah's pretty mouth gaped open so comically that he nearly laughed. "You spied on me?" she demanded. "You took time away from your juvenile romance to *spy* on me? You could have destroyed my cover!"

"You *have* no cover," he reminded her cruelly. "You have become exactly what you were pretending to be—a pathetic damsel in distress, living on crumbs of affection from Captain Moquet."

Rebekah bit her lip, and Klaus saw that his words had hit home. She really *did* love her dashing soldier-boy, at least as much as she could call any of those doomed infatuations of hers "love." Now that Klaus knew the truth, he had even less patience for his sister's tiresome affairs. As always, it would be his job to drag her, kicking and screaming, back into the fold. Did she never tire of resisting her fate and failing miserably at it?

"It's more complicated than you know," she murmured, then tossed her honey-colored hair back and raised her voice. "The army knows that supernatural beings exist, and they may even suspect that we are here in this city. I have *had* to move more slowly, to investigate and make sure that our secret is not exposed. I wouldn't expect you to understand caution, but this is what it looks like."

The strangest, most inexplicable part of it all was that she seemed to really believe what she was saying. The twit had just admitted that she was living among a bunch of armed men who knew of vampires. And she was so oblivious, so thoroughly lost, that she actually called that caution!

If anyone in the army knew of vampires, all the more reason to compel or kill them. What didn't make sense was to wait, investigate, and fall in love . . . and yet that was exactly the path Rebekah had chosen. How like her, and how entirely *unlike* caution.

"Rebekah," he reminded her, keeping the tightest possible control over his tone. He wanted her to understand that he meant every word, that this was no angry bluster. "Elijah believes it is crucial for our family to stay together, and I see merit in that belief. But if you insist on continuing to endanger our very existence, I have a silver stake with your name on it," he warned, stepping closer. She flinched away, the backs of her knees bumping into the tasseled coverlet. "Secure the army or destroy this threat or do both, for all I care. But do *not* fail. If you cannot be relied on, you will join Kol and Finn in a coffin."

"You monster," Rebekah hissed. Even in the warm candlelight, her face was ashen. "That you would *dare* to threaten me while prancing around the city with that—that—"

"Witch," Klaus finished evenly. "A witch who is also half werewolf. What advantages does your captain possess? That is, aside from the ability to reveal our location to your father?"

Rebekah laughed mirthlessly. "*Our* father," she corrected dryly. "He certainly hates us all the same by now."

"He hated me the same from the start," Klaus muttered, furious with her for turning the tables back on him so quickly. This sort of quick thinking was why she had always been a valuable ally, but he did not enjoy being the target of her wit.

Perhaps, though, it was a sign that she was not lost, that she could still rescue this disaster. Maybe her fear of his dagger would help her remember her responsibilities.

"I have no wish to fight with you," she told him more softly, as if she could read his own softening in his face. "Both of us want the same thing in the end, do we not? Love?"

It was just the slightest bit too far. He *would* not allow her to compare her schoolgirl romance with the extraordinary revelation of his feelings for Vivianne Lescheres.

"We do not," he reminded her icily. "I want you to put our safety above your feelings, and you want me to let some upstart werewolf marry a woman that he has no right to. I will not hesitate to put her well-being above yours, and you already know I will do the same when it comes to my own. So collect yourself and behave like a Mikaelson, or you will live to regret it. Eternally."

Rebekah's gentle expression turned murderous in the blink of an eye, and Klaus was glad he had held his ground with her. She was both the charmer and the snake, and he could not be too careful. "I will do what I must," she snapped, and he noted that she didn't explain what, exactly, that would be. "You will have no cause to fear from my behavior, but I warn you that I will not be bullied or threatened this way. Get your own affairs in order, Niklaus, before you presume to judge me for mine."

She gathered her full skirt in her hands, preparing to sweep from the room, when Elijah's abrupt appearance in the open door interrupted her. Klaus smirked—it served her right to have her dramatic exit so awkwardly canceled.

"What is this?" Elijah demanded, frowning.

He held a book close against his chest, and to Klaus's

keen eye it was one he had no business carrying around. "I might ask you the same question, dear brother," he pointed out pleasantly, nodding toward the book.

Elijah glanced down at it and frowned. Klaus could tell that he wanted desperately to know what trouble his siblings had been stirring, but he was reluctant to explain his own actions. "I have a plan that will ensure our safety in this city in the long term," he answered vaguely.

"As do we all," Klaus assured him. The early warnings of daylight caught the edge of the book in Elijah's hands, a volume of their mother's grimoire. Klaus knew that Elijah was up to as much trouble as the rest of them, and he felt almost proud at the deceitful trio they made.

"We will have to see who accomplishes the most in the next few nights." Rebekah blew dismissively through her lips and pushed past them, but Klaus aimed his next words at her back as well as Elijah's waiting ears. "You may be closer than ever to finding us some quaint little hovel, brother, and Rebekah may still win us an army. But I'm building us an empire."

FOURTEEN

*E*lijah knew that he had to outrace his siblings before they started more trouble than he could stop. He didn't fully understand the scene he'd witnessed this morning, but it was clear that both were up to no good. He wasn't their keeper, watching them to make sure they avoided whatever type of catastrophe to which they were the most prone. Time and experience had proved that totally impossible. The only thing he could do was complete his mission before they had gone too far with theirs.

For that he needed Ysabelle, and there was no time to waste. The sun was just rising over the glittering bayou as he ruthlessly kicked his horse toward her house. The steady beat of its hooves marked out the next steps in Elijah's mind, and he repeated the list to himself as they raced.

The spell to speak with Hugo's ghost shouldn't take long at all, not once Ysabelle had the grimoire in her hand. There was a protection spell in that book as well, and it was a powerful one. As soon as she saw that Hugo's house truly belonged to Elijah, he would throw her on the back of his horse and race her to the property, so that she could make it into a fortress. Something told him that any moment now, one or both of his siblings was going to need a stronghold.

Ysabelle's door opened before he could knock. She was ready for him. Her reddish-brown hair was pulled into a braid that coiled neatly around her hairline, and her cream-colored gown highlighted her elegant collarbones and chest.

"Are you in more of a hurry than before?" she remarked lightly, taking in his windblown appearance with a deliberately searching glance.

"I feel a new urgency this morning," he agreed, wishing he could simply drag her from her house. But she was safe from even his lightest touch until she chose to step across her threshold, and so he would just have to remember to be courteous. "I took time to read the spell and gather what you would need," he said.

Her lips pursed together, "I liked you better when you were a supplicant," she snipped. "But very well. If you have all that is needed, we can begin." She stepped out and meaningfully closed the door behind her. No matter how closely interwoven their interests became, he knew that he would never be welcome inside her home. At the very least he could prove to her that he wasn't a liar, no matter what else he might be.

Elijah opened the grimoire to the correct page, setting it carefully in the forked stump of one of the scrubby trees in front of the house. As if they had worked together before, he and Ysabelle arranged the spell quickly and efficiently. Contrary to his assumptions, it was no simple thing, and Ysabelle's inexperience with this type of power was evident. He never thought he'd miss the more powerful witches of Europe, but he did.

By midmorning they were ready, and she took her place in the center of the circle they had drawn in her front garden. Elijah stepped back, not wanting his presence to interfere. Ysabelle sat quietly, with her wrists resting loosely on her knees and her brown eyes closed, for what felt like a year. He was sure that the sun moved to its zenith during the time she struggled to master the forces at play within her circle. Clouds covered the sun, and the meadow darkened—taking on the feeling of twilight. The birds stopped chirping, and everything was still.

Then, from one instant to the next, Hugo appeared between them.

Elijah jumped back in surprise, then stepped forward, eager to see the ghost's face clearly. He could hardly believe it, but it had worked. His human friend stood in the shallow iron bowl at the circle's center.

"Well met, spirit," Ysabelle murmured, so low that Elijah barely heard her. "I am sorry to trouble your rest, but you guard truths I need to know. Will you help?"

Hugo's clever blue eyes found Elijah before he answered. He looked much younger than Elijah remembered him, closer to thirty than seventy. It made sense, he supposed, that a person would not be forced to spend eternity exactly as they had died . . . unless that person became a vampire. "Witch," Hugo said pleasantly enough for someone who had just been dragged out of eternal rest, "what is it that you want of me?"

Ysabelle's eyes flicked sideways toward Elijah, then back to Hugo. "This—Elijah has come to me with the deed to your former house," she explained, sidestepping whatever word she might have chosen to describe him. "He wishes me to place a protection spell around the land, but I have doubts about how he acquired it. . . . I cannot allow a murderer to profit from his crime," she clarified when Hugo did not immediately respond.

"There has been no murder," Hugo responded, and Elijah marveled to see an echo of the old man he had known in the young one who stood before him. "I knew death was near, and I decided to make it count for something. When that boy there arrived on my land"—he gestured at Elijah, who raised an amused eyebrow at his choice of words—"I saw a chance to do just that."

"You expected to die that very night?" Ysabelle's face was troubled, and her gaze flickered between Hugo and Elijah as if she was not fully satisfied.

Hugo's answering smile was genuine. He seemed to be enjoying some private joke of his own. "I certainly did," he agreed. "Predictability is one of the benefits of taking matters into your own hands. Or your own mug, as the case may be."

Elijah's head spun, and then he realized what Hugo must have done. "You drugged the liquor?" he asked in surprise.

"I was finished." Hugo shrugged. The sunlight glowed in the grass around his feet, but to Elijah it looked like Hugo was standing in a different light entirely. "I have given too many years to my conflict with the Navarros. With you, I saw a chance to vex them one last time." He smiled gently at Elijah. "It turned out to be a peaceful enough way to go—far more peaceful than the other opportunities I've had over the years."

"What quarrel did you have with the Navarros?" Ysabelle asked curiously. Her original question *had* been answered, but Elijah welcomed the opportunity to speak with Hugo a bit longer. It was becoming clear that he hadn't known his benefactor at all.

"For someone without supernatural power, I made them unusually angry," the ghost said. "I was once privy to their secrets, and they liked my pipeline to gunpowder, crossbows—I was an arms smuggler. But my business needed to expand. And the convenient thing about a war, for those who deal in weapons, is that there are at least two sides."

"Hugo Rey." Ysabelle frowned. "That name sounds familiar now."

"It should," he confirmed, looking quite pleased that she had finally recognized him. "I set up a side business dealing with your lot—even importing wolfsbane thanks to the high demand. The Navarros were less than pleased when they found out." He looked pensive for a moment, then shrugged. "I was their only reliable source for arms, so they had to let me live, but I knew too much—was living on the knife's edge. And from the sound of it, peace has come to my fair city, and I realized my era was over. I wasn't going to be safe for much longer."

Hugo smiled at Elijah again, his blue eyes twinkling. "You'll have to remind them of me when you can, my boy. I'm not sure just who you are, but I have no doubt that the Navarros do, and they won't be happy to see you're here to stay."

"They're not the only ones," Ysabelle reminded them both rather tartly, but Elijah ignored the barb. There was nothing she could do about it now—he had kept his side of their bargain, and now she had to keep hers.

"Is that so?" Hugo asked. "Good thing the cellar is stocked. In times of trouble you'll want to go looking there." He winked at Elijah, who couldn't stop himself from grinning back. Not even Ysabelle's stormy glare could check his spirits.

Soon he'd be able to jam his siblings down behind the barrier and smash their stubborn heads together until they both fell back in line.

"I am satisfied, nonetheless," Ysabelle admitted finally. "I am not entirely pleased with the direction this neighborhood has taken, but there's no denying that the house is fairly Elijah's. If there's no more, we can let you return to your rest now."

"I've earned it," Hugo grunted, but Elijah felt sure he saw the ghost wink again. "Take care of the place," he added. "The door to the smaller bedroom sticks when it rains, and there's a stump in the back I think is starting to rot."

"Thank you, Hugo Rey," Elijah offered sincerely, feeling as if there was much more he wanted to add but nothing that would really make a difference. "This means more to me than you'll ever know."

FIFTEEN

*R*ebekah wasn't sure if she felt like crying or kill-ing as she stalked past the drab tents of the army encampment. She wouldn't do either, having more self-control than Klaus gave her credit for. She had to handle this little problem diplomatically, or she was not the asset her family needed her be. Klaus might as well dagger her and be done with it.

So instead of giving in to her baser instincts and massa-cring the lot of them, Rebekah had decided to rededicate herself to the task at hand. She had fed in more than one alley last night, replenishing her strength and gathering her focus. It wasn't safe to try and co-opt the army as she had once planned, but she couldn't simply walk away.

Eric knew about vampires, and he'd accepted her presence too easily—he had to be searching for a deeper truth about her. His innocent questions and idle comments replayed themselves in her mind. He might have decided to keep her within arms' reach while he studied her, probing for weaknesses. Perhaps staking the werewolf had been nothing but a test of her resolve. But she was now determined to steer him off of his path in order to keep her family safe.

The soldiers were still laboring night and day to rebuild the damage the werewolves had caused. None of them seemed to notice her slipping into her tent, where she should have been all along.

She barely had time to make herself at home when she heard the sound of a throat clearing outside the walls. Crossing the piled carpets, she pulled open the flaps of her tent to see who waited outside.

Eric started forward when he saw her, gesturing for his guard to hang back. A clean white bandage, much smaller than the last one, circled his head at a rakish angle. Now that he was out of danger, the reminder of his battle scar made him look tougher, more rugged. The change was attractive, she noticed in spite of herself.

"Madame," he greeted her, as courteously as he could with his heart pounding so hard she could hear it. He was almost a foot taller than her, and he bent from his great height to kiss her hand. "Rebekah. I was becoming concerned about you. After your visit to the infirmary it was like you disappeared." His heartbeat steadied, and she stepped backward invitingly, encouraging him to follow her inside. "I hope it was nothing I said. . . ."

"I have been keeping to myself," Rebekah improvised. The distance between them felt much more intimate within the low cloth walls, as if the shadows of the tent were pushing them together. "With so much going on, I did not want to be in the way."

Eric's lean face smiled in understanding. "I have heard that you were extremely brave during the rebels' attack. It was also very selfless of you to visit with the wounded. But a battle is no minor thing, even for hardened soldiers. It shouldn't have surprised me that you would need some time to recover."

She couldn't argue, no matter how ridiculous that sounded to her. She had killed more men on her own in a day than had died in that little skirmish. She certainly hadn't huddled here, panicking like some weakling. "It took time to sink in," she agreed, trying to sound numb rather than bored, "and I did not feel able to face anyone once it had."

"I have just the thing to get it all off your mind," Eric responded crisply. He leaned his torso through the flap and signaled to the two men outside. They passed him some kind of folded cloth and a basket, but the only thing she could focus on were the vervain flowers he held out to her. "These are for you," he announced. "And I'd like to invite you for a ride out into the countryside to restore you to your former self. Our lunch is packed."

This time it was the sound of her own heartbeat that pounded in her ears. Was he trying to test her? To see what the poisonous vervain would do to her? The purple spikes were mingled with other blooms, and a matching length of ribbon (where had he found purple ribbon out here?) tied them all together. He was holding out a bouquet and inviting her on an outing—what new, twisted plot was this?

She struggled to calm herself. Did he know some of the flowers would burn her? He might suspect so, or even hope. But if she was to outsmart him, the best thing she could do was to continue playing her part. Flowers and a picnic lunch in the countryside. Why not? If she refused them it would look terrible. . . . Although if she touched them, the entire charade would be over.

Eric watched her curiously, but she couldn't tell if it was with eagerness or concern. "I wanted to thank you," he went on haltingly, as if her pause had made him nervous, "for your visit to my bedside. It must have been very difficult for you, but it was deeply moving to me." His smile was absolutely winning. The easy flash of his teeth, the genuine happiness in his hazel eyes. In spite of herself, Rebekah was dazzled by this man all over again.

If she wanted to leave this camp without a slaughter, she would have to pull herself together. "I love the idea of a day away from this place," she agreed, trying not to think about how appealing it sounded to spend the day with him. She was going along to avoid suspicion, after all. If she *wanted* to be alone with him, to see that smile meant only for her, to touch him . . . wouldn't that only help to make her pretense more believable?

"These are lovely," she smiled. "But when did an army captain have time to go flower-gathering?"

Eric had the grace to look a little abashed. "Fortunately, I have assistants who possess a wide variety of talents," he explained, although whether he meant that one of his men had chosen the vicious weeds or run the camp for him while he performed the task she couldn't be sure.

"How considerate." She improvised, leaning forward carefully and pretending to smell the bouquet he still held. She caressed his arm through the rough sleeve of his uniform, hoping he would not notice that she only touched him and not the flowers. She knew that if their positions were reversed, she would not have noticed anything but the stroke of his fingers. "Would you put them in the pitcher there for me until we return? I cannot carry them while we ride."

She could hear the unsteadiness of his breath. She thought she saw his eyes flicker briefly to the flowers before returning to hers, but she could not be sure. "Of course." He recovered his composure and set the bouquet gently in the empty earthenware pitcher she had indicated. "Safe until our return."

Without water, the flowers would wither in the heat of the day, and in the meantime, she could work on prying out every bit of information that she possibly could, free from distractions. And if she enjoyed his company while she did it, she could hardly help that. She would kill him if she had to, but her feelings in the meantime were no one's business but her own.

Rebekah remembered to turn her daylight ring around just before Eric helped her onto her horse. The site he had in mind for their outing was about an hour's ride away, through sun-dappled clearings and onto a grassy bluff overlooking the river. By the time Eric pulled up his horse, Rebekah found herself more relaxed and refreshed than she would have thought possible. No matter her real agenda—or his, for that matter—a day in the countryside with Eric Moquet was exactly what she needed.

He spread out the blanket with a flourish and set the basket in the center of it. Rebekah, whose appetite was already reasonably well sated from the night she had spent in town, picked politely at the cold lunch, biting a piece of cheese into smaller and smaller triangles and popping grapes against the top of her mouth.

There was wine and a tiny bottle of absinthe, and Eric imbibed freely—so freely that she began to wonder if he had really been intending to trap her with that toxic bouquet, after all. Would he be so careless if he truly thought he might be alone with a monster?

"I hated to be relieved of my duties these last few days," he admitted idly, taking a pull from the flagon of wine. "I could hardly stand not knowing what was happening in my own command."

"I know the feeling," Rebekah said, leaning her head back to let the breeze cool her face. "I was once—sick— for a long time, and it was maddening to wake and realize that life had gone on without me."

"I cannot imagine," Eric replied, gazing at her. "I think that the world *must* have stopped turning without you fully present in it."

Rebekah was not prone to blushing, but now she couldn't help it. To hide how flustered she was, she jumped to her feet. "Will you walk with me for a bit?" she asked. "I think the wine is going to my head in this sun." She had barely touched her glass, but he stood courteously and brushed the wrinkles from his clothing.

"I would be delighted to walk with you," he replied formally, taking her arm. She had to look away from his mouth. His lips were somehow both soft and firm. She could imagine them on her throat, on the hollow above her hip bones . . . everywhere.

Rebekah kept her eyes on the sparkling skein of river below them as they made their way along the edge of the bluff. It seemed as though she changed her mind from one minute to the next: She simply couldn't tell if he was hunting her, or courting her. She should be able to figure it out, after centuries of life. It was ridiculous that she still didn't know the difference between a man who wanted to bed her and one who wanted to kill her. Yet here she was, with all the evidence pointing one way and all of her instincts pointing the other.

"Do you know who the men were, who attacked us?" she asked, turning the conversation back to her strategy.

Eric waved dismissively. "Rebels." He shrugged. "Well-enough organized for what they were, but there was no sign that they were connected to any larger group. There are always malcontents when a lawless land submits to formal government. I expected nothing less, but we're now closer to a safe, peaceful New Orleans."

Rebekah wished that were true. Klaus was about to plunge the whole region into another chaotic civil war, and it would be one the army was not prepared to combat. Rebekah had once imagined the French soldiers as cannon fodder, as a horde of faceless, struggling bodies between her family and the other clans. She had to admit now that their leader had become something entirely different to her. "It is a city eager for peace," she replied neutrally.

"Yes, and I want to protect other citizens from the fate that befell you," he explained, avoiding her eyes.

She wondered if his awkwardness was due to conflicted feelings over her widowhood or any suspicions about her true identity. "That's very noble," she told him, because it was true either way.

They reached the first scattering of trees that signaled the thicker, wilder forest ahead. Enough sunlight shone through to nourish glossy green grass, and birds sang. Rebekah could feel the teeming life surrounding them, almost pressing in on them.

He walked so close to her that she could feel the heat of his skin. Suddenly, he grabbed her wrist, stopping her. Was he about to try and fight her? No . . . he was turning her to face him. He paused, muttered, "I hope you'll forgive me," and then he stepped even closer and pulled her in by her waist to kiss her.

It was light at first, questioning, and then his mouth found hers again with fresh urgency. He pressed against her until her back came up against the trunk of the oak tree whose branches spread above them. Then she pressed back, driving her body against his, knowing only that she could not be close enough to him.

Minutes or hours or days later he broke off their kiss, taking half a step back and holding her by her shoulders. "I have wanted to do that since the night we met," he told her, his mouth curving into a satisfied smile. "I was just afraid it would be too soon. Then I saw you beside me in the infirmary, and I knew that I could not let you go."

"I'm glad you did," she whispered, wishing that he were kissing her again already. The wrongness of it— that he might be dangerous to her, that she should not risk trusting him, that Klaus would stake her if he knew how much she was enjoying this—made it even more appealing. Perhaps she had more in common with her brother than either of them would have thought. "It was . . . not too soon."

"I know your loss is still recent," he said, and she tried to find an expression somewhere between sad and vixenish. "But I also know that life is terribly, impossibly short. I have not felt this way since my . . . since—"

"Since Marion died," she finished for him, wishing that she had never inadvertently pretended to share the same kind of loss as he had experienced. It felt like cheapening his grief somehow, to have faked her own.

"Since then," he agreed, seeming relieved not to have to say it himself. "We are both alone in the world, Rebekah, and both living with the reminder that even those closest to us can be taken at any time. There is no time to waste." She could see that there was more that he wanted to add, but he hesitated. She could still taste the sweetness of his mouth, and felt almost drunk off it.

"Do not waste any, then," she urged him, realizing that she was not afraid of whatever he might say. He could tell her all about vampires, or even ask her if she was one. At that moment he could have said anything at all, and she would have accepted it.

"There is no time to waste," he repeated softly, lifting a calloused thumb to trace her lips with an expression of wonderment on his face. "Whatever years or seconds or decades are left, I want to spend them with you. And so I hope you will understand that, and not simply assume I am mad, when I ask you to be my wife."

SIXTEEN

Vivianne had been crying. She had cleaned her face and concealed the signs expertly, but Klaus could see a tightness around her mouth and faint traces of swelling below her eyes. He reached out to stroke her face, his hand lingering along the fine line of her jaw.

"Whatever it was, it doesn't matter now," he told her softly. "You know you have only to say the word and I will take you away from this pain. You don't have to continue with this double life any longer than you choose to."

Vivianne glanced back at the elegant mansion on the far side of the garden. Its windows were all dark, as they always were at this hour. And yet she seemed keenly aware of the witches within, of the family she was betraying by meeting him night after night.

"I had a fight with Armand," she admitted, slipping herself into Klaus's arms with the ease born of practice. "A terrible fight."

"Terrible enough that the wedding is off?" he asked optimistically, nuzzling his face against her hair. It smelled of lilacs.

She pretended to shove him away reprovingly, but her heart wasn't in it and he didn't retreat an inch. "He has said all along that it was my choice if I want to become a full werewolf, that he would make his family respect my decision either way."

"He has the face of a liar." Klaus tugged her closer to him. "I assume he meant he would respect your decision either way as long as you made the one he really wants you to make, then."

Vivianne bit her lip and looked away. He could see from her face that she didn't know whether to cry again or laugh. He couldn't imagine Armand had ever seen this side of her—there was no way she was ever so freely herself around anyone but him. Eventually, she would understand the benefits of that and agree to be only his, but would she do it before the werewolves bullied her into joining their ranks? He hoped so, but she was proving impressively stubborn.

"I thought as much," he muttered, and she didn't need to speak to confirm his guess. "He won't make much of a husband at this rate. I understand that honoring one's word is generally expected in a marriage."

"You have no idea what a marriage requires," she snapped. "How many hundreds of years have you lived as a bachelor, again?"

Klaus smiled indulgently. Over the course of their nights together he had come to learn that the harder she pushed him, the more she wanted him near. It was a surprisingly fetching habit. "Until I met you, my dear," he reminded her. "I have not been a bachelor in my heart, at least, since the moment I first held you in my arms."

"That tedious dance," she muttered, but then she kissed him again, and he could think of nothing but her soft, supple lips until she pulled away.

"That boring party was the best night of my life," he told her, his voice low and hoarse with emotion, "except for every night since." He couldn't hold back the full truth of his feelings anymore, and he realized he didn't even want to. "Vivianne Lescheres, you must know that I love you."

She smiled up at him, and for once there was no trace of sadness in her face. "I know," she answered simply. For a moment he was taken aback—he had expected her to return his words. But that was classic Viv. . . . Everything in her own time.

He knew how she felt, and he could wait as long as she needed to tell him. "I am yours, love," he told her with utter conviction. "Command me and I will obey, except to leave you alone among the wolves. That I can't do."

"Leave me alone with *you*," she whispered, running her fingers lightly up his chest. "Take me away from here—now. I want us to be the only two in the world tonight."

He did not pause to clarify what she meant—he didn't even wait long enough to answer her. Instead he climbed to the top of the wall, then turned to take her raised arms and lift her up beside him. He held her tightly as he jumped to the ground on the other side, and then ran hand in hand with her through the cobblestoned streets until they reached the Mikaelsons' hotel.

Fortunately, the other two Originals were up to no good somewhere, and so Klaus was confident there would be none of the previous night's interruptions. He locked the door to his room behind them nonetheless, then turned to find Vivianne, fresh tears wet on her cheeks, gazing sadly at his most recent painting, which still remained on its easel.

Its tone was lighter than most of his work, begun just in the last few days. His blues were warmer, the greens that intersected them more vibrant. The trees suggested at its edges were alive, and the vast ocean inviting. Vivianne stood and stared at the proof that she was his joy, and she wept.

"It's something I do when I think of you," he told her, and she smiled ruefully.

"You don't just drink and carouse?" she asked, a slight edge in her voice. "I am not sure you live up to your reputation."

He chuckled. "I did try that, my dear," he argued pleasantly. Now that she was here, he felt giddy. There was nothing left to hide from her. She had made her choice and he could be exactly who he was. "It didn't work. There is no antidote to you except more of you. And more again after that."

He crossed the distance between them as quick as a strike of lightning, and then softly kissed the traces of her tears away. It must be frightening to choose the unknown over what she had expected to do her entire life, but he vowed that she would never regret it for a moment. His lips moved to her mouth, and she smiled, though her eyes remained serious.

"I'm sorry," she whispered. "I don't mean to be sad. I am so, so happy to be here with you, and would not choose to be anywhere else tonight. It is only difficult, to forget . . . everything. Everything else."

"Nothing else matters," he assured her, deftly untying her white silk dress as he spoke. "We are here tonight, you and I. In the morning we will—"

"Nothing," she interrupted firmly. "In the morning nothing. Just be with me now, tonight." In the morning *everything*, he knew, but if she was not ready to speak yet of their future, then he would not.

Her gown slipped to the floor, then all the layers beneath it, and she barely seemed to notice that it was gone. She looked slighter and yet somehow stronger without it. Standing just in her corset, her breath was steady and sure, and her bare arms gleamed in the moonlight. She already looked like the queen he would make of her.

Then she kissed him again, and her fingers worked among the fastenings of his clothes just as he tried to discover the secrets to hers. They raced silently, unhooking, unbuttoning, and untying, all while trying to keep their mouths connected, their bodies close.

His hand caught her raven hair and he tugged it gently, pulling her head back to expose her white throat. His tongue traveled from her collarbone to her jaw and then back again, and he felt the vibration against his lips as she laughed. "I'm not your meal tonight, vampire," she reminded him tartly, and somehow she shifted her weight while tangling their ankles together so that he fell heavily onto the bed beneath her.

"You are my everything," he agreed, and flipped her over so that her body was trapped under his own. "I will drink only you or anyone but you, as you command." He kissed along her collarbone, then paused to whisper in her ear. "But command me quickly, my love, or else I am bound to get ideas of my own."

Her laughter was a liquid ripple in her throat. "You think I would care what fool you drain, as long as your love belongs to me alone?"

"I do." He grinned and moved himself down along the length of her, so that his mouth rested on her creamy thigh. He could feel the beat of her heart through the artery there, and it was intoxicating. "I think that you will come to wonder what it would be like, to have that bond as well as all of the others we will share." He bit her playfully, not breaking the skin or even leaving a mark. She gasped all the same, her back arching up toward him. "I think you will be curious, and then you will beg me to try you, and then you will never want me to taste another."

She laughed again, more brilliantly this time. Her fingers wound through his hair, keeping him near. "You will suffer so, in this imagination of yours."

He ran his mouth up along her body, and she moaned softly. "Suffering is not my aim," he assured her. His lips moved lightly, teasingly, only touching her enough to make her ache to be touched more. "It is not mine, either," she whispered. Although the room was warm, goose bumps rose on the delicate skin of her abdomen. Klaus's body hummed with the anticipation of hers.

With a wicked spark in her black eyes, she took hold of his hips and guided him into her. He knew she was still pure, and he had intended to be gentle, careful. But she was as game and as fearless as ever, and he could feel himself nearly drowning in her desire.

From then until dawn he made sure that she could not speak another clear word.

SEVENTEEN

*T*he house was huddled so low to the ground that its silhouette barely made an impression against the night sky. Elijah knew that Rebekah would be livid and Klaus would be petulant, but at least they would be safe. Once the protection spell was cast, they would be able to weather any storm within its walls. Surely that was the only thing that really mattered.

Ysabelle's face looked tense and drawn. She must be nervous, he knew. The first spell had worked, and now she had a taste of what the grimoire's power could do for her. She needed this spell to go just as smoothly, though, or else she would be no better off than she had been before. The anxiety crackled around her like static, and he hoped it would motivate her to do her very best work for him tonight.

"We need to establish a perimeter around the land," she told him, and he could hear a little quavering in her voice. "With fire."

Working in opposite directions, they spread peat from the bayou in a thin line along the chalky ground. It was harder than he had thought it would be to keep it flowing steadily and evenly while trying to keep his footing in the dark, and he lost track of Ysabelle's progress before he had finished one full side of the large, uneven quadrangle of the land's border.

He could not help but smile, though, as he passed a large stump near the back edge of the land. He suspected it was the one Hugo had mentioned during their séance, the one that was rotting and would need to come out. Supervising repairs and improvements would be one way to keep his siblings busy, he decided, and Rebekah especially would have some choice things to say about the furnishings. There would be plenty for them all to do to make the place more comfortable.

Plenty to keep them out of trouble, and safe in the fortress. No one would be able to set foot on this little patch of ground unannounced. No witch or werewolf could enter without an invitation, and no weapon could touch the house or those sheltered within it.

No matter what happened this would always be a safe haven.

Ysabelle strode toward him, pouring out the last of her peat as she went. The perimeter was complete, and the two of them stepped inside. Ysabelle muttered a few words under her voice and a small flame licked up from the place where their two lines had joined. It took hold, and then it began to spread hungrily in both directions.

"Now the work begins in earnest." Ysabelle delicately touched the worn leather cover of Esther's grimoire. Elijah knew she had studied the spell and almost certainly memorized it, but they could not be too prepared.

She had mixed most of the required potion beforehand, but some elements had to be added at the last possible moment. Ysabelle rehearsed the incantation as she ground up some kind of dried insects with a pestle, then poured the resulting powder into the mix. She produced a small gemstone from a pocket of her gown and dropped it in whole, swirling the potion in its iron bowl and inhaling deeply through her mouth as if she was preparing for intense physical exertion.

"Ready," she announced tersely, and Elijah felt every muscle in his body tense.

Ysabelle began the incantation in earnest, and poured a thin trickle of the potion over the flames that danced up out of the line of peat. She took a moment to observe the result, then set off at a brisk but steady walk, pouring as she went. The fire spat and sputtered where she passed, although she was careful not to pour so quickly that she doused any part of it. He lost sight of her when she passed to the opposite side of the low house, and Elijah found himself counting off his heartbeats as if they matched her unseen paces.

It felt like forever before he spotted her again on the other side of the border. As she approached him, Elijah worried that she would make a mistake and they'd have to start over. Surely she would trip over a root or run out of her potion too soon or her hand would grow tired and shake . . . but the closer he came to fear, the more perfect her performance became.

She finished in the same spot where she had begun, and cut off her chanting. There was a stillness in the air—an oppressive, heavy presence. The silence grew louder until its pressure was so great that Elijah raised his hands to cover his ears . . .

. . . And then the spell itself exploded. In the force of the invisible blast, every single pane of glass in every single window of Hugo Rey's house blew outward.

Instinctively, Elijah threw himself in front of Ysabelle, shielding her from the shrapnel. He felt a sharp edge slice into his raised forearm, and a nasty puncture just below his ribs, along the sting of dozens of tinier cuts. But they would heal on him, and he needed his witch alive.

She had a great deal to answer for.

The flames around them were gone, and so was even the faintest tingle of magic in the air. The spell had ended, and there was no question that it had failed. Elijah rounded on Ysabelle, feeling his fangs extend. "Tell me what just happened," he ordered, "and I would advise you not to try to lay the blame on the spell."

"It should have worked," Ysabelle answered uneasily, but rather than his menacing face she was staring at the windowless house. Perversely, it seemed larger than when they had begun, nearly towering over them now like a face missing its eyes and teeth.

"It should have," he agreed furiously. "Unless you have the kind of death wish that leads a person to try to deceive an Original." He could not imagine what she thought she stood to gain from stringing him along with this charade, but he would make sure it cost her.

"Deceive—" She frowned, taking in the extent of his rage. "No, of course not." She crouched and picked up the grimoire from where it had fallen during the blast. She flipped through its pages, moving her lips as she skimmed and nodded, checking off directions. "It's not the spell," she muttered, but still her eyes roamed the pages, hunting for clues. "And it isn't the way we worked it, either." Then she snapped the book shut and looked at Elijah. "It can only be the land."

"The *land*?" he rocked back in surprise. "There can be no question of my claim to it."

Ysabelle nodded, her brown eyes far away. "It was transferred to you properly, and Hugo held the deed. But . . . " She pressed her lips together and crouched to touch the chalky soil at their feet.

"But?" he prompted impatiently. She almost seemed to have forgotten that he was there.

Ysabelle's long fingers dug into the dirt. She cocked her head as if she was listening to it. "This here," she murmured, her singsong voice far away, "this was once pack land. Werewolf land."

"It was Hugo's," Elijah countered, nearly growling in his frustration. "He had the deed." If the land had never been Hugo's, then it couldn't be Elijah's, and that was unthinkable. He would kill the entire werewolf pack before he would concede that his new home really belonged to the Navarros.

Ysabelle's hand was buried up to her bony wrist, and he wondered what strength she had found to force it down so far. "*Legally* the land was his, and now it is yours," she agreed absently. "There is no question of that. But magic and the law do not always agree.

The spell does not recognize your claim to ownership because by *natural* law, this is still pack land. I think that the reason Hugo Rey's name stood out to me earlier is because I vaguely recall that he was a werewolf by blood . . . but chose not to change. So the Navarros may have given him this land when they exiled him, but as far as the magic is concerned, it still belongs to the werewolves."

Elijah started to argue, but there was no point. The spell had failed, and Ysabelle certainly had no control over the finer points of supernatural land ownership. His wounds itched as they healed, and it only added to his annoyance.

"We cannot change what was done or not done," Ysabelle went on. "Now that I understand the problem, I can see what ingredient we were missing. It will not be simple to get, but it *will* make the protection spell work for you."

Elijah raised his head, intrigued. "Out with it," he snapped. It would serve her well to remember that she had *just* failed him, even if it wasn't entirely her fault. A little fear was a powerful motivator, and an angry vampire was a frightening sight.

Ysabelle licked her lips nervously, but her voice did not falter. "You need the blood of a pack member," she explained. "A Navarro werewolf." Elijah didn't think his problems could get worse, but suddenly they had. How the hell was he going to pull that off?

Her words hung in the air as she slid her hand out of the dry earth, brushing it off against her dress. It left a dark, dusty mark on the creamy fabric that stood out as starkly as blood. "More than a drop, although not enough to kill. But I suspect killing may yet be the only way to obtain it, and that will put you in a very precarious position before we can get the protection spell in place."

Elijah frowned. He was so close, and there had to be a way to overcome this setback. This one last obstacle could also be the easiest if Elijah kept an eye out for the right opportunity. Werewolves hunted, after all, and accidents happened in the woods. The moon was only a day away from full, so he could not hesitate. "Leave it to me," he told her, and saw Ysabelle's square shoulders slump in relief. "I will get the blood tomorrow night. Be ready to perform the spell again by the time the sun rises in two days, and wait for me here."

After he took blood from a werewolf, every second would count to get the spell in place.

EIGHTEEN

"*T*ake all the time you need," Eric urged her, pulling out her chair chivalrously. "We will speak about whatever you choose, and also . . . not."

He had said variations of the same thing so many times since his unexpected proposal that Rebekah knew it must be driving him absolutely mad that she had not yet answered him. But she wasn't looking forward to his expression when she said no.

She could still feel the heat of his lips on hers; she could still hear the passion in his voice when he had asked her to marry him. She had given him every reason to believe that she returned his feelings, and the truth was that she did. Which only made what she had to tell him more painful.

"Thank you," she said instead, sitting at the beautifully laid table. "You must know how flattered I am, but I appreciate having this time to think." It was difficult to believe that it'd only been a day since their ride into the countryside. Every moment she waited to give him her answer felt like another day in itself.

His love pressed right in the center of her pain. She *wanted* to marry him. If only they could ride off together into another life and dedicate themselves to nothing but making each other happy, and she could leave her tortured past behind.

Sooner or later, though, he would likely notice that she didn't age. And Mikael would not stop hunting her just because she chose to stop caring, and Klaus would probably stake her even if Eric didn't figure out her secret and do it himself. There were too many dangers and unknowns to ever accept his proposal.

But as long as he didn't know that, then she could almost convince herself, at least for this little while, that it might be possible. And so she could not answer him.

A boy who could not have been more than fifteen brought them a crusty loaf of bread and a pitcher of acceptable red wine, and assured Eric in a hoarse whisper that their dinner would be ready at any moment.

"The camp looks almost as good as new," Rebekah offered, to change the subject. "I heard that the armory sustained some damage, though, that will require new weaponry."

"Yes," Eric agreed, looking preoccupied. "We had a source of munitions in the area who has proved very useful for resolving that sort of shortage quickly, but he cannot be found. I have sent some messages up the river, and hopefully some of the other outposts are well supplied. If we have to wait for powder and cannonry from France, we may have trouble holding our position here."

"Has it been so dangerous?" she asked curiously. Aside from the werewolf raid she had caused, the only real source of entertainment for the soldiers seemed to be the bandits they encountered during their patrols. Cannons were hardly necessary.

"We have been well-armed enough to keep the peace until now," Eric explained. "If the word gets out that has changed, I expect the rebellious factions and criminal element in this region will grow bolder."

He wanted overwhelming force, and Rebekah approved of the tactic. It was, after all, the same policy to which she and her brothers subscribed. They had built their legend through a surplus of brutality, and made sure they were always prepared to reinforce the lesson. It was why neither she nor Elijah had tried too hard to slow Klaus's killing spree when they had first landed here. She believed in holding power at any cost. If Eric wanted artillery just to keep the peace, then he was the sort of man she would consider marrying.

If she could consider marrying.

She opened her mouth to tell him she would do it—damn the consequences. She wanted to be his wife. Years from now, when she hadn't aged and he wondered why there were signs of vampire kills everywhere they went and Elijah showed up every few months to try to drag her back into the fold . . . well, she would just figure those problems out as they came.

Her thoughts were interrupted by Felix's hooked nose poking through the flap of the tent, followed in a moment by his boringly handsome face. "Sir," he whispered, as if he were close enough to speak only to Eric without Rebekah overhearing the words. "Sir, you are needed. A message has come down from Baton Rouge, an answer to our—my lady"—he seemed to notice her at last—"I am terribly sorry to interrupt, but the captain is needed at the communications post down by the river. At once, sir," he added with a guilty glance back at Eric.

Eric sighed and rose. "I will return, Madame," he told her formally, refraining from anything more intimate in front of his lieutenant. Felix must know by now that there was something more than politeness between them, but he just nodded impatiently, eager for Eric to go to his work. As he approached the tent's exit, though, Eric hesitated. "Stay, please, Felix, and keep Rebekah company while I am gone." He glanced back at her one last time.

"Yes, sir," Felix answered smartly, saluting. "My lady."

Felix was pleasant enough to look at, she supposed, but in no way was he an acceptable substitute for Eric. *For my fiancé,* she tried out in her mind, and although it sounded strange she did not dislike it.

Felix did not sit at the table with her, but instead crossed the office to rummage in one of the drawers of the large rosewood desk. "I am sorry to interrupt your dinner," he repeated offhandedly, the main part of his attention on his search.

"It had not yet begun." Rebekah stood. "What is it you are looking for?"

Felix frowned and closed the drawer. "It is nothing, Madame," he assured her. "Just an item the captain will most likely want on hand when he returns. Please excuse me a moment."

Before she could stop him, Felix stepped into the inner chamber. She waited for a surprised gasp, but none came. It made sense, she realized—as Eric's right-hand man, Felix must have seen it all by now. That made

Rebekah distinctly uncomfortable. Just how many humans in this area had heard of vampires? How long before there was nowhere in the world where they'd still be a secret?

She stepped closer to the curtain and listened intently, trying to track his progress from the sounds of shifting and scraping within. "Madame," he called suddenly, and she startled. "Can I beg your assistance?" His voice had moved closer to her now as he approached the curtain from the other side. "I am sorry to ask, but I have need of some more delicate hands than my own."

Rebekah narrowed her eyes suspiciously. Why had Eric left so suddenly, and what was Felix up to? He had resisted her compulsion at first, she remembered with foreboding. Perhaps he somehow remembered the last time they'd been in Eric's tent together. Was he trying to catch her in some kind of lie? She felt her fangs come out.

"Coming," she answered sweetly. She stepped confidently through the curtain, and caught Felix's wrist as it swung down toward her. She twisted hard, and the wooden stake fell from his hand. The smile still on her face, she turned to him. "What was it you needed?"

He kicked at her and pulled his arm away, and she let it go. "Demon," he grated, and she rolled her eyes. That wasn't really the type of talk she was looking for, but it was a start.

"I think you have the wrong girl," she suggested, although her chatty tone was expelled through gritted teeth. She had been so concerned about what Eric knew that she had never stopped to think that he might have an accomplice. "I'm the one you rescued from the dark, scary woods, remember?"

He hissed between his teeth and lunged at her. She sidestepped, bringing her raised foot down on his leg for good measure. The splintering sound it made was deeply satisfying. But there had to be a reason he was so bold in his attack. . . . Had Eric set her up, proposed to her, and then left her to be ambushed? "I know who you are" Felix gasped, and she gave him some grudging credit for not screaming. He was a trained warrior, stronger than those in the French army, and he wasn't about to give up his fight easily

However, he was human, and humans broke. "I don't think you do," she disagreed as he hurled an iron railway stake from one of Eric's chests at her face. She caught it in the air and whipped it back into the foot of the leg she'd already broken, pinning him to the ground like a butterfly.

"I can see it," he hissed, pulling at the stake. It was stuck deep in the earth, and he wasn't going anywhere. "Your pretty face and your evil heart. In Europe, I was trained by the master of all vampire hunters, and I can see that you are filled with darkness to your core. The man who sent us wants your kind dead, and I want to do his bidding."

Rebekah's whole body went still as Felix's words washed over her. So it was her father—the master of the hunters—who'd sent Felix and Eric her way. Only Mikael would have men cross oceans to kill his children. But it seemed like Felix didn't fully understand who she was, or that her brothers were here as well. And that could be her saving grace.

"Your employer may want me dead," she agreed, "but I think if he had wanted you to do it yourself, he would have told you how to kill me."

Felix's brown eyes were starting to lose focus, and Rebekah knew she didn't have long to get coherent answers. "He taught me to resist your magic so that I could stand against you. He will reward me. . . ."

His words struck another chord of truth. Mikael *had* taught Felix to resist her, which was an impressive feat on its own. Only by repeating the compulsion over and over had she bent Felix to her will. Yet, through it all, perhaps he had still retained some hazy suspicion about the night she'd snuck into Eric's tent. It might have taken him some time to recall the pieces and figure out that she was a vampire—but what was Eric's role in this? Had he deliberately left them alone tonight? If only she'd left the army encampment—like she'd left Europe—and never returned.

Rebekah pulled a silver crucifix from the nearest chest, admiring the evenness of the blade that some lunatic had sharpened to a point. "Now the question becomes: Did you intend to surprise this benefactor of yours with all of the good news at once? Or have you sent messages reporting your discoveries all along?"

Felix's eyes refocused on the crucifix, and he watched it warily. "The captain sent everything we learned," he told her defiantly. He could no longer fight her, but he could still hurt her, and he knew it. "A report the morning after you arrived, and another when your monster friends attacked my soldiers." He smiled triumphantly in spite of the pain that lined his face. "We have known your kind was here for some time, and even heard rumors that you had made some foul nest nearby. Now I have seen the truth—that there has been one of you among us all along."

It was worse than she thought. She had known Eric was hunting her, that he was an enemy of her kind. So why did it hurt so much to hear it said out loud? Felix's strained voice spitting out her worst fears felt like actual torture. "Why now?" she asked, hating the note of weakness in her voice. The ache in her heart had cost her control, and now instead of questioning him she was almost pleading. "Why try to kill me now, after I've been here so long?"

"I followed you out of camp," he explained, his labored breath hissing in and out of his lungs. "When you snuck away without a word to anyone, I followed you into the city. And then, as I watched you feed, I remembered everything. I saw what you are, what you do. I am sworn to keep the peace in New Orleans, and there can be no doubt about my duty. The captain did not know the intricacies of my plan, but he will understand what I had to do. You're a murderer, and you deserve to die."

"And yet I won't." She shrugged coldly. There was no victory to celebrate in defeating him, especially now that fear and pain had driven him into delusion. But Rebekah hurt, and it made her want to hurt Felix. And Eric, especially Eric, but she could only worry about one hunter at a time.

"Killing me will accomplish nothing, demon." Felix's words carried conviction, but his eyes looked delirious. "The hunt is only beginning. Your days are numbered."

Rebekah bent down, enjoying the dread that grew on his face as she came near. It made her feel strong. "Killing you will accomplish a great deal," she disagreed, tracing the collar of his uniform jacket with her fingernail. "Your little plot interrupted my dinner,

Felix." She smiled so that he could see her fangs clearly. "Now I'm hungry."

He tried to fight her off even then, but it was hopeless. He died with a strangled cry, and she drank her fill. She didn't bother to try to cover the marks—there wasn't a point. Eric would find the corpse, and know that it was the work of a vampire. Even if he didn't know that Rebekah was the daughter of the very man he took his orders from, it didn't matter. Her father wanted to kill all vampires, and that he'd finally found his children again would just be a special treat. If it was true that Eric had reported that vampires resided in New Orleans, Mikael might already be on his way to the New World.

Every time the facts crossed through her mind, it was as if she were learning them for the first time. She couldn't absorb them, because then she would have to believe them. The ambush may have failed, but she had still fallen into the trap.

Eric was far more to her than just an attractive man, or even an opportunity to escape into a new life. She had *loved* him. She loved him still. The betrayal was more than she could stand, but the thoughts kept coming, reminding her over and over that she had let him play her for a fool. Had he flattered her, wooed her, begged to *marry* her, solely with the intention of keeping her close until Mikael could arrive to dispatch her?

Rebekah rolled beneath the back of the tent and broke for the river, running so fast that a human eye would see no more than a blur. She hoped that Elijah had gotten the protection spell working on that sorry old house he was always rambling on about. They were going to need it.

NINETEEN

*K*laus woke in the late afternoon, fully rested for the first time he could remember. He reached for Vivianne by pure instinct, needing to pull her closer again, to be touching every inch of her. But his hand found nothing but cold, crumpled bedding, and he jumped to his feet in alarm.

She was gone. Her dress, her shoes, even her scent was fading. She had been gone for hours and hours, and soon it would be as if she had never been there at all. What had happened to her?

He dressed quickly, thinking over what had happened. Whatever they had experienced together, something had obviously gone wrong. He had missed something . . . something she hadn't wanted him to see. When she had given herself to him, she'd also been preparing to take herself away, and he had misunderstood everything.

He circled her family's home, prowling like an animal with every sense attuned to the slightest change. He could *feel* her moving between its rooms, even when he could not see her. And so he knew when she stole out of the house, although her own mother had no idea she was gone. She was escaping his love and now her family's, believing they could never understand what she was about to do.

She was wrong. She was young and impulsive and sincere, and that combination made her incredibly vulnerable to the manipulation of the werewolves.

And people called Klaus a monster.

She wore a long, black cloak with a deep hood that hid her face, but he did not doubt for a moment that it was she. He followed soundlessly, pursuing her through the shadowed cobblestoned streets until they gave way to dirt tracks. She did not hesitate, and he did not take his eyes from her concealed form. He would have killed anyone or anything that troubled her, but he couldn't protect her from herself.

He knew Vivianne better than anyone. If she truly wanted to do this, then blocking her path was futile. If he didn't stop her he might lose her, but he would lose her for sure if he tried. So he could only watch, hoping against hope that he had misunderstood her intentions.

He had not. He smelled the werewolves before he saw them. Dozens and dozens, all waiting for Vivianne. Her first kill would not be some accident in a narrow back alley—they would make a production of her joining their ranks. They would draw her in with their celebration so that she wouldn't be able to stop, and then it would be done. Irrevocable. She would become the wolf that he could not, and then she would be allied with his bitterest enemies.

They had gathered in a semicircle near the edge of the forest, waiting for her with torches and the requisite human sacrifice. Klaus was repulsed by the makeshift altar, which tried to lend an air of legitimacy to the proceedings. An unconscious man lay across it, naked to the waist with his hands bound behind him. How could Vivianne not be revolted by it? That she could believe she was amongst her own kind turned his stomach.

Vivianne threw back the hood of her cloak, and Klaus closed his eyes for a moment, remembering every single emotion he had seen on that lovely face the night before. There was no hint of a smile on her bloodred lips now. Even in the soft golden light of sunset, she looked pale and serious. Armand stepped forward to greet her, but stopped halfway, apparently reading her expression. Vivianne was obviously in no mood to be comforted. She had come to kill.

"Welcome, all," Solomon Navarro bellowed, tugging his son back into the semicircle. "And welcome, Vivianne. We are here to welcome you into our ranks, and to celebrate the union of our families. It will be formalized at the wedding, but we all know it begins here, with this bridge between our two worlds."

"Thank you," Vivianne answered. "As a girl I never gave much thought to my werewolf heritage, and I certainly never expected to find myself here. But there is no denying what I am—the common ground between the witch and the werewolf clans. And tonight I will fully embrace both halves of myself in order to make this city whole."

Klaus longed to shake sense into her, but a rumbling of approval rose from the werewolves. Their energy was high, yet so was their tension. So far, Viv had said the right things, but she hadn't actually killed anyone yet. The real party wouldn't start until she had backed up her pretty words with murder.

"Who is he?" she asked, gesturing to the man on the rough wooden altar.

"A criminal," Armand Navarro assured her. "This death is better than the one he deserves."

Vivianne lifted her chin. "I would prefer to be the judge of that," she told him. Klaus smiled in spite of himself—she couldn't bring herself to be sweet to Armand so soon after being in Klaus's bed. "What was his crime?"

A female werewolf stepped forward from the pack. She was young, with long blonde hair that was pulled back severely. "He attacked me," she answered, her voice full of steel. "He said I wasn't the first, there'd been other women before me."

Solomon crossed the line of werewolves to rest a heavy hand on Vivianne's shoulder. "He has committed innumerable crimes against humanity," Sol continued for the woman, "but it is for the crime against a pack member that he dies. You will grow used to our ways in time, and they will protect you as fully as any one of us."

Vivianne considered those words, her gaze level with Sol's. Finally, she unfastened the clasp of her cloak, letting it fall in a puddle of darkness at her heels. Armand offered her a knife, and in the flickering torchlight Klaus could see strange carvings running the length of its blade. Vivianne took it, shifting the hilt in her hand as if to test the balance. "It is for all of his crimes that he will die," she countered.

Sol nodded his consent, and Vivianne walked slowly to the altar. She seemed to be studying the man who lay across it, but Klaus wasn't sure. He hoped that this was harder for her than she wanted the wolves to know, and he wished that she would just turn and run. They would pursue her, but Klaus would be waiting. She only had to feel Klaus's presence.

Instead, she lifted the knife.

A howl rose from the werewolves, and they closed in around her and the man. There was no chance left to hesitate, and so the knife flashed down, slicing the man's throat in two just as neatly as if Klaus had done it himself.

There was a moment when the man's blood spurted out and the air meant for his lungs bubbled through the gap and nothing else happened at all. Klaus watched, stunned. The split second lasted longer than the rest of his entire life. He had been *so* sure that she would run. He had imagined spending lifetimes with her, and in one brutal moment she had thrown it all away. Thrown *him* away. She wasn't the person he thought she was, not at all.

The response from the werewolves was deafening, like they had all gone mad. The howling drowned out any individual voices, overwhelming anything Vivianne might have said. She was lost to him now, just another member of the pack. She might as well have cut his heart apart with her knife.

And then the pack was changing, shifting, crying out in an agony that matched their ecstasy. The sun had fully set, Klaus realized, and the full moon was rising over New Orleans. Vivianne would greet it as a wolf.

All around her, men and women turned into wolves one by one, but she writhed on the ground in her shuddering, breaking human form. No matter what pain this transition caused her, though, her feelings about what came after would be worse. She didn't have the luxury of shutting off her emotions the way a young vampire might have. She would have to live with her condition long after the werewolf change had grown easy for her.

It was the least she deserved.

Disgusted, Klaus turned his back on the increasingly wild scene. Their celebration would go on until morning, but there wasn't a reason for him to stay. He'd leave her to her new family and find some other way to drown his sorrows.

TWENTY

*I*t seemed impossible that there were no werewolves to be found on the night of the full moon. Elijah had been sure there would be at least one prowling the woods near Hugo's house. Eventually, he had wandered out into the forest in the hope of crossing their path, and finally had begun tracking in earnest when he had realized that dawn might come without him finding a single wolf. At this rate, he thought, he might not even need the protection spell—maybe all of the Navarros had simply left town.

He was almost on top of them before he realized his mistake.

On a curved plain between two wings of the tangled forest, hundreds of werewolves reveled. They fought, mated, and tore into raw game with their bare teeth. There was a dead man lying on a wooden platform in their midst, surrounded by sputtering torches, and Elijah could guess what they were celebrating. He couldn't remember ever seeing a changing ceremony this large before, and the game they were sharing was coming from somewhere.

Even as he watched, four wolves split off from the celebration. They had to be a hunting party, and Elijah crouched in the underbrush. Before he could overthink the consequences he put his head down and ran.

Their trail was wide and clear, with broken branches and trampled leaves leading straight into the depths of the forest. Elijah followed cautiously, trying to understand and predict their movements. The largest of them, a massive silver beast, nearly surprised him once. It paused as Elijah quickly slipped between the trees, lifting its angry yellow eyes straight at him. Elijah didn't blink or breathe, and after a moment the hulking silver monster took off at a run to rejoin the hunt.

Elijah picked up the track of one of the two smaller wolves, a quick-footed brown creature with nervous, alert ears. It hunted intently, and he pursued it with the same kind of focus. When the rest of its friends were a good distance away, he crouched in the soft dirt, measuring the werewolf's steps with his eyes.

There was no more time to lose, and so he sprang.

He wrapped one hand around the werewolf's muzzle, both to avoid being bitten and to prevent it from alerting the others. The wolf bucked and twisted, but Elijah sank his fangs into its shoulder like a cobra striking. The brown werewolf squealed through its closed jaw and fell awkwardly to the ground, trapped beneath Elijah's weight. He could feel warm, sticky wetness on his hand, and he pulled out the handkerchief from his breast pocket and pressed it to the spot.

The werewolf thrashed again, but halfheartedly this time. Elijah suspected it was wondering why he hadn't killed it already. He would if he had to, but all he needed was some blood, not the creature's life. He rolled off the injured werewolf, releasing its muzzle at the last possible instant before backing out of range.

"Run," he yelled, hoping it wouldn't try to fight back.

But instead, it crouched low and growled . . . and so did a chorus of other wolves. Elijah realized he was trapped. The giant silver werewolf was there, its hackles up, along with the rest of the hunting party.

Except there had only been four of them in the beginning . . . and now Elijah couldn't count them all. Yellow eyes stared out from every side, and the growls vibrated through the woods. The whole pack was there.

He had been recognized. They had caught an Original vampire attacking a werewolf, and now their fragile truce would come to a bloody end.

He launched himself over the brown wolf and straight at the big silver one. They tumbled one over the other, snarling and snapping, and then the other werewolves moved in. There were too many of them, and Elijah knew better than to stick around and try to defeat them one by one. He disentangled himself from the silver and sprang forward again, kicking another werewolf in the jaw as he passed.

He was faster than them, and stronger, but they were everywhere. He lashed out with fists and fangs, and, above all, kept moving forward, but he felt a sharp set of teeth rake across his forearm. It stung like fire, and broke his concentration just long enough that another werewolf's bite caught the back of his thigh, trying to sever his hamstring.

He tried to ignore the pain and forced himself onward. There was no chance for him to fend off the attacks, and he was bitten again and again. After what felt like hours, he staggered out into the emptied plain, where the dead man still lay across their makeshift altar.

His vision was starting to blur, but he could have sworn that he saw a snowy white werewolf, female by the size of her, lying beside the altar with her head on her paws. Her yellow eyes stared balefully at him, and the stars swam and swung overhead. She did not attack.

Elijah gained a little speed as he crossed open ground, and the werewolves were losing interest in their pursuit as dawn neared and the change came upon them again. The sun would be rising within minutes, and Elijah's strength was fading nearly as fast. Now and then there was a nipping at his heels, almost mocking, but most of the werewolves seemed content to let their venom do its work. With the wolves' poison burning in every inch of his body, his last thought was that he should have let Klaus kill them all. Then he saw the sun's first rays glittering off the water of the Saint Louis, and he threw himself in.

TWENTY-ONE

*T*here was no one at their "new" house, and it was even less glamorous than Elijah had described. Rebekah's clothes were soaked from her flight out of the army's camp, and she was not amused that the windows lacked glass. The sun was still not up yet, and the wind made her clothes stick to her body. And her brothers were missing.

She added her swim in the river to the list of insults visited on her by Eric and his late lieutenant. Felix had paid his share, but the tally was still rising. She wrung the musty-smelling water out of her long hair, tugging at its tangles with restless fingers.

From the evidence of whatever disaster had occurred

there, it was clear that the house was not protected. She was no safer inside than anywhere else in New Orleans. The one place she *would* be safe was with her family, and so she had to stop pacing the tiny drawing room and go find them. She pulled a musty cloak off a hook, and slammed the door shut behind her, ignoring the squeal of hinges letting go of the wood. They were already out of windows—what was one extra door? She had far more important things to worry about.

There had been a full moon, and she had heard an unusual amount of howling from the woods to the north. In her heart, she suspected that her brothers were probably right where the worst of the trouble was, so she made her way back to the river, intending to follow its line as closely as possible in case she needed to make a quick retreat. She could still cover large sections of the forested land that way, and save the depths of the forest for a last resort.

The sun rising over the bayou touched it with fire, waking some living thing everywhere it reached. For a brief, dizzying moment Rebekah saw what Elijah had seen in this place: It was as wild and confusing as they were. It would shelter them and protect them, and it could be their true home.

Then the strange, almost sourceless dawn light gleamed off something white in the river, and Rebekah stepped closer, trying to ignore the way the mud sucked at her shoes. She certainly had not thought to dress for this sort of thing while flirting with Eric, but her clothes were already ruined by her first dip in the river, so a second couldn't do them any more harm.

The floating thing didn't look like driftwood, and animals didn't wear starched shirts—not even the stained and shredded kind. With a soft cry, Rebekah dove into the water, striking across the lazy current to reach the limp body of her brother.

Elijah had been mauled. It wasn't just his shirt that was in tatters: His skin was a bloody map of slices and tears. One of his eyes was so bruised that she could not see how it could possibly open, and a bloody welt on his lip was swollen and raw. But worse than anything she could imagine was the sight of his one open, staring eye. It looked straight up into the rose-and-amber sky, seeing nothing, not even noticing that she was beside him.

The werewolves had done this to him, and she bit back a scream of rage. Under the full moon, the beasts had torn at his flesh and filled him with their poison. But why? Werewolf venom would kill a normal vampire, but not an Original. An Original could live through anything, at least anything that didn't involve a white-oak stake. Still, the pain and hallucinations were almost as bad as dying a second time, and Elijah must have headed to the river with the hope that some of the poison would seep out into the water.

So much for the supposed truce. She hoped that Klaus was eloping with the little trophy bride right now.

She pulled him close and dragged him to shore, feeling relief at the faint sound of his heartbeat. It was easier to carry him once she reached the shore, although the sucking mud and tangling grasses did their best to hold her back. She was concentrating so hard that a shout rising up from the bayou caught her completely by surprise.

A man in a wide-brimmed hat and drab hunting clothes gaped at the pair of them, then lifted his hand and called out to her again. He must want to help, and Rebekah was happy to take him up on the generous offer. Setting Elijah gently down among the reeds, she sprang on the hunter before he could even lift his rifle. She struck him hard in the head, struggling against the wild, anxious energy in her body that urged her to knock it clear off his neck.

But she needed his heart still pumping, and so with an indrawn breath she stopped herself after the first blow. She dragged his limp body back to Elijah and split open the hunter's neck with her teeth. The thick red blood flowed freely, and she turned and adjusted the gash until it was spurting more or less into Elijah's mouth. She waited, hoping that he would revive enough to feed, but whatever blood he swallowed was still better than none.

Eventually, the hunter's heart gave out. Elijah was still as vacant, but she thought there was a little more color in his pale cheeks. He must be deep within the hallucinations of the venom, and she didn't envy whatever demons he fought—he'd come back to her in time. She lifted him again and ran for all she was worth.

Back in the house, she felt unnaturally exposed. Without windows, anything or anyone could come inside. She prowled the structure's two levels, trying to find a place that felt safe enough to harbor her wounded brother, but everywhere she went, she felt *seen*. It was as if someone was lurking just out of sight, watching her progress from room to room. Part of a windowsill in one of the second-story bedrooms had splintered and skewed upward, and viciously, she tore it off and threw it outside.

Anger would not help her brother, though, and so she dug her fingernails into her soaked, muddy wool gown and started again, this time working from the top of the house downward. When she reached the ground floor again, Elijah moaned softly, and she leaped to his side to check his pulse. It still sounded terribly faint, but to her keen ears it was a bit steadier. He would recover, she knew, but she had no idea what so much venom would do to him. He needed to rest in peace.

She searched the first floor again, trying to find any protected area, no matter how humble. She threw open closets and even cupboards, looking for any enclosed space big enough for Elijah to lie down comfortably. She had crossed the living room floor three times during her hunt before she realized that her footsteps sounded different in the center of the cheerfully red woven rug. She tore it aside and beneath it she found a trapdoor.

The cellar below was damp and more than a little musty, but she didn't smell anything rank or unclean. Crates and barrels lined the walls. She pried open one and then another, finding musket balls and artillery shells and wicked-looking swords. There was an entire armory below their new house—it was a bit more defensible than she had initially believed.

The cellar was spacious and not much light filtered down through the hole in its ceiling, but Rebekah found short wooden doors in each of the four dirt walls. She moved aside a large whetstone that half blocked one of them and pulled it open, to the loud protest of its tired hinges.

Beyond lay a narrow tunnel, and, more curious than concerned, she followed it. Through another low door lay a smaller cellar, with a set of uneven stairs leading up to where another trapdoor must be. She climbed the stairs and pushed hard on the ceiling. It swung open, letting in fresh daylight. This second cellar had been hollowed out under the stump of what must have been an enormous oak tree, some distance from the house itself. Five large barrels took up most of the small space, and Rebekah vaguely remembered something about Elijah moving barrels to shelter for the owner.

The sunlight also revealed two other closed doors leading out of this smaller chamber, and she realized that there must be an entire network of tunnels and trapdoors. From the house, one could access every corner of the land without being forced to step outside and be seen. Elijah had done well for them, perhaps even better than he had realized.

A small sound came from the nearby trees, and Rebekah froze, her eyes scanning back and forth. Nothing looked out of the ordinary, and of course there were all kinds of sounds on the very outskirts of civilization. But something *felt* wrong, and she couldn't ignore her instincts. She ducked back underground, closing first the trapdoor and then the ones that blocked the tunnel behind her. It wasn't perfect, but it was certainly the most sheltered part of the house.

She carried some bedding down first, and then Elijah,

who moaned again but still stared in that blank, horrible way out of his one good eye. She decided that he was as comfortable as she could make him, so she left him to heal.

The best thing to do, of course, would be to go out and find him some more blood, but the unseen, unknown *something* outside made her afraid to leave Elijah alone. She knew it was most likely just her overexcited nerves that kept screaming that they were being watched, but she wouldn't be able to forgive herself if she walked into some trap.

She busied herself with straightening up the house, sweeping up the dust and leaves that had blown in through the missing windows and nailing the billowing curtains over their empty sockets so there was at least some kind of barrier. It made her feel a little better once she couldn't see outside, but at every noise and shadow that shifted across the fabric she jumped.

No sane person would attack a vampire blind. No one, no matter how foolish or how angry, would approach this house and burst into it knowing that she was somewhere inside. No *one*, but what if there were many? Elijah had marks on him from dozens of werewolves. The entire pack could be out there, human now but desperate to finish what they had started. Or perhaps Eric Moquet had somehow tracked her here, with his army at his back.

The Mikaelsons had come to New Orleans in search of a haven. It was supposed to be their home, their shelter. But the city had turned into a trap. They were exposed, surrounded by enemies, constantly on their guard. There was no safe harbor.

Rebekah peered out between two green canvas curtains, but the sunlit grass was undisturbed. Try as she might, she could not catch one single glimpse of someone hiding among the trees. The only thing to do was wait it out.

She rearranged furniture, chose the largest bedroom for herself, and tried to comb the remnants of the river out of her hair. She hung her gown out on the ramshackle front porch and sampled some of the previous owner's surprisingly acceptable liquor in nothing but her damp cotton shift. She waited, watched, and fought against her paranoia for all she was worth.

When the sun finally began to dip back down toward the horizon, she decided that it was time to check on Elijah again. He might be strong enough to speak, or at least to share a drink with her. He might be able to tell her what had happened, and what they should fear was coming next.

There would be no need, though, to burden him with the news of *her* recent disaster. Eric's first dispatches wouldn't reach Mikael for weeks yet, so there would be plenty of better times to break that news. They would have to leave, but it didn't really matter where they went. Rebekah understood now that trouble would follow them everywhere.

She poured some of the liquor into a flask. When Klaus arrived—if he ever got around to it—she would be free to go find some plump farmwife to help speed Elijah back to health. And Klaus always felt like he was being watched, so the eerie feeling she suffered from wouldn't bother him.

Rebekah pulled open the trapdoor and dropped down. There was a stirring of movement from the blankets where Elijah lay, and her heart leaped with the hope that he was finally awake.

Then her eyes adjusted, and a feral hiss escaped from between her teeth. Elijah was still unconscious, lying exactly in the same position, except that his one eye had finally closed. He breathed shallowly and sweat beaded on his broad forehead. His body was fighting the poison, just as it should be. The movement she saw had come from another source entirely.

Eric crouched in the dank basement, a wooden stake in his raised hand. She prayed that it wasn't made of white oak, but she could not rely on that hope. Eric was positioned over Elijah's limp form, threatening his life even as Elijah barely clung to it. Eric gaped at her in surprise, and she experienced every feeling of his betrayal again in fresh, sharp detail as she threw her body against his.

They rolled together, away from Elijah, and the weapon fell from his stunned hand. His body was as hard as steel beneath hers, every muscle taut and tensed. He tried to speak, and part of her wanted to listen. Even now, the sight and feel and smell of him drew her in, made her want to be weak. But Eric had done more than enough damage already thanks to her traitorous feelings.

She wrapped one hand in a vise around his throat, cutting off his breathing until his hazel eyes fluttered and closed.

She fantasized a thousand brutal ways of repaying him for her broken heart, but her family's safety hung in the balance, and so pragmatism won out. There was no need for another *violent* death, or for a mysterious disappearance that coincided so neatly with her own flight. His body would be found, drowned in the sea on the far side of New Orleans. It would be a mundane, ordinary death, and that would have to be vengeance enough.

TWENTY-TWO

After two full days of pouring cloying amber liquid down his throat, Klaus was starting to feel nearly drunk enough. If he could just maintain this inhuman level of intoxication for a few years, he might—*might*—start to forget the sight of Vivianne turning her back on him. As always, the kind ladies at the Southern Spot had done their best to take his mind off his troubles, and one healthy-looking, bouncy brunette in particular had made it her mission to ease his pain. She had kept him supplied with good whiskey, charming banter, and every ounce of the expertise with which she plied her trade.

Best of all, she didn't remind him of Viv in the

slightest. Except when he noticed how dissimilar the two were, and then he called for more whiskey, and the dance began again.

Sooner or later, he suspected, he would have to step out of this happy haze and return to real life, but there was no rush. He liked it here, and this was a place that could never let him down. His siblings probably needed rescuing by now—they were talentless when it came to staying out of trouble—but surely they would rather have him at his best. He needed a few more days of restoration before he was ready to dust off his trademark swagger.

The brunette refilled his glass, and Klaus caught her around her waist and pulled her, giggling, onto his lap. "I've missed you," he told her lustily, and she snuggled her ample bosom conveniently closer to his mouth. He sampled the whiskey, and then he sampled her. A week would be best, he decided. The world could do without him for a week.

Vivianne Lescheres obviously could.

It had never once occurred to him during their night together that she was saying good-bye. It should have, perhaps, but every clue had had an alternate explanation. A *better* explanation—one that fit Klaus's way of looking at the world so that he had ignored the obvious. He hadn't wanted to see that her relentlessly stubborn streak could work against him as easily as for him.

The brunette had an adorable sprinkling of freckles across her snub nose, and Klaus devoted all of his mental energy to counting them. He had everything he needed right here, and Viv could go to hell for all he cared. She didn't appreciate him, anyway. He had been willing to reorder his entire life for her, to become a new and better man. If that wasn't enough for her, then she hadn't been worth it after all.

The belled curtain across the door chimed merrily, and a few of the whores squealed. Klaus's girl didn't so much as flicker her eyes toward the sound, and he made a mental note not to get so drunk that he forgot to pay her handsomely.

"Of course I found you *here*," a voice snarled arrogantly, and Klaus furrowed his brow in concentration. It was a familiar voice, and it was attached to a pair of legs in dark leather boots. He followed the boots upward, then continued along a line of gold buttons that edged the waistcoat. There was a long neck above that, with a juicy pulse beating beside a large Adam's apple. Klaus acknowledged he might be a bit drunker than he'd thought as his eyes finished their lazy trek to rest on Armand Navarro's smug face.

"A likely story," Klaus slurred carefully, "claiming

you walked into a brothel because you were looking for *my* company."

Armand's answering smile really *required* a punch in the mouth, but Klaus's hands were otherwise occupied and his head felt a bit fuzzy. He suspected that his best chance of winning a fight right now was to stay out of one. Perhaps if he sat very still, Armand would get bored and leave him alone with his cheerful brunette friend. Everyone would win in that scenario.

"Stand up and face me like a man," Armand demanded. "We knew it was only a matter of time before one of you vermin went too far, and I wanted to be the one to ensure that you pay for it personally." Perhaps a fight was unavoidable, then. Klaus had been ready to empty the city of werewolves once they learned about his affair with Vivianne, but having to do it without her seemed joyless and dull.

The smile had drained from the whore's face, and Klaus patted her pleasingly rounded thigh reassuringly. "You should go check on our room," he suggested, feeling considerably more sober already. "I'm sure you remember how I like it."

She nodded and rose, shrinking away from Armand as she passed by. Klaus watched her shapely rear fondly as she walked away, then returned his attention to the annoying werewolf in front of him. Armand's breathing was rapid, his pupils dilated. He was keyed up and ready for a fight, and Klaus could only imagine one reason why.

"We don't *have* to do this," Klaus offered magnanimously. He certainly wouldn't mind pummeling Armand into a pulpy corpse, but just this once he should give the werewolf a pass. He had, after all, spent a glorious and extremely thorough night with Armand's fiancée, and that was probably injury enough. If Armand was willing to walk away, Klaus would let him.

"Stand up," Armand growled menacingly. "You'll answer for your brother's crime whether you want to or not, so meet your fate like a man."

The intoxicated wheels in Klaus's head turned slowly around that new piece of information. It seemed possible this wasn't about Vivianne after all—maybe Armand still didn't even know about what had happened between them. Maybe Viv had kept their secret. Maybe she cared for him even now. . . .

"What has my dear brother done to you?" Klaus asked, rising to his feet. He was pleased to discover that he did not sway.

Armand's smirk was tainted by the ugly yellow gleam in his eyes. "He attacked us in the woods," he explained, sounding both murderous and a little bit triumphant. "On his own, during the full moon. The fool died in the Saint Louis River, and now you're going to join him."

Well, good for him, Klaus thought. Elijah had taken on the entire werewolf population of New Orleans. Klaus realized that he must have interrupted the changing celebration, and for whatever reason he'd decided to fight off the wolves. In spite of Armand's cocky assurance that Elijah had not survived, Klaus knew differently— mere werewolf venom wouldn't kill an Original. Klaus felt a slow burn of pride for his idiot brother.

Klaus didn't hesitate. He cocked his fist back and punched Armand squarely in the nose, and the werewolf's hot blood spurted out in a sudden torrent of red. Armand looked surprised for a moment, and then his eyes went fully yellow and he struck. Klaus heard the sound of wood splintering as Armand knocked him first into a grandfather clock, and then downward through a low table. Klaus would pay for a lot more than the whiskey and his brunette's time before he would be welcome back in the Southern Spot again, and the thought enraged him even further.

He drove his knee up into Armand's stomach, pressing his advantage when the wolf gasped. He used the distraction to grab one of the shattered legs of the coffee table, and bashed it into the side of Armand's head. The blow dazed him for a moment, and Klaus seized the opportunity. Driving his arms and legs upward, he threw Armand off of him and against the wall behind their heads, which made a dry cracking sound when the wolf hit it.

Armand fell heavily to the floor, but somehow managed to pull all of his long, awkward limbs into order and rolled to his feet with improbable grace. Klaus was still half crouched when he was knocked to the floor again, and the two of them struggled for a moment with neither getting the upper hand.

Elijah had struck at the werewolves when they were strongest. Drunk or no, Klaus could certainly do his part. And while Armand might not have realized it yet, he had Vivianne to pay for as well.

Klaus trapped one of Armand's legs with his own and twisted, putting the tall werewolf flat on his back and rising up to sit on his chest. He lashed out with his fists, hitting Armand again and again. In his mind, Klaus saw Elijah wounded, Vivianne changing. Blood flowed freely until Armand's face was barely visible through it, and then his eyes returned to their normal, dull blue and rolled back in his head.

Klaus watched him for a moment to make sure he would really stay down, and then staggered inelegantly to his feet. "Ladies," he offered politely to the few whores who had remained cowering against the walls. "I apologize for any inconvenience this brute has caused you. Rest assured that I will always be available to defend your honor, just as I have today." He tried to smooth his shirt, and realized that it was soaked with Armand's blood.

He reached into his pocket and grabbed the hand of the nearest girl to drop in a handful of gold coins, folding her fingers closed around them in case she was too stunned to do so herself. He kissed her on the cheek for good measure, feeling more like his old self than ever. Whiskey, the company of half a dozen good women, and beating a werewolf unconscious: *That* was the recipe for Niklaus Mikaelson.

With a spring in his step, he left the brothel and turned his feet toward the house Elijah had acquired. He couldn't wait to hear his brother's side of this bizarre tale. If it was half as entertaining as Armand had made it sound, it was past time for the Original vampires to catch up.

TWENTY-THREE

*E*lijah had given up on trying to figure out what was real. Rebekah had been gone so long that he wasn't sure whether she had been there to begin with. Esther had walked in and out of the cellar more than a few times, which probably hadn't really happened, but the man in the blue soldier's coat with the wooden stake in his hand seemed almost as improbable.

Certainly, Kol and Finn had not stepped out of their coffins to visit with him, and his two mortal—and long-dead—brothers had not stood vigil at his bedside. But that meant it was possible Niklaus was not there, either. The werewolves' poison had spun wild dreams and visions that he was sure were more meaningful than true, and yet Elijah could not quite grasp their message. Perhaps that was all a part of the hallucinations—the conviction that the nightmares must be trying to tell him something.

It had been hours or days or weeks since Rebekah had pulled the unconscious blue-clad man through the ceiling, and yet she had never returned. So that may not have been real, either. Except how could Elijah have gotten here, in this dank cellar on a bed of soft blankets, if Rebekah had not first brought him, and then inexplicably abandoned him?

There was something about a sunrise across the river and a bleeding man in the bayou, but it was confused with the conviction that he had flown away from the wolves and then nested here like some strange, unlikely bird. He had no sense of what had happened since he'd been attacked, but each hour was a little less confusing than the last, and so Elijah suspected he was drifting toward lucidity.

He ached all over. His wounds itched as they faded into smoothness, and with every tiny movement he discovered a new source of tenderness. But there was no doubt that he was healing, and Esther's magic had served its purpose once again.

He opened his eyes and blinked, trying to distinguish the faint difference between the darkness in the cellar and the kind behind his closed eyelids. There was the slightest outline of light around the edges of a trapdoor, and he stared at it intently until it was all he could see.

When the trapdoor was suddenly thrown open, the flood of light behind it nearly blinded him.

"Brother," an amused voice called down, and Elijah wondered if he was hallucinating again. Klaus was haloed by sunlight and covered in blood, hardly the most encouraging sign of his mental recovery.

"Brother," he replied cautiously, lifting himself gingerly onto one elbow and discovering with relief that it did not hurt as much as he had expected. "Did you bring me here?"

Klaus jumped down into the cellar and stared at Elijah, his eyes appraising. "You look well," he remarked, sounding grudgingly impressed. "I heard you took on the entire Navarro pack under a full moon, but if that's true I would hate to see how they fared."

Elijah pulled himself up to a sitting position and sighed. "It's true," he assured his brother. "A few of them will certainly remember me."

Klaus crouched companionably beside the blankets, looking totally unaware that his clothes were soaked with blood. It must not have been his, but that stirred something troubling in the back of Elijah's foggy brain. Someone else's blood had been the point of this fiasco, and he felt around frantically to find . . . something. Something that was missing.

"All your parts still there?" Klaus grinned, and Elijah glowered at him.

Blood! That was what he had needed—werewolf blood. And despite all his cuts and bruises, he had succeeded. So where the hell was his handkerchief? He patted his clothes again, rifling through the tatters, but the bloody cloth was gone. It'd been the one thing he'd needed to work the protection spell, and he'd failed.

Elijah closed his eyes and breathed. He would have to regroup and come up with a new plan—that was how it always went. There were setbacks and then there were solutions, and then there were more setbacks. His next plan would have to wait until he absorbed the magnitude of this failure.

"Where have you been?" he asked Klaus, rather than answering him. "Is all that your blood?"

Klaus grinned happily. "None of it, as far as I recall. That idiot Armand decided to bother me during an otherwise lovely morning. He was under the impression you had been killed, and that he was capable of doing the same to me. It ended bloodily for him."

Elijah opened his mouth, then closed it again, momentarily stunned. If he hadn't felt his healing wounds so acutely, he would have sworn he was still dreaming. But when he reached out and grabbed Klaus's soaking-wet shirt, he knew this was really happening. Suddenly, his grin matched his brother's. "You did well," he told Klaus, whose blue-green eyes widened in surprise. "Now give me your shirt."

Ysabelle stepped back from the fresh line of peat and muttered as the flames sped around the perimeter of the Mikaelsons' land.

"Nice trick," Klaus remarked good-naturedly.

Elijah elbowed him in the ribs. "Concentrate," he reminded Ysabelle, with a warning glare at his brother.

"I remember how this goes," the witch assured him. She mixed her potion deftly, this time swirling in the blood she had coaxed from Klaus's shirt. She rehearsed the incantation one final time before she began to circle the land and pour out the liquid.

"That will take forever," Klaus grumbled, kicking at a tuft of grass. "Was she this slow the first time?"

"I don't really care as long as it works," Elijah countered. He watched Ysabelle reappear on the far side of the house and waited, barely daring to breathe. She did not look at them, instead keeping her eyes fixed on the potion spilling onto the long line of fire. She allowed herself a ghost of a smile when her iron bowl emptied just when she had reached the end. This time, there was no boom, but the world seemed to ripple and the pressure mounted. Then, it seemed to Elijah that the house absorbed the brutal, urgent silence into itself, and the walls swallowed it whole.

She'd done it—and now his family was finally safe.

He would have to arrange for their belongings to be brought from the hotel. He had dreamed of seeing Kol's and Finn's coffins in the basement with him, but that was an illusion. It was odd, actually, that Rebekah hadn't moved them, unless he'd only imagined her as well. That part of his memory still felt hazy. Trying to put events into their proper order only made him feel like he was sliding back into the venomous fever.

He blinked in the sunlight, trying to put his finger on what had changed. The house looked exactly the same, although that was already an improvement over their last attempt.

Klaus wandered closer to it, climbing up onto the low porch with his head cocked, looking for a sign that the spell had really worked. Ysabelle moved the other way, stepping across the extinguished line of peat. She fumbled in her bodice for a moment, then withdrew something that flashed silver in the lazy afternoon sunlight. With an agile ripple of her shoulder, she threw it squarely at Klaus's back.

Elijah didn't bother to move. If she had failed a

second time, she might as well kill them. But the knife bounced back, landing on the grass as if it had been dropped rather than ever thrown. Ysabelle's face was lit with her triumph, and Elijah clasped her shoulder appreciatively.

"Thank you," he told her, but his mind was already elsewhere. The deadly point of a weapon . . . He had seen that before, and recently. Wading through the hallucinations, he could distinguish the memory of a blue-coated man with a stake.

He'd crept in from one of the passageways, his weapon held at the ready. He'd said something, hadn't he? Something about Rebekah. About *taking* Rebekah. And then she appeared, attacked the man, and pulled him out of the cellar.

So why had she not returned? He was now sure that she'd rescued him from the river but that had been at least a day or two ago. Who was that man, and why had Rebekah not simply disposed of his body and returned?

TWENTY-FOUR

*R*ebekah stared out at the ocean, watching the waves chase and break across one another. She could have stayed there forever. She felt finally, totally at peace.

Eric joined her on the little terrace, resting a warm, possessive hand on her shoulder. She smiled up at him, remembering the feeling of safety she had experienced the first time they met. He was waiting, and he must feel like his entire life depended on the choice she had to make. But he looked relaxed, simply happy to be with her in this little abandoned cottage facing the sea.

Rebekah had fully intended to make good on her plan to drown him, but she had been overcome by fear and curiosity in the end. She'd wanted to know the details of his messages to her father, and she'd needed to understand why he'd gone to such lengths to deceive her. He could have pretended to shelter her *without* pretending to love her. He certainly didn't need to propose to her, and so why had he? What had been the point of his twisted game?

Once she had reached the seashore, she had waited impatiently for him to wake up so she could kill him. And then, with his first breath, he'd said that he was so relieved *she* was safe.

It was too much, that he would try to keep up the charade even now. But something in the softness of his lips, the trusting look in his eyes, gave her pause.

"How did you get away from that monster?" Eric gasped, and then he looked around them in confusion. "What is this place, and how are we here?"

"'That monster'?" she repeated. "*You* were the one who was trying to kill *him*."

Eric nodded then winced and rubbed at his throat. "He killed Felix," he explained, grimacing. "I returned to find Felix murdered, and you gone. I knew the creature was punishing us for our curiosity. We had heard that there was a nest of his kind near here, and so when I realized you had been taken I searched the area. I found the tracks where he carried you from the river. A piece of your dress had snagged on the reeds and so I knew you had been there. I followed your trail to this house. I watched from the trees, and finally I saw you."

Rebekah tried to make sense of his halting speech. He had found their house, and must have seen her come up through the trapdoor while she had been exploring the tunnels beneath it. And then, believing her to be Elijah's prisoner, he had used that same door to try to set her free.

It was a ludicrous explanation, but she found that she still wanted to trust him. The way he stared up at her, as if he were drinking in her presence, she could actually believe that he had thought her a helpless victim all along.

Except that Felix had said otherwise before he died.

She could not stand the layers of lies between them anymore. It was not serving her purpose to keep pretending. And the only way to figure out the truth was to reveal what she was. There, in the light of day, where Eric could see.

"The man in the cellar is a vampire," she told him bluntly, and then she concentrated for a moment so that her own fangs extended into view. "He is my brother. I am a vampire, too, and so you understand why I couldn't let you hurt him."

Eric remained sprawled out on the sand, carefully

thinking over her words. Even if he had known all along, she hadn't expected such composure from him. "You were not kidnapped," he said finally. "You . . . you killed Felix." He did not sound angry or afraid— but amused.

"Felix tried to kill me," she said. "He tried to ambush me with the same stake I found you holding over Elijah. *You* attacked *us*. Felix said you had been hired to find us, and that you'd sent reports back to my . . . to your employer."

Eric sighed and closed his eyes. "The man who hired us wanted only information, not murder. He chose me because I had education and resources, which Felix did not—he only had a fervent desire to hunt down monsters. Our employer hoped that would lead me to you. But I deceived him, and I lied to Felix as well. I didn't want anyone else to find vampires—I wanted them to be all mine."

"You sent no reports," Rebekah interpreted. "Or you sent false ones. And if he had no education, then Felix could not write any himself, nor read what you wrote. Then no one but you now knows where we are. But why?" It made no sense, but he stood to gain nothing from inventing that tale—and if he was the only person who knew her secret, then killing him would keep her safe.

Felix had promised Rebekah that she would be

hunted down, and Eric could have told her the same story, trying to bluff his way into some kind of negotiation. The chance he would survive would be slim, but it would have been smarter than saying that her exposed secret could die with him, right there on the beach. As bizarre as it seemed, she found herself inclined to believe what Eric was telling her. She sensed that, like her, he was ready to simply tell the truth.

His hazel eyes had opened again, and lingered on the smallest details of her face. "Your brother," he repeated. "I did not know."

"He was lying half dead," Rebekah snapped, irritated by her own confusion on top of everything else. "How did you think he could have carried me away in that state? He hardly looked a threat."

"His injuries confirmed that he had fought with Felix." Eric coughed and rubbed at his throat again, then tried to prop himself up on his elbows. With a firm hand, Rebekah indicated that he should stay where he was. "And I thought that even a wounded vampire could manage to kidnap a frightened widow."

In spite of herself, Rebekah laughed aloud. "You were wrong on every count." Really, the idea of Elijah's gruesome wounds coming from a tangle with some human was ridiculous. Rebekah hadn't gotten a scratch in their brief struggle.

To her surprise, Eric smiled at her. "I knew you were extraordinary," he murmured. "And yet I find myself embarrassed by how thoroughly I underestimated you. And equally as ashamed that my lieutenant picked up on the truth before I did, when I could not be there to protect you."

Of course she *was* extraordinary, but it seemed like a rather odd reaction to everything she had just disclosed. For a human. "You don't sound as alarmed as I would have expected," she pointed out, showing her fangs again for emphasis.

"I am hopeful that you'll let me live, in a sense," he admitted. She scowled, but her eyes roamed to the lean chest that his ripped shirt exposed. His strong hands, and how capable they looked . . .

"If you didn't want to report our whereabouts back to you benefactor, then what did you want?"

"I've been hoping to meet a vampire for years now, but not because I wanted to kill one," he replied.

"I don't understand, Captain. If not to kill him, then what was the point?" She remembered the sight of the dead werewolf with the wooden stake protruding from his chest, and shuddered. "You cannot tell me you have not hunted us, and a hunt should end with a death."

"*My* death, though," Eric argued urgently, pushing himself up into a sitting position. This time, she let him.

"Since Marion died so suddenly, so senselessly, my own death is all I have been able to think about. It haunts me to know that I will simply end, between one breath and the next. I stood before her grave and vowed that I would not follow her so easily. I would not let some sickness, some wound, some *accident* rip me out of the world. When I discovered writings about your kind, I knew that you held the keys to life and death. I need those keys, Rebekah. I have searched for years so that I could beg you to make me like you. Kill me, so that I cannot die."

She recoiled, hope and fear warring together in her heart. She had assumed his obsession with death was morbid, that he hated having to live in a world from which every trace of his wife was gone. Death was indeed his enemy, she realized, but only because he loved being alive. She wanted to believe him so badly that it was almost physically painful. "Next you will say you never intended to kill my brother," she hissed, her voice even harsher than she expected. "You were just trying to threaten a vampire into turning you?"

"I thought he had *taken* you," Eric shouted and then winced and lowered his voice again. "I saw you emerge from that tunnel, too afraid to run away. I knew I had to act before the sun went down, and the vampire woke up.

"When I saw no further signs of you or your captor, I tried to follow you inside," he rasped on. "It was foolish, but when I found him lying there, I thought the risk had paid off." He frowned, his brow furrowing deeply. He raised one hand to run a rough finger down the side of her face, and the small touch sent shivers through her body. She found herself at a loss for words. "I will not deny I planned to kill him for his sins against you. I intended to kill him if it cost me my life or even a chance at eternal life. What would any of it matter if I lost you?" he said.

She lifted her hand to cover his, and he wove his fingers between hers. "Once I met you, I began to want more than just immortality. I wanted to share it with you," he finished.

Rebekah felt a sudden heat flushing her skin. She bent down and kissed him passionately, and he wound his fingers in her long hair to keep her close. In that moment she knew she wanted to stay that way forever.

They had found the abandoned cottage and lost track of the time. They had talked about everything—learning each other from the beginning, with no secrets between them this time.

He told her what he knew of Mikael's plans and whereabouts, which naturally wasn't much at all. They had met only once in an inn outside of Paris, and after that meeting Mikael had handled their business through associates. In turn, Rebekah told him about her father's past, and he held her while she cried at the most bitter parts. She talked about her short life as a human, and he reminisced about the brief time with his beloved wife.

Most of all, though, they made love. Even when they had to pause, their bodies remained in constant contact. They could not stop touching: hair, shoulders, lips, back, ankles, everything. Her fingers traced the scars from his battles, and his calloused hands explored the flawless silk of her skin. They clung and collided, entwined and caressed. She drank her fill of his blood, and he begged her to take more.

She could not, though, not yet. She had made a promise to the witches of New Orleans nine years before, and her brothers' bargains were tied to her own. As long as she remained in the vicinity of the city, she could make no new vampires, or else they would all be cast out.

Elijah and Klaus would not forgive her for that disobedience, but they would not absolve her for leaving them, either. She spent hours weighing those two choices, because the only other option she could think of was refusing Eric, and that she would not do. After all of her long life she had found a true mate, and she fully intended to keep him.

Eric's hand slid down from her shoulder to drift along her collarbone, and he bent to kiss the side of her throat. He had extraordinary stamina for a human, and she could only imagine what he would be like as a vampire. She reached up and pulled him down closer, always closer, her mind made up. "We will leave together," she told him softly. "I will make them understand that you are my family now, and we will go."

TWENTY-FIVE

*K*laus was restless. It had taken him only a night to discover that he was not made for life in the countryside. It was boring, and the sounds from the bayou were downright disturbing. The house, with its formidable new enchantment, was obviously the best place to be when every werewolf within fifty miles was probably out for their blood. But the confinement chafed, and so he paced and complained and made his brother miserable until dawn came and Elijah sent him outside to take care of the rotting old stump near the back of the property.

It would almost certainly have to be removed, but their explorations revealed that its roots framed one of the several underground caverns that dotted the property. They had strategic value, the brothers had agreed immediately, and it would be unfortunate to lose one of them if they could help it. Klaus examined the lacework of the roots, trying to see where they gave the most support. The dead and rotting wood would not hold up forever, but if they worked carefully they could probably replace it without caving in the chamber entirely.

A strange keening came from the direction of the house, and Klaus straightened. It sounded mechanical, but he couldn't think of anything in the house that might have made such a noise.

"I thought I might find you here," a familiar voice said, and Klaus froze. Of course . . . the protection spell. Someone had stepped onto their land, and the spell had tried to warn him. He had not understood quickly enough, and the price of his mistake stood before him, watching him with haunted black eyes. "I came to see if you were all right."

Vivianne looked more fragile than he remembered her, as if something vital were slowly being drained from her body. She wore a deep, heavy cloak of ivory wool that should have been sweltering in the heat of the day, but she pulled it close around her as if she still could not get warm enough.

Klaus found himself unsympathetic.

"You've seen me now," he pointed out sharply. He slammed the trapdoor closed and turned his back on her, marching toward the house.

She followed him through the ankle-high grass, but he refused to slow down. "I saw Armand, too," she called after him. "He said you were the one who hurt him. Your brother was in the woods the other night, and he attacked us, too. Is this all happening because of us? Klaus, is it because of . . . me?"

He reached the shelter of the porch, and turned so that she could see the bitterness on his face when he laughed. "You!" he exclaimed. "What could *you* have to do with these squabbles, Viv? What might *you* have done that could possibly cause all this fighting?"

She bit her full red lip, looking even paler in the sunlight than she had in the shade of the trees. "Armand wouldn't tell me anything," she admitted, "except that it was you he fought. But the way he looked at me, I think he knows. What we—what I did."

Klaus shrugged nonchalantly. "If he does, he didn't learn it from me. I don't go about bragging about being abandoned at sunrise by the woman I had loved all night."

Vivianne looked as if she had been slapped. "I thought it would be the best way to say good-bye," she whispered. "I thought I had to change, and I wanted to have one last night as myself. Can't you see what that meant to me?"

"You 'thought,'" Klaus repeated slowly. "You 'thought' you had to activate the werewolf within you." Had she changed her mind already? What a cruel twist of fate that the full moon had brought if she was so inconstant in her conviction. Another few days and she might have forgotten the whole idea. Just as she had forgotten him.

Vivianne's black eyes glowed hopefully. "You were right all along," she breathed eagerly, hurrying to close the gap between them. "I should never have done it. You were the only person who has ever cared about what was best for me, and I was foolish not to trust you."

Klaus watched, amused, for the moment when she would run into Ysabelle's barrier. Vivianne was about to lift her right foot onto the porch when she rocked back, almost losing her balance. She gaped at him in confusion. "Your aunt was here," he told her spitefully. "She helped us guard ourselves against unwanted visitors."

Vivianne pushed curiously at the invisible barrier, moving sideways a few steps to see how far it extended. "You need to invite me in," she guessed, looking stunned.

Klaus deliberately misunderstood her meaning. "I don't, in fact," he reminded her harshly. "You're welcome to sit out there until your new pack comes along and drags you home. I assume that if you knew where to find us, they do, too."

Guilt was written all over her face. Elijah had gotten their house in order in the nick of time, because the Navarros had figured out where they were. Then the guilt changed to anger, and Vivianne tossed back the hood of her cloak. "I shouldn't have bothered to worry," she snapped. "You're obviously *exactly* as you always were."

Klaus smirked. "If you thought an encounter with one werewolf could somehow change *that*, love, you underestimated me."

She stared at him, and as furious as she was there was something calculating in her look. Klaus could see her gathering her emotions back under control, and in spite of his resentment he respected her for it. She might be a fool, but she was an impressive one.

"I must have," she agreed coldly. "When you told me you loved me, I believed it. When you said you wanted nothing more than to be with me, I believed it. When you insisted that there was no part of me"—she held her hand up to forestall his interruption—"*no* part of me you did not want to know, I believed it. Obviously, I underestimated your capacity for empty words."

If he were not so furious, he would have laughed.

"You *chose*," he nearly shouted. "You crept out of my bed and chose to become a vicious *thing* that is my mortal enemy. You can't twist that to make it seem that I never wanted you enough, when——"

"Then you do!" she exclaimed, moving as close to him as the magical barrier would allow. "You're angry; of course you're angry. But you meant all those things you said, and you still want me, even now."

Klaus Mikaelson was rarely at a loss, but Vivianne's outburst left him wordless. It was bold—he could not imagine being so brave in her position. But most of all, it was true. He had tried to drink, fuck, and fight her away, but the sight of her standing before him had brought everything back.

He still loved her, and he wanted, desperately, for her to say whatever would set him free to say so again. "Why have you really come here?" he asked, knowing that he could not answer her accusation until he had answers of his own. "I don't believe for a second that you were worried about my health. We know each other too well for that sort of charade."

She nodded and bit her lip again. He remembered the taste of it perfectly, and he wished more than anything that it were between his teeth.

"I made a terrible mistake the other night," she said, her voice low with emotion. "I knew it as soon as it was done. I didn't think I could live with half of myself locked away, but now I would give anything to seal that doorway closed. I can't, but I will do whatever it takes to make things right with you, and that's why I have come." Her luscious mouth twisted up into a wry smile. "I knew perfectly well that one werewolf would hardly leave a scratch on you."

He wanted to reply so scathingly that he would be able to see the marks his words left. He wanted to drain her where she stood, make her a vampire, and then stake her. In the red haze of his rage, he knew that he would not be so furious if she were not right.

She had done something beyond stupid, but no matter how angry he was, he *did* still want her. Now that she stood before him, full of remorse, Klaus found his anger slipping away. He realized his battered heart would never leave him in peace if he didn't at least try to forgive her.

"Enough," he told her, his voice rough with the things he would not say. "I believe that you regret what you've done, but that does not make it any less final. I cannot live with the uncertainty of your loyalties, Viv. This wavering between the Navarros' side and mine has to end."

She lifted her eyes to meet his, disbelief showing in every line of her delicate face. "I'll end my engagement.

I would not have come here if I wanted to marry another man." Her smile was like the last flare of the sun setting, like the sight of the first stars beginning to show in the sky. "I know every part of myself now, Klaus. Mortal enemies or no, there is no part of me that does not love you."

"Come inside," Klaus whispered, and she burst forward into his waiting arms. He kissed her and folded her tightly against him, and then he tipped her head back to kiss her again, more deeply this time. There in the shadow of his home, with the warm breeze grazing their skin, he allowed himself to believe that it might be just that easy.

"I will break off this madness today," she mumbled into his chest, "all of it. I can be back here by nightfall."

He stroked her raven hair, the wheels of his mind turning. This revelation would change the political landscape of the city—if he could choose when to make this news public, it could be a powerful advantage. And the cynical, wounded part of Klaus longed to know, would she really keep her word once she had more time to think things through?

"Not today," he disagreed, pushing them gently apart and kissing her palm reassuringly. "Viv, if you want to throw in your lot with mine, I want proof that your mind is made up."

She frowned quizzically. "But I just said I would—"

"Not that." He shook his head. "I need you to do as I ask, not to simply run off and do what feels best to you." *Again,* he did not add, but he knew that they were both thinking it.

She looked uncertain, but not entirely unwilling. "You want me to hide this," she translated. "You want me to lie, so that you can control how the truth comes out."

"We have a foothold now," he explained, as much to himself as to her. "We can use this information to carve it deeper. And if you mean what you say today, you will wait until I tell you it is time." A week ago, he hadn't cared about Elijah's plans—he'd been blinded by his overpowering feelings for Vivianne. But now Elijah's line of attack was taking a shape and Klaus found himself being caught up in making it a reality.

But most importantly of all, Klaus's love had already blinded him once. He would not be so reckless a second time. Not even for her.

TWENTY-SIX

*T*he council met every month on the night of the new moon. Klaus had discovered the location of the meeting somehow, and Elijah was pleasantly surprised to see his brother's renewed dedication to their family's cause. Working with Klaus was infinitely easier than working against him. Whatever had convinced him to tread more carefully, Elijah approved.

The handful of witches and werewolves in the room—the most senior, the most respected—did not look pleased to see him. They sat in a wide semicircle in the nave of a church on the eastern outskirts of the city, which had been abandoned when the congregation had grown to need a larger space. Every candle holder in the room had been put to use, and Elijah could detect the lingering smell of incense.

At a glance, he could tell that none of the councilors had expected to see him there, and Solomon Navarro and his two sons looked like they were seriously considering trying to throw him out.

"You should have died," the broad-shouldered younger one snarled. Elijah remembered him pushing other werewolves aside to join the little skirmish that had broken out during the engagement party.

"I would have, I'm sure," Elijah replied coldly, "if any of you were strong enough to kill me."

"What is the meaning of this?" Ysabelle demanded, rising to her feet. Her auburn hair shone red in the candlelight, and her face was tense and afraid. Elijah suspected that her conflicting loyalties must not seem like the wisest idea now that she found herself in a room with the vampire she had helped, the werewolves who wanted him dead, and the witches who would require an explanation for all of it.

A black-haired woman, as tall as Ysabelle and similarly featured, laid a restraining hand on Ysabelle's wrist. "It is not the first time that this vampire has come before us," she reminded the assembly in a carrying voice. She didn't stand, but she didn't need to. It was obvious from the stillness that came over the room that she had a great deal of authority. "It is possible that he may have further business here."

"What I would like," Elijah told her, ignoring the glares from other parts of the semicircle, "is a seat at this council. I believe that it's time my siblings and I had a voice in this city's affairs."

The reaction from the werewolves was so violent that for a moment Elijah thought that they had somehow changed. "He attacked us!" Armand's reedy voice shouted above the crowd, and Elijah saw some faint cuts and bruises still healing on the young werewolf's face.

Klaus must have beaten him quite thoroughly, Elijah decided with a satisfied smirk. He would have to make sure to tell him; it might be a small consolation to his brother. Elijah had been delighted when Klaus had told him he was giving up his pursuit of Vivianne, but he also respected how painful that decision was to make.

"A simple misunderstanding," Elijah lied. "I find it difficult to communicate nuance to werewolves under the influence of a full moon." He glanced at the witches, and risked a sly wink at the dark-haired one. He thought he saw her lips twitch in response. "Doesn't everyone?"

"That misunderstanding should have cost you your life," Louis Navarro growled. "I'm sure we could arrange to correct that oversight right now, if you would like."

"Sit down," the witch told him sharply, without

even bothering to look his way. To Elijah's surprise, the Navarros sat. "State your case," she ordered, "but do it quickly. We have other matters to attend to tonight."

Finally, he could place the powerful witch: She was Sofia Lescheres, née Dalliencourt. Her husband had been Quentin Lescheres, a werewolf who had been too far on the periphery of the Navarros' clan to build peace on the strength of his marriage. He had died young in any case, killed in a hunting accident before Vivianne had reached a year old.

His widow was one of the main architects of the alliance with the werewolves, of course, since it involved her own daughter. But Sofia did not seem overly fond of them, and Elijah made a mental note to shake Klaus until any scraps of information about Vivianne fell out. Their own doomed romance was over, but if the girl's mother was a key player, then Klaus might know something useful without even realizing it.

"Madame Lescheres," he acknowledged politely, and then nodded in turn to the rest of the assembly. "It is a simple enough matter. I represent a faction of supernatural beings who reside in this city. We have been here nine years, and now we are landowners. We intend to stay, and we deserve a place among you."

This time, there was no quelling the reaction. Shouts and accusations echoed off the vaulted ceiling, and

Ysabelle Dalliencourt looked so pale that Elijah thought she might be sick. She was certainly regretting her help now, but Elijah wasn't going to give up over some yelling.

"Who sold you land?" Sol Navarro demanded. Although it was not loud, his voice cut through the general uproar like a knife. His face was so beet-red that its scar stood out. His hands were clenched into meaty fists, and Elijah saw the wisdom of holding these meetings as far from the full moon as possible.

"I inherited it"—Elijah smirked—"from a werewolf." He held up the deed to Hugo's house proudly.

Sol's eyes flashed yellow. "He was no true werewolf," he muttered, but to Elijah's surprise—and Ysabelle's obvious relief—he did not press the matter.

"Just because some outcast left you his land, that doesn't mean you belong here," Armand chimed in weakly, but he seemed to run out of things to say beyond that.

Elijah waited, emphasizing the lack of argument with his own silence. When it was painfully clear that Armand would not go on, he shrugged. "We are here nonetheless." He smiled coldly at the fuming werewolves. "Your entire pack has already taken a good try at killing us, and failed. What is left to do but find a way to coexist?"

"We could try again," Louis suggested, cracking his knuckles.

Sofia Lescheres laughed, ignoring the dirty looks the Navarros and a number of her fellow witches cast her way. "As I said, wolf, we have other business to attend to tonight. We will never get to it if we are forced to waste time watching this vampire slaughter you and your family. There is no violence at these meetings by design, and so if you want to keep *your* place here, you will leave off these empty threats and focus on the matter at hand."

"The matter at hand is preposterous, though," an elderly witch argued, his palsied hands resting on a heavy, jeweled cane. "We made an arrangement with these creatures nearly a decade ago, and now this one has the audacity to barge in here and tell us it has changed." He frowned at Elijah. "Your gratitude leaves something to be desired, vampire."

"I will express my gratitude through strengthening this city, along with the rest of you," Elijah told him politely. "Working together for peace and prosperity."

"You know nothing of peace," Armand hissed, and Elijah decided that he was starting to see why the lanky young werewolf so irritated Klaus. "You still haven't answered for attacking us under the full moon."

Sofia Lescheres stared at him intently, and then at

his father. "What was your entire pack doing together in the woods that night, Sol?" Her tone was conversational, but her black eyes were narrowed suspiciously. "Just what was it that this vampire stumbled upon?"

It was a fair question, and from the look on the werewolves' faces, Elijah wondered why he hadn't thought to ask it himself. The dead man and wooden altar swam in his vision for a moment, along with a small white wolf huddled below it. Who was she that the entire pack had turned out to witness her transition? The answer that came to him was absurd, impossible . . . but if it was true, then the Navarros would not risk giving him a reason to share what he had seen.

"It was a misunderstanding," Sol conceded gruffly, not quite meeting Elijah's eyes. "The sound of the fighting carried, and more wolves arrived. Certainly, the thing got out of hand, but everyone involved has recovered. We should not speak of it again." He glared pointedly at his two sons. Sofia steepled her fingers together, but did not pursue the question.

"Perhaps," Ysabelle croaked, then cleared her throat and began again. "Perhaps it would help to avoid future misunderstandings such as that one—whatever it was— if we granted the Mikaelsons' request." She looked so nervous that it took him a moment to register that her words were supposed to help him.

Of course, things were already swinging a bit more in his favor, but he appreciated the gesture. It certainly didn't endear her to the rest of the councilors, who murmured in various degrees of outrage.

"There is some truth to what my sister says," Sofia mused, ignoring the angry looks that were directed toward her. "If the vampires are willing to respect the peace in this city, perhaps it is time to make them a part of it."

"We will not only respect it, we will celebrate that peace," Elijah added quickly, ignoring the scoffing sound that came from Armand's direction. "We have longed for a home of our own, and an end to the violence can only benefit us. In fact"—he improvised—"we would like to throw a ball to demonstrate our enthusiastic support of the upcoming wedding. Let that be our part in the truce, to show that we will honor it as sincerely as the rest of you."

Even Sol seemed somewhat mollified by that offer, although Armand continued to look bleak and unconvinced. "A seat among us in exchange for a party?" Louis muttered, and a few heads around the semicircle nodded in agreement.

"In exchange for *peace*," Sofia emphasized. "We know now what the Mikaelsons want from us. What we want from them is their promise that there will be no more violence . . . and no more 'misunderstand-ings.'" She raised an eyebrow at Sol, who inclined his head in agreement. "It is easier to place conditions on those who are under your roof than on outsiders. If we want to ask them to join in our treaty, then we must be prepared to invite them inside."

"Your words are both wise and fair, Madame," Elijah replied, gliding forward to kiss the hand she offered after a tense heartbeat. "The party is merely a sweetener to a deal that will benefit all of us in the years to come. I can think of no better way for our kinds to begin anew than to come together and celebrate such a happy occasion."

The council rose as one, and the triumph of his success was almost dizzying. He had done it, and the Originals would never be drifters or outcasts again.

TWENTY-SEVEN

Sooner or later, Rebekah knew that she would have to face her brothers. The harmony she had with Eric had stretched on blissfully, but it couldn't last forever. She was still an Original, with ties and obligations. And he was still a human, with all the dangerous vulnerabilities that entailed. Eric was ready to become a vampire, but she couldn't change him in New Orleans, and they could not leave until she made things right with her family.

Eric had managed—barely—to contain his frustration, but she could still sense it. He had been forced to accept her judgment, since he couldn't deny that he didn't understand the complexities of being an ancient, immortal vampire. But she could see how the rules annoyed him, and how eager he was to leave and be free with her.

But it was time to visit Elijah and Klaus, in order to set her future in motion.

She heard a strange wailing sound as they approached the house, as if an animal were crying out. *The protection spell must finally be in place,* she realized. Her brothers would be safe behind its barrier. . . . And they would have been warned that a guest was coming: Eric.

Sure enough, as they reached the front porch, the door banged open. "Sister," Klaus greeted her broadly, extending his arms to indicate the entire quadrangle of land around them. His muscular frame filled the doorway, and his amused smile gave way to a dangerous gleam in his pale eyes. "You have returned to our happy home at last." Klaus was still mad at her—weeks later—for their encounter in his hotel room, and now she had walked Eric straight into the lion's jaws.

"Not now," Rebekah hissed, pushing him aside and dragging Eric through the door, and Klaus followed gamely. With Klaus in this kind of mood, she'd need a cooler head to mediate.

Elijah was at the rough-hewn table, and he put down his set of papers when he saw her. She was relieved that there were no lingering traces of the terrible attack he had suffered. Then he saw Eric's uniform and jumped up in surprise. "You have returned our cousin to us," Elijah guessed, his brown eyes darting from Eric's to Rebekah's and back again. "We had heard her husband was killed in the woods, but—"

"He knows," Rebekah interrupted, unwilling to cope with layers of lies. It had not been easy to explain the wagoner to Eric, but he understood that the price of immortality was blood. "He knows everything."

Klaus and Elijah went completely still, staring at her as if she must be joking. "He knows *what?*" Elijah asked incredulously, and his serious face pleaded with her to go back to being the wagoner's widow, or to show him that this was just some further deception.

"Perhaps I should give you a little time with your family," Eric suggested, and beside his composure, her brothers looked to her like a pair of thugs. Rebekah nodded, and he gently disengaged her hand from his arm, passed Klaus without flinching, and returned to the solitude of the front porch. Rebekah steeled herself for what was next.

"My dear sister," Klaus shifted his weight to block the doorway, "it seems you have been keeping things from us. Elijah, do you remember 'Tell the good captain everything' being part of her plan?"

"She didn't mean *everything*," Elijah insisted stubbornly, still trying to read Rebekah's expression.

"Explain yourself, Rebekah, because at the moment it sounds like you've betrayed our deepest secrets to the humans you were meant to recruit."

Put that way, it sounded even worse. She decided in that moment that her brothers didn't need to know about Eric's brief involvement with Mikael. It was going to be hard enough to convince them not to kill him as it was. "It's true that I have abandoned my mission," she told them, keeping her chin resolutely high. "And I have also revealed our deepest secret, but only to *one* human, not all of them. He already knew of our kind, and desires—more than anything—to become a vampire. And I love him, and intend to do as he asks."

Klaus made to follow Eric outside. Rebekah intercepted him, taking a hard blow to her stomach before Elijah pulled them apart. "He's a liability now," Klaus snarled, baring his fangs at Elijah in turn. "I'll kill him and stake her. Get out of my way, brother, or I will be forced to question your loyalty along with hers."

"*Loyalty,*" Rebekah scoffed. "To our family's cause, or to you, Niklaus? How are things going with your little witch?"

"That's over," Klaus replied, his eyes darting away from her for the briefest moment. "You have no right to even speak of her, traitor."

"Really, Klaus? And what have you done for us, except for meddle in the affairs of the witches and werewolves, and put us all at risk in the first place? And as you seemed determined on bringing everything down on our heads, I found something more. Something *real*." She turned to Elijah, hating the tears that sprang to her eyes. "I love him," she repeated. "And he loves me. He asked me to marry him before he knew what I was, and now he feels I'm the answer to his every prayer. I am going to turn him, and I am going to be with him. I'm sorry to tell you this way, but no matter how or when I say it, it will happen."

Klaus lunged for her again, but Elijah held him back. "Rebekah, what you want is impossible," he reminded her gently. "We have made significant progress with the local factions in your absence, but the fundamental rules of our presence here remain unchanged. If you make a new vampire, there will be hell to pay."

"I know," she whispered, and she saw Klaus stop struggling. He watched her intently, and although she spoke to both of her brothers, he was the one she wanted to reach. "There is no future for Eric and me here, and so we will have to leave."

"Leave," Klaus breathed, as if he thought he must have misheard. He shook off and straightened his collar, the motion practiced and automatic. "*Leave?* After everything we have done in the last few weeks—did you know how seriously Elijah was injured in the fight to stay here?"

"I found him and brought him home," Rebekah reminded them, and Elijah's jaw softened a bit. "I wish that I could always be there when you need me. Both of you," she emphasized, laying a careful hand on Klaus's sleeve. "I promised to be with you forever, but forever has still barely begun. I know we will meet again, but I can't stay here with Eric. And you have built too much to leave now."

"It's just the way it is, then," Klaus sneered. "Circumstances have gotten in the way of your vow—oh, well. When I fall in love, I'm a dangerous madman who needs to be brought to heel, but you're just some starry-eyed romantic whose abandonment we're supposed to accept."

"You want other things, Klaus," Rebekah reminded him. "You want power and admiration and notoriety in addition to love, and you will not be happy without all of them. My life is the *only* thing I have truly wanted since it was ripped from me. I have longed for the love I should have had for centuries, and finally, I have found it. Outside is a man who loves me, who never wants to be without me."

Perhaps having heard her, or perhaps simply impatient with waiting, Eric reappeared, standing squarely in the doorway. He looked fearless, ready for any blow that might come.

"I am sorry to meet you under these circumstances," Eric told the Mikaelson brothers. "I was under the impression that Rebekah had no living family when I proposed to her, or else I would have courted your approval first."

"What an odd turn of phrase," Klaus remarked, one eyebrow raised. "You said *living* . . . and you did not say *ask*."

"I did not," Eric admitted, ignoring Klaus's ruse. "Your sister knows her own mind. She loves you dearly and would rather go with your blessing, but I will not demean our love by pretending that she can't live without your permission."

Klaus looked wrathful, but Elijah chuckled. It was a low, strange sound in the tense air of the house, and Rebekah wondered how many times she would get to hear it again. Because she knew, before Elijah stepped forward to clasp forearms with Eric like a brother, that they were going to let her go.

As if Elijah's reserve had been the last thing shoring up his own anger, Klaus's glower dissolved into a rueful smile. He nodded grudgingly toward Eric first and then Rebekah, who impulsively threw her arms around him and held him tightly. He kissed the top of her head the way he had when they were children, and she stretched onto her tiptoes to kiss his cheek in return.

"We should drink to your happiness," Klaus said, smirking suggestively at Eric's throat before stalking into the dining room to pour some whiskey into four glasses.

They drank and talked until the sun was low on the horizon, its red final rays drifting in through the homespun curtains. Once the tension between them was settled, Rebekah realized with a bittersweet pang that her brothers and Eric got along well. She could tell that Elijah liked him, and Klaus was considerate and well-behaved enough that she understood he was signaling his approval. If only they could have stayed here.

"This does not need to be forever," Elijah reminded her when the green glass bottle on the table between them was empty. "We have a voice here now, and we will use it. The witches' prohibition against making new vampires cannot stand eternally. In time they will waver, and we will send for you."

"We will return," Rebekah promised, and Eric pressed her hands lovingly between his own.

"We will," Eric agreed. "And if we find another place in our travels where vampires are welcome and safe from hunters, we will send for you."

The words hung in the air for a long time before Rebekah realized that there was nothing else left to say. Her brothers would throw their glittering party to cement their place in New Orleans while she left it. There was nothing to keep her, now that she'd said good-bye to her brothers. She and Eric could sail that very night.

Looking at her brothers' faces, she knew that if she stayed even one more day, the guilt of separating their family would break her heart.

TWENTY-EIGHT

"My love," Klaus murmured, whisking Vivianne aside into an empty corridor. "Are you ready?"

She looked magnificent in a long silver gown that trailed away into unexpected shadows of lace. So far she had held up her end of their bargain, which required her to keep their secret while the Mikaelsons maneuvered for power. But the next steps would probably be harder.

"I have been ready since the morning after the full moon," she replied. A peal of laughter filtered in from the main hall, and Vivianne's head swiveled toward it for a moment. Beneath the powders, curls, and silk that made up her elegant armor, she was tense. "But they are all so happy tonight. I can't imagine many of them will want to see my side, once I tell them."

Klaus lovingly ran his thumb along the line of her jaw. "I am on your side, Vivianne," he reminded her. "What the rest of the city does is of no concern to us as long as we are together."

She swayed closer to him, her entire body seeking contact with his own. "I know you would *rather* fight your way out of a banquet hall full of enemies," she teased, a smile playing on her lips. "But as you say, we are our own allies now. And so I will be your ambassador in this, and keep you safer than your own instincts would."

"A bit," he conceded with pretend reluctance. "I won't give up all my fun, but it's true that the Navarros have far more to answer for than your witches. If they are prepared to accept the new order, so much the better."

He pulled her face up to his, kissing her in earnest this time. She responded eagerly for a minute, then set her hands on his chest and gently separated them. "Let's wait," she told him seriously. "Just until I have officially called off the wedding."

"You want to be free of Armand, to tell him first," Klaus interpreted.

"You understand, then," she said, looking so relieved that he hesitated to tell her no. "Whatever else he is, he is technically my fiancé. It is only decent to tell him first, before making a spectacle of the news."

A spectacle was just the sort of surprise that Klaus wished on Armand Navarro, but Viv looked resolute.

"Very well," he agreed, "Tell him, then announce it to the rest, and we'll deal with whatever comes. Things could get out of hand quickly if he has time to spread the news."

"What's the hurry?" she purred, wrapping her arms around his neck. "We still can have a few more minutes of peace." Klaus folded her against him, inhaling the lilac fragrance of her hair.

"I knew you were a faithless whore, but to betray me with this *thing*?" Armand's voice was thin and strangled. "How could you, Vivianne?" Vivianne gasped and spun around in Klaus's arms.

While Klaus had kept half an eye on the door to the banquet, Armand must have approached stealthily from the other direction. He must have noticed that they were both absent and begun a calculated search. It was a dreadfully inconvenient time for him to have grown a mind of his own, and Vivianne looked absolutely stricken by the development.

"Armand," she cried, straining forward while Klaus held her back. "I was going to tell you tonight. Within minutes. You should not have seen this."

"Tonight?" Armand asked, his tone bitterly mocking. "And what about all the other nights you have spent 'taking air' in our garden, or sneaking out through your bedroom window? You never thought to tell me then?"

"You knew," she breathed, shame flushing her cheeks to a deep red. "All this time, you knew."

"I didn't know it was *him*," Armand spat. "I had nothing but gossip and rumors. No one knew you've been spreading your legs for a dead man."

Before either of them could answer—although Klaus certainly had a few things to say about *that*—Armand ran in the other direction, making for the lights and music of the party. Vivianne squirmed out of Klaus's grasp and hurried after him. Klaus saw a few heads turn their way even before they emerged from the relative privacy of the corridor. He was losing control, but he could not intervene without doing even more damage.

Vivianne caught Armand's arm just inside the brilliant pool of candlelight, where everyone could see Armand shake it off and slap her across the face. Klaus could have slit his throat on the spot for that insult, but he had promised to try to avoid a war. Quite a few eyes had turned toward the supposedly happy couple already. It was unlikely the brutal murder Klaus had in mind could go unnoticed.

The music faltered, and Klaus saw Elijah gesturing

furiously to the band. Elijah had arranged a spectacular party, Klaus noticed belatedly. The room glowed with thousands of chandeliers and candelabras, and every bit of space was packed with flowers and vines. The music was lively, the wine flowed freely, and up until this unfortunate interruption, everyone had seemed to be having a good time. The musicians resumed their cheerful reel, if a bit shakier than before. Klaus stepped between Vivianne and Armand, ready to defend her from another blow if he couldn't avenge her for the first one, but Vivianne was only getting started.

"We were never in love, Armand," she shouted recklessly. "You coveted me, and I was willing to do my duty. But once I understood what you demanded of me, what you let your family put me through . . . I never loved you, Armand, but after that I could not even bring myself to respect you."

Armand laughed coldly. "You lost your respect for me? It's mutual, Vivianne. You have been smitten with this abomination since the night we announced our engagement, so you'll have to forgive me if I'm not too concerned with your opinion of me."

"If he's an abomination, what am I?" she asked, and Klaus could see real despair on her face. He had not thought about the next full moon, but he realized that it must be always on her mind. "What did you make me?"

"Nothing you weren't before." Armand shrugged. "Nothing like what your undead lover will change you into."

Klaus saw the light glitter off Vivianne's eyes as they flicked toward him. Armand had touched on the one topic that still divided them. Vivianne was tremendously powerful now, but she was still mortal. She would want to become a vampire eventually, he was sure of it . . . but she wasn't.

"He has asked nothing of me," Vivianne retorted, showing no further sign that Armand's blow had hit home. "He loves me for what I am, not for how he can use me."

Armand's laugh was bitter. "And when he does? Will you change your mind again, and slink around behind his back, too? I'm sure you will. It hardly matters what else you call yourself, Viv: *That* is what you are."

She slapped him in turn, and now any pretense of a private argument had ended. Guests stared openly, curiosity and suspicion mingled on their faces. Vivianne noticed them too late and froze, caught in the glare of the attention. The music stopped, and this time it did not resume.

"They might as well all know now, Vivianne," Armand remarked, letting his voice carry, twisting the knife. "I think this farce has gone on long enough."

He stalked away, and the crowd parted to let him through. Vivianne and Klaus remained alone, exposed, with every eye on them. It was not the announcement he had hoped for, not by a long shot. If he had to fight his way out of the ball he would, and he would enjoy it thoroughly. But he cursed Armand for setting him up.

"Ladies and gentlemen," Vivianne began bravely, and though Klaus would have preferred to stand proudly beside her, he knew he had to separate himself, to look more like part of the audience than a player in this disaster. If they thought it was her choice, if they had missed some of Armand's words or mistook their meaning, perhaps this still could be contained. "I want to thank you all for coming tonight, but I also owe you an apology. As you have perhaps guessed, Armand Navarro and I have ended our engagement tonight."

Whispers became an angry buzz of conversation. Klaus deliberately avoided looking in his brother's direction, as no good could come from seeing Elijah's expression.

"Have *you* nothing to say, vampire?" Sol Navarro prodded, his voice deceptively mild.

Klaus had a great deal to say, but in a moment of inspiration he decided that Captain Moquet had already said it best that same morning. "She knows her own mind," he said, wishing that Rebekah were here to hear him say it. "I am no part of this alliance—that is for you to sort out among yourselves."

"No part of the alliance, but you cannot deny your part in ending it," Sol countered, some heat creeping into his tone.

"I ended it," Vivianne said, "although *you* have played your own part in that as well. I am done being a pawn in this conflict, and I will not sacrifice one more part of myself for it."

Sol's beady eyes narrowed, and beside him, Louis's irises turned dangerously yellow. Vivianne stared them down, and then spread her hands wide to include the entire crowd. "Please continue to enjoy the party," she announced in a loud, clear voice. "And I am sorry again for any damage my behavior may have caused."

Deliberately, she turned her back on the crowd. From where Klaus stood, he could tell that her eyes were so full of tears that she must be barely able to see. Vivianne made for an exit, but Sol came toward her so quickly that Klaus had to throw himself in the big werewolf's path.

"She has said all that needs to be said," he warned Sol, but he heard Vivianne hesitate behind him. He willed her to just go, but she was proud and stubborn. She had been prepared to leave, but she would *not* flee.

It was what he loved about her, and it was also what could get them both killed.

TWENTY-NINE

*I*t was happening all over again. A party full of witches and werewolves, a lovely young bride-to-be, and Klaus. Always, always Klaus. Elijah let himself fantasize for a moment that, when the fight inevitably broke out, he would simply kill his brother himself. It would make everything so much easier.

Rebekah should have been there—this debacle wouldn't have gotten so far out of hand under her watchful eye. She would have diverted Armand, contained Klaus, and still had time to terrify the three servers who'd snuck out with one of the better bottles of wine.

But there was no time to think about what might

have been. In the blink of an eye, Elijah inserted himself between Solomon and his brother. "Get her out of here," he ordered Klaus. *"Go."*

He could see that Klaus wanted to argue, but for once in his life he listened. He must really love that poor girl if he was willing to forego a fight to keep her safe. The two of them ran into the narrow corridor, Vivianne's silver gown gleaming until they were finally out of sight.

In the hall, the chaos had escalated to pandemonium. Sol's furious snout was just inches from Elijah's own, and it took all of Elijah's self-control not to bury his fist in it. "You tried to kill me once already," Elijah reminded him, keeping his voice quiet and brutal. "I don't think it'll go any better tonight."

Sol gritted his teeth, but backed off. "You played us for fools," Louis Navarro shouted. "You came to us with all those fine words about peace, knowing that your brother destroyed the alliance behind our backs."

"No one ever knows what my brother is up to until it's done," Elijah said. "I negotiated with you all in good faith, and I'm prepared to keep up my end of the bargain. I want there to be peace."

"But now your brother has run off with our prize," Sol growled. "And I want her to be returned to her rightful place."

"Your prize," Elijah repeated, rolling over a worrying thought. It couldn't be true, could it?

Sol took another step back, unsure if he'd said too much. Elijah scanned the crowd to find Sofia Lescheres, wondering if she'd stumbled upon the truth before him. That small white wolf he'd seen . . . Those damned wolves must have convinced the girl to change. Her mother would never have allowed it if she'd known, but it was too late for that.

It dawned on him that Klaus must have already known about Vivianne's change. Naturally, Klaus wouldn't have bothered to mention something so important, busy as he was sneaking around with the one woman the entire city seemed to have a claim on.

"And why is Vivianne's rightful place with you, Sol?" Sofia demanded, stepping closer to Sol. "She has no desire to marry your son, so why do you think she still belongs to you? *What* did you do to my daughter?" She was watching Sol's face intently, waiting for him to say what she already knew.

"She made a pledge," Sol argued, frustrated that Sofia was backing him into a corner.

"Obviously the alliance isn't that important to her," he went on, "or to any of you. If you don't intend to follow through with your part of the contract, there is no contract."

Louis grinned maliciously, and a crackle of energy rippled through the werewolves around him. *Their part in this peace has never been more than halfhearted,* Elijah realized—probably why they had been so willing to risk it. *A war could break out right now, and they'd welcome it.*

"If the alliance is dead," Elijah suggested, lifting his voice over the menacing thrum, "then I hope this time the witches will be smart enough to want us on their side." If he could not have a peaceful city, then at least the vampires could have one of the factions at their backs this time. And if Klaus was set loose to resume his old hunting practices, the fighting would be quick.

"You?" a white-haired witch demanded shrilly. "What could you possibly have to offer us that would replace the good will of the werewolves?"

"The werewolves' allegiance was never yours to begin with," Elijah told the witches, although he kept a careful eye on the pack as he spoke. "They've gone rogue. All that's left to do is decide whether you want to deal with them alone or with help."

"They are only turning against us again because of you!" another witch shouted.

"Because of your brother," another said. "If he hadn't been in Vivianne's ear, convincing her to break her word, we would still be celebrating tonight."

That was probably true, Elijah reflected, *but their happiness would have been short-lived*. Klaus, as mind-numbingly selfish as he was, might have accidentally done the witches a favor.

"And yet the werewolves had already violated the terms of the alliance before the wedding could even take place," Elijah declared, deciding it was time to reveal the truth—his ace card against the werewolves. "At the last full moon, they convinced Vivianne to take a human life, so that she would be more theirs than the witches'. They were not content with a marriage of equals—they wanted to own her."

There was a renewed outcry, but this time Elijah let the cacophony build without trying to interrupt. Sofia Lescheres, pale, reached out to clutch at his arm. "So it's true?" she whispered.

"I saw her," he replied softly, and then he raised his voice again. "I saw her after she had changed, and the werewolves tried to silence me." That was not exactly true, but it was close enough.

"You attacked me unprovoked!" a petite brunette werewolf cried, straining to be heard over the others. "You struck first."

But it didn't matter. Elijah's version of events had already caught the imagination of the crowd. "There can be no peace if you made my daughter turn," Sofia shouted back.

Elijah pulled Sofia back into the ranks of the witches, who closed around them protectively. Elijah could feel a strange energy in the air, and he saw some of the witches' mouths moving in a steady, focused pattern. "This is who you thought you could ally with," he reminded them ruthlessly. "These filthy, faithless creatures broke the contract and turned Vivianne, and wanted her to marry Armand against her will. They want to enslave you, not govern with you. There can be no peace in a city where they are allowed to live."

"Enough!" Solomon bellowed, but before he could say more, a wineglass was hurled at his head. His eyes, and dozens of others, blossomed with murderous yellow, and Elijah could hear the deliberate chanting of the witches around him.

"Let's go," Elijah urged Sofia, who stared at him in shock and shook his hand off her arm.

"I'll kill them all," she hissed in a strangled voice, her black eyes wide and round.

This betrayal must be doubly bitter to her, a woman who had once loved and bore a child to a werewolf, never dreaming that one day his kin would return to claim her. Sofia had every right to her anger, but it would not do anyone any good if she died defending her daughter's honor.

"Vivianne needs her mother now," he said with

urgency as snarls and screams began to fill the banquet hall. "Let me get you to safety."

Ysabelle appeared on Sofia's other side and grabbed at her arm, trying to pull her toward one of the exits. Sofia yanked herself free just long enough to cast some spell at a werewolf Elijah hadn't even seen coming. The werewolf fell to the ground with a high-pitched whimper, and Elijah dragged both women—one much more willing than the other—to the door.

It was strangely quiet outside. The sounds from within the hall could almost have been the remains of the party. Witches and werewolves alike fled in twos and threes, but they did not linger or make any sound to draw attention to their exit. They simply lost themselves in the maze of moonlit streets, disappearing down cobblestoned alleys and over the walls of gardens.

Elijah relaxed his grip on the two witches, and Sofia slumped miserably against her sister. "I knew it was a mistake," she sobbed. "But she thought she was one of them already. She wanted to trust that they wouldn't hurt her, and I wanted that to be true."

Ysabelle stroked her sister's black hair and gave Elijah a pointed look. He understood—this was a time for family and he had his own family to attend to. He needed to find Klaus.

THIRTY

*R*ebekah had never expected to feel so guilty as the sea spray misted her face and seagulls barked over the harbor. Back when she'd promised to stay beside her brothers forever, she had barely tasted immortality. Who could really expect such a promise to be kept for centuries? But they'd all believed in it, and what made the separation worse was that part of her truly wanted to stay. She had fought for a life of her own, but after all this time she hardly even knew what freedom meant.

Eric came up next to her at the bow of the ship, and put a protective arm around her shoulders. His warmth was comforting, but he wouldn't be warm—or mortal—for much longer. With him beside her, she owed it to herself to find out what life was like when you were unshackled from your past. She had to explore this love, this passion. She snuggled closer to his side, enjoying the way her body molded itself to his. She deserved this happiness, even if it came at the expense of an eternal vow.

As long as she and Eric kept to themselves, they could move through the world undetected—something that had always been impossible with Klaus around. She could be safe and anonymous, while Elijah and Klaus continued their endless work of building, negotiating, fighting, and fleeing. She could not imagine seeking more when she already had Eric.

She could hear his steady heartbeat, and she ran one hand up along his lean chest. It was strange to see him without his captain's uniform on, but she found him just as handsome in civilian clothes. The army would miss him, no doubt, but it wouldn't be the first time that an officer had gone missing in the New World. Men disappeared all the time, in search of gold, women, and land, and Eric's disappearance would be written off soon enough.

"The captain says the tide is turning," he told her gently. "If we wish to leave tonight, there is no more time."

In spite of her convictions, Rebekah had found herself hesitating, procrastinating, checking their luggage and the ship's charts long after it was obvious that every-thing was in order. They planned to sail to the West Indies and lose themselves among the islands, making good use of both her daylight ring and the one Eric had managed to come across during his studies. She could picture it vividly: endless white beaches, locals full of fruit and fish, and a little hut where they could shelter from the wild, hot thunderstorms.

But they could not have those things if they did not go. She didn't know what she was waiting for. Someone to stop them? Of course not, but it felt so strange and unfamiliar to set sail without her brothers . . . or at least without them chasing after her to bring her back again.

They had their own lives to attend to now, though, as did she. "Tell him I am ready," she said softly, kissing Eric lightly on the mouth.

He smiled, his happiness uncomplicated and pure. After he left to find the ship's captain, Rebekah moved to the stern of the boat and looked out at New Orleans for what she suspected would be the last time. From that distance she couldn't pick out the hall where Elijah's party was surely a raging success, but she chose an espe-cially bright pool of light and decided to believe that was it.

"Good-bye," she whispered to her brothers—who had once been her everything—as the lines were cast off and the ship began to move through the dark waves.

Then Eric returned to her side, a new everything that was worth the loss of the old. The night breeze was light but steady, and the trim ship made good use of it. They were making good time and had left the small harbor for the star-littered expanse of the lake beyond. The tide would give them plenty of time to reach the narrow passage to the next lake, and then out into the open sea.

She pressed against Eric's side, and wrapped her fingers through his. "I feel free, Eric—finally, I feel free."

He bent his head to press his face against her neck. "We are free," he agreed. "The city is behind us, and we can do as we please."

She hesitated, moving her hands to grip the smooth wood of the ship's rail. She knew what he meant. Knowing how badly he wanted to be immortal, she appreciated his patience all the more. She longed to begin their new life together as soon as possible, but she could still see the lights of New Orleans, and she had this one last obligation to her brothers.

"When we are at sea," she said. "It may seem safe enough here, but we're not truly away yet. As long as we can see the city, as long as we remain in the waters that border it, the witches will know when a new vampire has been made."

"The witches . . ." Eric mused, and she heard the familiar spark of his relentless curiosity in his voice. "My world has become full of magic thanks to you, Rebekah." He kissed her lightly along her jaw until he reached her mouth, where his lips lingered. The wind had tugged some locks of her hair loose from their pins, and he tucked one tenderly back behind her ear. "So, let us wait until we are out of range from these witches, so that your brothers don't come to any harm. I never want you to regret giving me this gift."

"I always called it a curse," she whispered, so softly that he might not have even been able to hear. "Until I met you."

The black sky above them was covered in endless layers of stars, and the waxing moon had just begun to rise above the clouds to the east. Rebekah leaned against Eric's solid body and watched the bayou slide by. The thousands of torches, candelabras, and chandeliers in New Orleans blurred together into one bright, shining island that grew smaller as she watched. Soon it would be out of sight entirely, swallowed up by the shadowy, teeming swamp on either side.

"We could go and wait below," he suggested after a short while. When she tore her eyes away from the shoreline to look up at him, his smile was suggestive. "I'm sure we can find a way to pass the time."

Of that there was no doubt. She took his hand and led him to their little cabin, her heart pounding as she descended the narrow ladder. For a brief moment she remembered another ship, on her way to yet another new life, with nameless men dying in front of a ladder just like this one. But there would only be one death on this ship tonight, and it would be a beginning rather than an end.

Although it was true that the sailors would not reach their destination alive. Eric would be ravenous after the change. Compulsion would keep the survivors from noticing their missing comrades, and by the time they sailed into port there would be no one left to notice. She had paid extra for a captain who ran with more than the bare minimum of crewmembers for just that reason.

In their cabin, Eric reached behind her and took her by the waist, and she forgot one kind of hunger for another. She began to turn around, but he held her where she was, kissing her neck lightly at first so that she shivered. Then his mouth grew more ardent, and he deftly untied the long line of bows that ran down the back of her dress.

Impatient with even his quick work, she tore the last of them to simply remove the thing, then did the same with his starched white shirt. The rest of their clothes followed onto the floor, and Eric lifted her by the hips and threw her gently onto the bed. The ship rolled a bit as he moved to follow, and she laughed as he over-balanced and fell on top of her.

He smiled, with a mischievous glint in his hazel eyes, but he did not laugh. Instead he took full advantage of his position to taste every inch of her skin, drinking her in as if he were already a vampire tasting his first blood. His mouth explored her collarbone, then moved across her breasts and her belly, working lower while she sighed in pleasure. He did not linger long, although she wished he would. . . . He continued to explore along her thighs and even her ankles, appreciating each new landscape of her body in turn.

Then he rose again, attending to her pleasure in such thorough detail that she thought the sailors on the deck must hear her cries. And when he finally entered her, it was with the desperate need of a man who knew it was the last thing he would do in his life. She welcomed him and moved with him, swaying with the roll of the boat and rising up against it until they were both entirely spent.

THIRTY-ONE

*K*laus was glad of Elijah's ridiculous pursuit of safety as he spurred their horse onward. Vivianne clung tightly to his waist, and together they struggled to keep their seat on the agitated animal. Klaus could not hear the sounds of the chase yet, but it was only a matter of time. Not even Elijah's diplomacy could hold off the wolves for long.

The house rose up before them, and their skittish horse shied away. Klaus jumped to the ground, pulled Viv down after him, and slapped the beast on its rump. It cantered away gratefully toward the forest, eager to leave its supernatural charges far behind.

Inside, Vivianne scanned the door to bolt it shut, but

Klaus took her arm and led her to a chair. "No one can get in besides the two of us and Elijah," he reminded her, then added, "and our sister as well, but she is no longer in the city." He wondered if there was a way to exclude someone from the house after they had once been allowed in. If Rebekah no longer wanted to call this her home, then she should not be able to simply walk in unannounced. Perhaps Vivianne knew some tricks—it was handy having a witch around who actually liked him.

He could hear shouting outside, still a long way off but moving closer. Rebekah had nailed the curtains down over the missing windows, and Klaus tugged apart the ones by the door. He couldn't see any werewolves yet, or witches for that matter. But some ugly-looking clouds were rolling in fast, blotting out the stars, and Klaus felt the hairs on the back of his neck stand up when he saw them.

They were moving *too* fast. The night had been dry and peaceful, with nothing but a light, warm breeze to stir it. The clouds did not belong, and they seemed to be coming for him just as quickly as the werewolves' cries were. It might well be him and Viv against the entire world at this rate. "Let them come," he whispered aloud, and Vivianne startled to attention at the sound of his voice.

"They will," she warned him hollowly. "They are."

He turned swiftly and kissed her, unable to tolerate the empty sound of her voice. He would do anything to keep her safe and with him, but she needed to *stay* with him. She could not succumb to fear or doubt. He would not allow it. She was slow to respond to his kiss, but after a few moments her lips parted and he could taste some of her usual fire returning.

By the time he gently disengaged, the first torches were visible among the trees. Soon there were dozens of people outside, and the shouting was near enough that he could distinguish a few words here and there. *Traitor* featured heavily, along with *monster* and *vengeance*. It would seem that the time for negotiation had passed, although even Elijah would see that coexistence had never been a real possibility.

Werewolves had been hunting their family since they were human, and Mikael's furious rampage had made the blood equally bitter on both sides. Mikael had started this war over his wife's betrayal, Klaus remembered with a sneer, not from any noble intention. Even after the werewolves had killed one of his sons—one of his *real* sons—he hadn't dreamed of attacking them. It wasn't until he learned that Esther had strayed that he'd finally gotten murderously angry.

Perhaps Armand felt the same betrayal now as Mikael

had so long ago, Klaus realized, and the possibility tied a grim little knot of satisfaction in his chest. A point to the Mikaelsons, even after all these years. Because no matter how angry the werewolves were, they could not exact the same kind of revenge that Klaus's stepfather once had. Killing one Original vampire had proven to be too much for the entire pack. Killing two would be impossible, and the attempt would cost them dearly.

They were surrounding the house but looked more cautious now. They couldn't know about the protection spell, but they had to know that rushing the home of a vampire was unwise. They milled about, the light from their torches gleaming oddly off their formal gowns and coats. Most of the fine fabric showed some staining and tears, and Klaus noticed more than a few injuries among the throng. It would seem that the witches had held their own, at least for a while. Until the werewolves had remembered that their real enemy had already left the party.

Solomon Navarro prowled around the perimeter, looking more animal than man under the moon. He must know the house was defended, but he was reluctant to attack without knowing exactly how. Klaus could only imagine Sol's outrage at the irony; a witch could have told him everything about the protection spell—if it had any vulnerability, if there were a way to attack it without losing half of his wolves to some invisible trap. But that very night Sol had lost the goodwill of the witches.

Still, Klaus did not like his position in this fight any better than Sol seemed to be enjoying his own. There were enough wolves to set an extended siege around the house, and eventually Klaus would get hungry. And of course they would do whatever they could to chip away at the protection spell while they waited. Most important of all, Vivianne *could* be killed. Klaus would do whatever was necessary to protect her, but the werewolves would know that, and he was sure they would try to use it to their advantage.

The first werewolf stepped onto their land, and a wail seemed to emanate from the barrier itself. It was an eerie and unnatural warning, and Klaus was relieved when it stopped.

"They cannot come inside," he reminded Vivianne, who went deathly pale at the sound.

"They will not need to," she said, and he knew that her thoughts had run parallel to his own. "They will starve us out or smoke us out. All they have to do is wait, if they even have to wait that long. Spells can be broken."

For a moment, he wondered ruefully if he had really *needed* to fall in love with such an intelligent woman, but there was nothing to be done about that now. She was right: They needed a plan. Something better than just sitting in the dark room and waiting for something worse to happen.

The werewolves had an army, which they most certainly did not. Rebekah had failed completely in that minor task before sailing off to wherever it was she had gone. But they were not, he remembered suddenly, unarmed. The house's previous owner had traded in weaponry, and Klaus had seen evidence of that thriving business when he had found Elijah in the cellar. Perhaps they could thin the pack's ranks without having to leave the safety of the house, which would improve their odds considerably.

"We need to inspect the cellar," he announced, glad to have something to do. He did not like the way she sat so still; it made him uneasy. Thunder rolled in the distance, but not so far in the distance. "There are things we can use."

He lifted the iron ring set into the floorboards, and an even blacker patch of darkness opened at their feet. Neither of them needed candles to see in the dark— Vivianne now had the sharpened eyesight of a wolf—but Klaus lit a taper anyway. Its light would be comforting to her.

Her silver dress gleamed gold in the light, but it could

not warm the drawn whiteness of her face. "We should talk to them," she suggested, barely more than a whisper. "If they understand that I won't go back, that it has nothing to do with you . . ."

"They will have no further use for you," he explained, prying the lid off a case of musket balls. The muskets they belonged to must be around somewhere, and he kept an eye out for a box that would be about the right size. "Viv, they have only wanted to use you all along. Convincing them would be no better than throwing your neck onto their claws."

"I'm *one* of them," she pointed out, sounding angry rather than scared now. "Even after my father died, Sol always told my mother—"

"Lies," Klaus interrupted brutally. He hated to hurt her, but he needed to fuel that anger, to keep her ready to fight. Fear and numbness were every bit as dangerous as the wolves outside. "Being half one thing and half another makes you neither, not both. Sol lied to your mother because he wanted you to be a werewolf instead of a witch."

He could hear the breath hiss in through Vivianne's teeth; he had been harsher than he meant. "Cynicism is probably easy when you know you'll live forever," she snapped, and as absurd as it was to be lectured by a woman a fraction of his age, he was pleased to hear some life returning to her voice. "The rest of us have to live and die *with* each other, and so we cannot afford to simply slam doors the way you do."

He had finally located a cache of muskets, ready to load and fire. But he set them aside and took her firmly by the shoulders. They felt so slight between his hands, and he was reminded of how fragile she was. "I admire your faith in people," he conceded. "I suspect I have been the beneficiary of it. But if you want to remain alive, you will stay inside. If you bring up this idea of negotiation again, I will lock you down here until I've killed every single werewolf waiting outside to tear you to shreds."

She stared defiantly at him for a moment before jerking her chin into a nod. "I understand." It was not quite the same as agreement, but it would have to do for the moment. He could make good on his threat, although he would rather not have to fight a war on two fronts.

"Good." He shifted his hands to draw her close, kissing each of her eyelids first and then her unresisting lips. "Because this unending life of mine is meaningless without you."

She softened a little then, knowing that he truly meant it. She would never admit that he was right about the werewolves, of course. Her pride wouldn't allow it, and maybe she really did believe that a peaceful solution could still be found. But he knew she could see how deeply he loved her. Perhaps she could even glimpse how terrifying it was for him to watch her walk through the world, vulnerable, like a child who had not yet learned to be afraid of the dark.

"I will be here with you," she vowed, resting her forehead trustingly against his cheek. "I would never leave you, Klaus. I love you."

In that moment, whatever waited for them outside, whatever they would have to get through next, would be worth it as long as they were together.

THIRTY-TWO

*T*he werewolves poured out of the banquet hall first, looking worse for the wear but with their rage still unquenched. Elijah waited for the last of them to leave, then crept inside. He was half sure he would find all of the witches dead, but he hoped against hope that some had survived.

There were more alive than he had expected, and he wondered what had lured the werewolves away. There was still more fighting to be done here if that's what they wanted. But then he realized what might be waiting for them elsewhere, and he clenched his jaw in frustration.

Klaus would almost certainly need his help soon. He

would have taken Vivianne to their house to regroup. Elijah would join them, but he would have to fight his way in through the wolves.

Elijah could see casualties scattered around the hall, but the witches didn't look beaten. The ones who were left standing, in fact, looked downright warlike. A few of them chanted in the center of the long, candlelit room, and even as Elijah watched, more were gathering to join in.

He grabbed the arm of a short blonde witch as she made her way toward the circle, but she shook him off angrily and moved on. A few others passed Elijah without a glance, so focused on their spell that they didn't care about the presence of a vampire. He could not understand the words they were chanting, but all of their energy and attention was devoted to this one spell, and he could feel their power building in the hall like static. Whatever they were doing, his instincts told him it was something bigger than simple revenge on the werewolves.

Thunder rolled in the distance, and several heads turned toward it. Elijah had not expected a storm that night, but it looked to him like the rest of the hall's inhabitants knew it was coming.

He caught a tall young witch with a prominent Adam's apple by his crisp, purple coat. The young man tried to shake free, just like the blonde girl, but Elijah was ready this time, and he held on tightly. "I don't want trouble," he explained, seeing the witch begin to whisper something under his breath. "There's no need for that."

The man hesitated, but the prospect of an angry vampire was enough to get him to agree with a nod.

"What are they doing?" Elijah demanded, jerking his head toward the growing circle of witches.

The young man glared at him with renewed hostility. "They are cleaning up your mess," he said, and Elijah relaxed his grip on his collar just a little. "They are doing what needs to be done."

"That's vague," Elijah growled warningly. "You can do better than that."

"They're cleansing the city," the young man explained reluctantly. "We've had enough of you, the werewolves . . . all of it. The foundation of this place is rotten; there's nothing that can be saved here. We're going to raze New Orleans to the ground and start over." Thunder pealed again, much closer this time, and the witch grinned morbidly. "Nothing will be left but the swamp."

"The storm that's coming," Elijah realized. "That's your work?"

"No ordinary storm," the young man sneered,

pulling free of Elijah's unresisting hand. "What's coming now is a hurricane like this city has never seen. And I'm going to help," he added, straightening his coat and joining the chanting throng of witches.

Elijah didn't know if Ysabelle's protection spell would guard against a hurricane, but they had no better place to weather the storm. He turned and ran.

Outside, he could tell that the clouds were rolling in unnaturally fast. Elijah tried to outrace them, plunging between the trees at breakneck speed. But the first drops of rain struck his back just as he saw the werewolves around his house.

Elijah gritted his teeth, remembering his last fight with these same wolves and the seemingly endless pain that had followed. But their backs were turned to him now, giving him the advantage of surprise, and they were trapped in their human forms. He threw himself on the nearest werewolf, tearing his throat out before the body could hit the ground.

They turned and howled, rushing toward him in an indistinct, snarling mass of brandished torches and yellow eyes. Elijah was a blur, breaking limbs, snapping necks, and avoiding teeth and fire alike. They could not hope to kill him, but they could slow him down, and he couldn't allow that.

Without the levelheaded influence of Vivianne, her

mother, or her aunt, the witches would make good on their threat to level the city. If their house could not survive the hurricane, he wanted to stop the werewolves before they were completely vulnerable again.

He snapped and hacked his way toward the small porch, unable to guess how many werewolves he'd maimed or killed. He did register Louis's broad shoulders and meaty lips at one point, and paused long enough to snap his burly neck with his bare hands. The Navarros had caused him more than enough trouble, and their clan should feel the price of that. Elijah had done his best for *years* to be understanding and accommodating, but if they could not appreciate his efforts they could start losing sons.

He noticed Armand near the back of the pack, shouting with the rest, but keeping a safe distance from the actual fighting. He would have his turn, but not now. Instead Elijah spun, his fist crashing into a redhead's jaw and breaking a young woman's silk-covered thigh with a vicious kick. She screamed and fell, and Elijah stepped over her writhing body and onto the porch.

Another howl went up when the werewolves realized they could not reach him anymore, and Elijah smirked. However long it lasted, Ysabelle's spell was a work of art. Then an arm shot out from the front door and dragged him inside, and he found himself staring into his brother's blazing eyes. Their blue-green fire, along with the jutting set of his jaw, showed that Klaus was livid. Elijah was supposed to be the one who was angry at Klaus, but his brother had a knack for rewriting history. Klaus always liked to see things his own way.

"About time," Klaus complained, and Elijah inhaled and exhaled deeply to keep from hitting him. "We're surrounded, and Viv had all these ideas about *talking* to them."

"It could work," Vivianne sniped sullenly from the living room, and both vampires turned incredulously toward her. Her silver gown made her look unearthly in the dark room, like the ghost of some long-forgotten queen. "They're only here because of me in the first place," she began, and Elijah decided he had already heard enough of that.

"They're not," he informed her tersely. "They're here because Klaus killed a few dozen of them nine years ago. They're here because our father killed dozens more a lot longer ago than that. They're here because it's in their blood to hate us, and because Armand was humiliated and Louis is dead. This is much bigger than you now, Mademoiselle, so you'll help us fight or the three of us may well die tonight. But if not all three of us, then certainly *you*."

Vivianne blanched and bit her bottom lip, but did not reply. Elijah could see that Klaus had not had the heart to spell things out quite so bluntly. It *must* be true love, which, bizarrely, made him feel better about the entire wretched misadventure. His brother was the only family he had left now, and their predicament might almost be worth it if Klaus had found a partner as worthy as Rebekah had.

The thought of Rebekah nagged at his mind for a moment—her ship had been leaving that night. The witches' hurricane seemed to be coming in from the ocean, and Elijah hoped that she had made it to open water in time. But there was nothing he could do to help her now. She had chosen to strike out on her own, and she would have to handle hurricanes and worse without her family to back her up.

"There's an arsenal in the cellar," Klaus informed him brightly, his mood improved since Elijah had taken his side against Vivianne. "We can pick them off from inside the house for a while, although we'll need a better plan while we do."

"They won't wait outside forever," Elijah agreed. "And the house might not last the night, so that plan will have to come to us in a hurry."

Vivianne's head snapped up. "What do you mean about the house?" she demanded. "Klaus told me it was protected."

"Against weapons and intruders," Elijah reminded

them both grimly. "I doubt the spell will hold against the weather, and your people, my lady—your *other* people—are raising that against us as we speak."

A crash of thunder punctuated his words, and the other two flinched. "The *weather*?" Klaus said incredulously.

"The witches," Vivianne understood. "They could do that." Her black eyes searched Elijah's face, and he could see her hope fading fast. "Are you sure?"

"I have it from the source," he confirmed. "We must deal with the werewolves now, before the hurricane hits us."

Klaus whistled appreciatively. "A hurricane," he repeated, grudgingly impressed. Then his manner shifted, and Elijah knew he was preparing for the fight at hand. "I have some ideas, brother," he said. "But you'd best not run off again to play politics."

"Politics are done," he assured his brother. "We have done what we could, but now we fall back on your skills rather than mine."

Klaus grinned, and Elijah found himself grinning as well. "I knew you'd come around," his little brother said, and Elijah cuffed him affectionately on the shoulder.

"An arsenal in the cellar, you say?" he asked, feeling confident despite the circumstances. They were on familiar ground now, and they had each other's backs. "Show me."

THIRTY-THREE

*T*he storm came in faster than any Rebekah had ever seen. The captain was caught completely off guard, stammering that it couldn't be happening. They lost precious minutes to his stupidity, but it didn't matter. They were never going to make it to open water before the hurricane reached them. It wasn't even going to be a close race.

"We have to turn back," Eric urged, his brow furrowed with concern. "The captain is putting everyone in danger. We need to tell him there's no need to take such a risk."

"We can outlast this," Rebekah said, gripping the rails as lightning forked the sky. There never should have been a storm that night, and it couldn't possibly be as bad as it looked. "It's just a bit of rain. You'll see much worse than this if you stay with me."

Eric looked away from the hurricane to pull her near for a kiss. "Of course I will stay with you," he said into her hair. "Through this, through worse—through anything. But the ship's crew have made no such vow, and this is far more than just a bit of rain to them." She realized that he was leaving his entire life behind to go with her, but he couldn't leave his habits. He was a leader. Of course he thought of the common sailors, even at a time like this.

"They are all being paid as well, and they understand the risks," she replied, but she was not so sure. The sailors looked alternately green and pale, clinging to the rigging and watching the clouds anxiously. The captain, who stood to gain the most by leaving and arriving on schedule, was the only one who seemed to think that they should press on. Aside from Rebekah, of course, who had not been afraid of storms since she was a child.

"We can go back," Eric persisted, "After this, we'll have every night together, my beloved, so what does it matter if that begins tonight or tomorrow?"

No, she wouldn't go back—she couldn't. If they hesitated, they might be lost.

The water was growing wilder by the minute. As

they watched, a wave broke just over the bow of their ship, and a few of the sailors shouted in alarm. Wave after wave pummeled the ship, and the wind groaned and whipped about them in an incessant fury. They were tossed about like toys, and the ship spun in the water's brutal current. Even the captain looked nervous. Finally, Rebekah realized that a broken boat and a drowned crew wouldn't carry them far, and that they had to turn back.

"Wait here," she told Eric, kissing him as she left his side. "Please, where I can see you, and hold on." Another wave broke over the rail, higher this time, and a line snapped free of its mast and whistled through the air above their heads.

When he nodded his assent, Rebekah ran forward to the bow, where the captain struggled to keep control of the wheel. The ship was less and less inclined to respond to his orders, much like his crew. The storm was slowly taking ownership of them all, and she cursed the time she had lost to her stubbornness.

"Not to worry, Madame," the captain shouted, his voice barely audible over the shrieking wind. "It's just a trifle. Looks worse than it is."

Rebekah positioned herself before him and ruthlessly caught his eye. "Turn the ship around," she ordered, her voice humming with compulsion. "We'll return to

New Orleans and sail again when the weather is clear."

"We'll turn back now," he agreed numbly, then shook himself into action. He began barking orders, which the sailors struggled to obey. By then, one wave out of three was soaking the deck, and the crew was fighting just to stay on board.

Lightning struck down out of the sky near them, and a tree just past the shoreline exploded into a shower of sparks. It was too close, Rebekah realized—they were too late. The ship would never make it back to the harbor, not intact. Just as the thought occurred to her, a crewman was washed overboard, his hands groping for the rail until they disappeared below the white-capped waves.

"Eric!" Rebekah screamed. It had been a terrible mistake to leave his side. She had to get back to him. She tried to run, but the deck tossed and rolled. Another wave washed over the boat, tugging hungrily at her ankles. She wiped the spray from her eyes and found him again. He was holding fast to the central rigging, just as she had asked him to do, but even then she had underestimated the hurricane's fury. Eric's feet skittered across the wooden boards of the deck, the strength of his grip the only thing keeping him on board.

In the back of her mind, Rebekah counted between each wave. She would make it; he could hold on. She would reach him before he was swept into the water, and she could carry him safely to land. She would turn him the second they had solid earth beneath their feet, pact be damned. She could not live with the thought that she might lose Eric.

She could predict the swell and crash of each wave, but the next bolt of lightning caught her completely off guard. It struck the mast, and the sound of splintering wood and booming thunder was deafening. She staggered as the deck beneath her feet shuddered.

It cost her two seconds at the most, perhaps only one. But one was enough. A beam the width of her torso collapsed across the ship, splitting the deck from the prow to the stern. And she could not see Eric anymore.

Her cry was lost in a second peal of thunder. She could not believe the violence of the storm, and for a moment she allowed herself to believe that Eric had only been hidden by the bracing curtain of rain.

But she knew, even before she reached him. She had thought she could escape her fate—running from her family to make a new one. For a few short days, she had believed that an Original vampire could be entitled to a life of her own choosing, but it had all been a girlish fantasy. Her crime and her punishment was Eric Moquet.

He lay, limp and lifeless, beneath the heavy beam.

His glassy hazel eyes stared vacantly, and his mouth was slack. There was nothing left but his body. Everything else, everything that made him real and human and hers, was gone.

"Eric," she cried, "Eric, come back to me."

She bit viciously into her own wrist, tasting the tears that ran down her face as she ripped into the pale, blue-veined skin there. She held the bleeding wound to his lips. Each beat of her heart sent blood coursing down his throat, and she willed it to move and swallow.

She could feel water rushing into the hold below her feet, and fewer voices shouted around her now. The sailors were dead or dying, or else they were abandoning the ship. They were sinking and she needed to get Eric to safety so that her blood could work. She needed to save him so that he could rescue her.

She tugged at his arms, but his body was trapped. She pulled again, harder this time, and felt one of his arms pop out of its shoulder socket. She risked a closer look at how he was stuck.

His stomach and pelvis were completely crushed, and there would be no extracting him without lifting the beam. That would speed the breaking up of the ship, she knew, but it might still be worth the risk . . . if Eric were not so finally, completely dead. She had known it before she'd given him her blood, but the truth was too hard to comprehend. He'd been beside her just a minute ago. She had kissed him.

Desperately wanting those last sweet moments back, she kissed him again and smoothed a hand down over his eyes. The lids closed, and she choked back a hysterical sob. He looked less dead now, as if he might only be sleeping. She could remember him sleeping a dozen different ways, and she rested her head next to his, trying to capture her happiness again.

There was no breath, no heartbeat, no miracle. He was gone, and he stayed gone. The ship broke apart beneath them, the water pulled them down, and the wreckage surrounded and covered them. They fell into the cold, swirling water together, him dead and her unable to die. She couldn't feel the storm at the bottom, but it raged on inside her.

Eventually, she had to kick, to swim, and he remained on the bottom. It broke her heart to let him go, but she knew that it would be better there, in the silent depths. If she carried him back with her into the miserable night, she might hold his corpse forever, waiting for it to come back to life. She would lose her mind with the grief of the mistakes she had made and the chances she had missed, and in the end it would do her no good, anyway. Eric would not come back no matter how long she waited.

She broke the surface with a gasp, and made for the shore. Once she thought she saw a sailor clinging to some driftwood, waving frantically at her, but she ignored him. She dragged herself into the shallows of the bayou and sat on a muddy hillock for a while, her arms wrapped around her knees, crying like both a lost child and a grieving widow.

She would have to stand up eventually, she knew. She would have to make decisions again. She would have to rejoin her family and perhaps even speak about this terrible loss. The wound would be covered over and then hidden under fresh ones until she could barely remember the shape of it, because she would have to live with this pain forever.

But for now, she just sat, battered by the rain and whipped by the wind, sobbing.

THIRTY-FOUR

*J*ugo Rey had been brilliant, and Klaus wished that he had managed to meet the man before he died. The network of tunnels and chambers that radiated out from the main cellar allowed them to move unnoticed beneath the werewolves' very feet. Unfortunately, none of the tunnels seemed to extend beyond the borders of the property, so they could not escape, or even properly flank their besiegers. But there was an opportunity there, Klaus was sure of it. They needed only to decide how best to take advantage of it.

Klaus was partial to the idea of springing from one trapdoor while Elijah leaped out of an opposite one, surprising the wolves on two fronts and hopefully creating enough casualties to convince them to leave. But Elijah pointed out, quite reasonably, that once the trapdoors were open, the werewolves might manage to get into the cellar. Its far-flung chambers could not possibly be covered by the protection spell, and once the wolves had found them their only advantage would be lost.

Vivianne was no help, as all of her suggestions involved as few deaths as possible. She seemed convinced, in spite of the taunts and threats shouted through the missing windows, that a peaceful solution was possible and even desirable. Klaus fumed at the pointlessness of his earlier threat—he couldn't very well lock her in the cellar when they needed access to the arms stored there.

Klaus preferred if Vivianne didn't watch the slaughter, and put her in the upstairs bedroom, where she agreed to wait out the battle and storm.

"Stay safe, my love, and I will be back soon," he said with a kiss that was more of a bite of her full red lips. She gave him a smile that melted him from the inside, whispering a yes into his chest. Damn, he'd never get enough of this woman.

Back in the cellar, they scanned the ammunition. "This isn't everything," Elijah declared, his sharp brown eyes scanning the boxes. "The day Hugo died, I brought some barrels down for him, but they must still be in one of the outer cellars." He turned slowly, muttering something about "the southeast corner" and seeming to mentally check off each door in turn.

"That one," Klaus told him decisively, pointing to the one on their left and then crossing the dank dirt floor to throw it open. He let Elijah go first, then followed.

The barrels waited at the end of the tunnel, five of them, each nearly as tall as they were. Elijah was already prying the lid off one of them by the time Klaus caught up to him. He looked up with a strange gleam in his eyes. "Gunpowder," he said.

"In all of them?" Klaus demanded, but he didn't wait for an answer. Instead, he yanked up the lid of the nearest barrel while Elijah moved on to another. He could smell it even before he could see it. All five barrels were packed with gunpowder. There was enough to last them a year if they fired at the werewolves night and day the entire time, but Klaus felt that would be a terrible waste of such an extraordinary supply of the stuff.

"Each of these would make a powerful blast if we left it as it is," Elijah mused, and Klaus knew that they were thinking along the same lines.

"Four of these chambers and four barrels," Klaus agreed, "and a fifth from which we could pour out fuses. No blast will damage the house, but we could blow up the ground beneath their feet."

"I always did envy the number of werewolves you managed to pick off when we first arrived," Elijah grinned, positioning one barrel on the rough earthen steps and stepping back to examine the effect.

Klaus tipped his barrel over at the base of Elijah's and began to pour heavy black powder in a steady stream. When the thickness looked right for a makeshift fuse, he began to back away down the tunnel from which they had come. Elijah picked up a second barrel and took the easternmost door toward another of the outer cellars. With a full barrel in each corner of the property and the loose powder from the fifth barrel connecting them all to the center, they could turn the tables on their attackers with one simple spark.

Klaus ran his fuse into the very center of the main cellar, just below the open trapdoor. He counted his paces as he continued in a straight line to the door. By Klaus's estimate it would take less than a minute for the lines to burn in every direction, reach the full kegs, and blow them up through the earth.

Elijah met him below the central trapdoor, grinning. Klaus hadn't realized the extent to which they'd been at odds during the last nine years until they were on the same side again, fighting shoulder to shoulder—just as they always should have been.

"No point in waiting," Klaus pointed out, striking

a spark and waving Elijah toward the ladder. "We can clear out the werewolf infestation before the worst of the storm hits, then come back down here to ride it out if we have to."

Elijah cast a wary glance at the tinder in Klaus's hand before climbing up into the house. Klaus crouched down and touched the flame to where the four trails of gunpowder joined. It popped and caught, and he watched for a moment to make sure that it spread in each direction before following Elijah up the ladder.

"I'm impressed, brother," Elijah told him as he closed the trapdoor and stamped it firmly shut.

"It's a good plan," Klaus agreed smugly. "But it's fortunate we were so well supplied." It was easy enough to spread some of the credit around when there was so much of it and they were about to take out the entire Navarro pack from the comfort of their own home.

"That as well," Elijah said. "But I meant that Vivianne stayed put when you told her to."

Klaus chuckled and nodded, but then he felt a sudden stab of doubt. Why *had* Viv obeyed so placidly? Elijah was right—it wasn't like her at all. He raced up the stairs, calling her name and throwing open the bedroom door.

She was gone. She was gone, but she had not come down to the cellar to debate with them. He had not heard, seen, or even smelled her anywhere on the ground floor, and now there was no trace of her on the upper floor, either. She was simply gone.

It took him seconds—he could not have said exactly how many—to understand. She was not in the house, and so she must have left the house. She had defied him and departed the one safe place left to her, to go out into a crowd of angry werewolves under a bewitched hurricane. If she survived the night, he would kill her himself.

He crossed to the window and a flash of lightning showed him everything. Armand held her white arm in a vise grip, his face inches from hers. Sol stood directly behind her, his forehead beaded with sweat as he shouted something unintelligible.

"Viv!" Klaus shouted, and a few of the closest werewolves turned his way. The main ring of them was a good distance from the house, settling in for what they thought would be a long wait.

It would not, though. Klaus could picture the burning fuses and in the next brilliant bolt of lightning he even thought he could make out the trapdoor beside Vivianne's beaded shoes.

He dove from the window, but the first of the barrels went up even as he fell. There was another deafening crash just as he hit the ground. He rolled immediately to his feet, but before he could take a single step, the last two explosions went off together. Vivianne stared at him, her mouth open as if she wanted to speak, and then she disappeared as the ground beneath her erupted in shrapnel and flames.

The concussive blast of the explosions slammed Klaus hard against the wall of the house behind him, and fire bit into every inch of his skin. For a long time he could not see anything but light and smoke, and then he wished he could not.

Through the deafening ringing sound in his ears, Klaus thought he heard moans here and there around the house, but the destruction had been nearly total. The house stood untouched, in the center of a ravaged plot of dirt, crisscrossed by tunnels that lay open like waiting graves. Corpses lay everywhere around them, a triumph that left Klaus completely, utterly empty.

One of the bodies was hers. He knew before he looked, and so he could not bear to look too carefully. A shred of blackened lace, a stretch of blistered skin. She had been standing directly above the keg of gunpowder. He found that his arms were around her, that he held her as close as he ever could have. She had met a quick, brutal end to her short, charmed life, and Klaus knew it was far more his loss than hers.

Vivianne Lescheres had lived every moment fully

and passionately, and now Klaus would have to live the rest of his without her. It was unbearable, unthinkable. It was cruel, and it was at least a little bit his fault. He had seen how far she was willing to go to defend her faith in her people, and he had understood the profound depths of her naïveté.

And yet he had left her unprotected, because no matter how well he knew her, he had never once managed to put himself in her place. He had never predicted the intensity of her need to do the right thing, and so he had lost her again and again until there was nothing left to lose.

"Run, if you can," he shouted hollowly to any wolf left to hear him. "Run now. There will be no amnesty, no peace. Run."

A hurricane was coming to level the city, and nearly all of its werewolves were dead. The ones who remained would do well to heed his warning, because Vivianne was gone and Klaus had nothing else to protect. He heard a few miserable survivors scrambling into the brush. Klaus found himself alone, the world around him as barren as his own heart. A sudden sheet of rain drowned out the fires from the explosion, and Klaus held Vivianne's body closer, guarding her as the storm came upon their exposed scar of land.

THIRTY-FIVE

*T*he storm forced the door closed again as soon as Elijah managed to yank it open. The wind had a life of its own, thrashing and dancing around the house, and carrying along bits of debris. The storm had blown in across the water and reached them at last, and Elijah was not at all sure the house would stand against it.

He dragged Klaus inside, fighting the wind the whole way. Klaus stubbornly held a body in his arms, a corpse Elijah recognized as Vivianne. He cradled her tenderly against his chest, and Elijah was awed by the endurance of his love.

"You should have told me, brother," Elijah said, but Klaus did not seem to hear him. He slammed the door behind them. Perversely, now it did not want to remain shut, and Elijah found a wooden bar to hold it closed. "I would not have liked it, but I would have understood."

"You were dead set against it," Klaus said, but there was no bitterness in his tone, there was just nothing. "Everyone was against us, and yet she never stopped wanting to explain. She died trying to make the rest of the world *understand*."

"I would have," Elijah repeated, resting one hand on his brother's shoulder. Klaus flinched a little, but he did not pull away. "If I had known you felt this way, I would have stood behind you."

"We will never know," Klaus answered, setting Vivianne's body down on the floor and stroking her dark hair. "With her gone, I do not think my happiness will ever depend so entirely on one woman again."

Elijah rocked back on his heels, stunned at the raw, vulnerable loss in Klaus's voice. Vivianne hadn't simply been a conquest or a delectable piece of forbidden fruit; Klaus had been in love. He could not remember the last time he had seen his brother look so empty, his usual fire not just dampened but nowhere to be found. It was almost unbearable to see Klaus—irrepressible, impossible Klaus—defeated.

Rebekah was gone and Klaus was broken, and the storm had come in earnest. Elijah could tell that the witches fully intended to make good on their threat, and as the night went on it was clear that Ysabelle's protection spell was the only thing that kept the house standing. Perhaps it actually did defend against the weather, or it could somehow tell that this was no natural storm.

The hurricane howled through the window frames, shredding the curtains and throwing books, plates, and even furniture around the room. Lightning crashed down around them, splitting whole trees down to the ground. The pounding rain turned the earth into rivers and waterfalls, flooding the tunnels and certainly the cellar beneath them. But the house itself did not yield. When morning arrived, the new day brought the faintest hint of sunlight along with it.

Elijah convinced Klaus to take a ride with him, promising that they would pass by the witches' cemetery along their way. A place would need to be made for Vivianne, and making that kind of practical arrangement might lift Klaus's spirits a bit. He would want to feel he could do *something* for her.

They caught a couple of horses that were running loose in the forest. From the look of them, Elijah guessed that they had come from the French army's encampment. He doubted they fared well in their tents and makeshift buildings, especially with their commander and his lieutenant gone.

Where the houses were closer, the damage was even more pronounced than in the ravaged outskirts. Elijah barely understood where he was at first, now that all the landmarks were missing. It seemed he no longer knew his way around New Orleans, with this house gone and that villa collapsed, with that magnificent tree now lying sideways across that stately manor. It was as if he had entered an alien place, and he hurried his horse along.

Klaus followed behind, not seeming to notice what had become of the city. He held Vivianne's body before him on his horse, and only looked at her.

The werewolves' quarter had been beaten just as badly. Even though most of the pack had been at the Mikaelsons', it was obvious that the witches would have been willing to do the job for them. Any werewolf who had not taken part in the siege had been drowned or crushed.

Hardly anyone but the two Originals moved among the devastated houses, and of the few survivors he saw, at least half were packing up their possessions into carts. New Orleans was no place for the werewolves now— they were surrounded by enemies and without a pack. They'd all be gone soon enough, and Elijah felt a twinge at the bitterness of his success.

Yet in spite of the solemnity of the destruction around

him, Elijah could feel the wheels in his head turning. It certainly had not been their intention, but the witches had created a great deal of space . . . and left vampires to fill it.

They turned west, toward the cemetery. Elijah had an ulterior motive, of course—he was curious to see if Ysabelle had survived the night. She and her sister had taken no part in the raising of the hurricane, and he would be sorry if it had killed them.

Klaus dismounted in the graveyard and waved him onward. Elijah left his horse beside Klaus's and continued alone. He found Ysabelle and Sofia on the porch of Ysabelle's house, blinking in the daylight as if they had just come outside.

Sofia Lescheres saw him first, and she touched her sister's elbow and went into the house without a word. Ysabelle watched her go, then stepped down off the porch to meet Elijah halfway. "She is grieving," the tall witch explained, wrapping a mauve shawl tightly around her body. "There was a great deal of death last night, and in their anger the fools did not think to protect our people. Witches are dead, and she believes that her daughter is one of them."

"She is," Elijah confirmed simply. He considered trying to explain how she had died, but there was very little he could say that would not make it worse. He and Klaus had survived, and Vivianne was dead. Even surrounded by werewolves, the ground exploding, and a magical storm bearing down, the brothers had lived, and the witches would hold them responsible for failing to protect Vivianne.

And perhaps they would be right. If Klaus had not been so deeply, blindly in love, he would have tied her to a chair and been done with it. "It was quick," Elijah offered. "Vivianne did not suffer."

Ysabelle shuddered, and he could tell that she was holding back a sob. "Thank you," she whispered. "I will tell my sister." She clenched her hands, blue veins standing out angrily. "Those fools," she repeated, and in those two short words Elijah could hear all of the raging she refused to do in front of him.

"My brother is in the cemetery now," he told her. "We would like to help with the arrangements, if we may." Even better if they could get Vivianne's remains safely into a casket before anyone thought to ask why she was burned. "I understand that Vivianne's father rests elsewhere, but we thought this place would be most appropriate, if her family agrees."

Ysabelle hesitated, glancing back at her house again. It looked untouched by the storm, Elijah noticed. He guessed that his was not the only house she had used Esther's grimoire to protect. "Sofia will be staying with me for a while," she replied. "Her roof was lost, and she doesn't want to see anyone. But it is a kind offer, and I think that if it were simply *done* . . ."

Elijah nodded. "We will take care of it," he assured her. "We can begin work on a suitable tomb this morning. If Sofia will come to the cemetery two nights from now, I will make sure that she has a chance to say a proper good-bye. Alone, if she wishes it."

"I think she will," Ysabelle agreed. "Thank you."

He left her there, unable to do more. Ysabelle and her sister would just have to live with their anger and their grief. Elijah guessed that it would be some time before they thought about the rebuilding and running of the city, and that suited him quite well.

He found Klaus still in the witches' graveyard, looking sober and intent on his task. "I was thinking here," he said at Elijah's arrival. "You can see a bit of the river from right here."

Elijah clasped his arm, then walked with him back to where their horses waited. He explained his conversation with Ysabelle, and they discussed whether they were likely to find a tradesman left in the city to build a casket and a little mausoleum.

Klaus seemed somewhat cheered by the news that a number of witches had perished in the storm, and Elijah was glad that he was beginning to look beyond his gloom. It would take Klaus time to heal, but forever was a long time to carry such a raw wound—and eventually his brother would start to let go of the pain.

As they returned to their home, Klaus's horse snorted and shied in surprise. Elijah tightened his reins instinctively, looking around for any potential source of danger.

She was right in front of them. Rebekah sat on their porch, with her bare feet dangling carelessly in the muddy water. Her golden hair was plastered down against her skull, and her clothing was so soaked and filthy that he could not have guessed at its original color. Her beautiful face was dirty as well, but he could see where fresh tears had carved out tracks of bare skin.

She didn't need to speak—it was obvious that she had also lost her true love last night. She would not be there, alone and weeping, if Eric had survived. He would never have wished that kind of a loss on her—or on Klaus, for that matter. To see both of them bereaved in one single blow was the worst kind of sorrow.

"It will be all right," Elijah told her, then nodded to Klaus so that he would know Elijah spoke to them both. "There can be no replacement for what you have lost, but you have not lost everything. No matter who else is gone or missed or remembered, we will always have one another. We will always have family."

The untold story of THE ORIGINALS
has only just begun.

Read on for a sneak peek of
THE ORIGINALS: THE LOSS

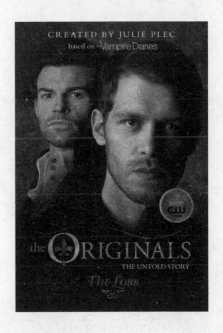

Coming soon from creator Julie Plec,
Alloy Entertainment and HQN Books . . .

PROLOGUE

1766

*L*ily Leroux had promised herself that she wouldn't cry. Her mother would never have forgiven her for crying. Lily's job was to look strong and poised in her fitted black dress, to accept the community's condolences without seeming to need them. She was in charge of New Orleans's witches now, or whatever was left of them. She had to lead them, not lean on them.

They could certainly use some leading. Lily's mother had done her best to hold them together after the hurricane they'd created had razed the city to its foundations more than forty years ago, but their losses had been catastrophic. And the guilt of having caused so much destruction . . . the guilt was even more devastating.

In the meantime, other players had stepped into the void of power left behind by the witches. The French had recently handed New Orleans over to the Spanish, who had chosen to wholly ignore their new territory. Instead, it was the vampires who had taken the reins.

The Mikaelsons—the Originals, three of the very first vampires in existence—had made their move at an ideal time. Elijah, Rebekah, and, worst of all, Klaus now ruled the city. The witches hated them with a passion, although Lily suspected that her mother had always nursed some kind of soft spot for them. She had categorically shut down any talk of retaliation or reprisal by reminding them that their own hands were responsible for their current sorry state. If they hadn't tried to seek reckless revenge against the werewolves for betraying their truce, they wouldn't be sequestered in the backwaters of the bayou.

And the result of that policy was that Ysabelle Dalliencourt's funeral was a sorry shadow of what it should have been. She had led her people out of the ruined city and kept their community together, she had counseled them against a destructive path of war, and taught them to focus on themselves and their craft rather than on the walking abominations that sat on their former throne.

She should have lain in state in the heart of New

Orleans, not in the sorry little clapboard meetinghouse the witches had built in the midst of a swamp.

The Original vampires were responsible for this slight, Lily knew. They could have forgiven the witches' weakness, as the witches had once looked past the brutality of the vampires. Instead, the Mikaelsons had tasted freedom and run with it, creating an army of new vampires from the humans of New Orleans and driving the witches out.

Everyone stood, and Lily rose with them, numbly. Six witches lifted her mother's wooden casket on their shoulders and she heard Marguerite sob as they carried it past. Lily rested a comforting hand on her daughter's thin shoulder, and fought the burning behind her eyes.

But she would not cry. Ysabelle had done well by her people, but her death was a sign to Lily that it was time for a new era, a changing of the guard. Lily was sick to death of subsisting under the vampires' tyranny. The Mikaelsons needed to answer for their sins, and Lily Leroux intended to make sure they paid in full.

ONE

1766

*I*t was Klaus's kind of night. Wine and blood flowed freely, and the relaxed company and summer heat had led to an easy loosening of everyone's clothing. He could only guess what was going on upstairs, but he didn't intend to leave it to his imagination for long.

There would be time enough to take it all in. That was one of the nice things about being both a king and an immortal: He could do whatever he wanted, whenever he wanted. Elijah took care of the running of the city, Rebekah took care of the running of the Mikaelsons, and Klaus was free to take care of Klaus.

Carousing vampires filled every room on the ground floor, and Klaus could hear the party continuing through the ceiling above. In the forty-odd years since they had taken possession of a dying smuggler's modest home, the Original vampires had done a great deal of adding on and improving, but even so it was filled to capacity. To effectively rule over a city full of eager young vampires the Mikaelsons might need to move to a larger home, but finding more land wouldn't be the problem it once had been for them. New property was easy to come by in a metropolis empty of werewolves and witches.

Most of the werewolves who managed to survive the hurricane and explosion of 1722 had straggled away, and the ones who remained kept their noses down. The witches had fared a bit better, but not much: They squatted out in the bayou, their taste for power broken. New Orleans was essentially free of vermin.

It still made his gut twist in pain to think of what they'd done to Vivianne, even decades after her death. The way the witches had offered her hand in marriage to the werewolves, as if her only value lay in her heritage as the child of both clans. After signing her life away in a treaty to bring peace, the werewolves had demanded more of her mind and heart at every turn. She had died terribly young, still trying to make everything right between the factions.

"You're so quiet tonight, Niklaus. Should I get you

another drink?" A buxom young vampire fell into Klaus's lap with a giggle and interrupted the dark turn of his thoughts. Her long, strawberry-blonde hair smelled like orange blossoms. *Lisette*, he reminded himself. She was one of the newest crop of recruits in their little army, but she carried herself with the ease of a vampire who had lived for centuries. She did not seem intimidated by the Originals, nor did she strain herself to impress them, and that indifference had won Klaus's approval.

He smiled, blowing strands of her long hair away from his face. "Would you like me to still recognize you by the end of the night?" he asked her airily.

"I'd lay odds that your memory can stand up to more liquor than you have in this entire house." Lisette returned his fond smile with a saucy wink. "But you could just join me for some air, if you like. It's a beautiful night, and I'm restless. Helping you keep your wits about you could be my good deed for the day."

"You want to leave my party?" Klaus asked, curious in spite of his bleak thoughts. "I never thought of you as the solitary type." He could not, in fact, remember ever seeing Lisette alone. Perhaps he had confused her with another new vampire after all. He had been drinking liberally, trying his best to truly join in the revelry around him. Forty-four years, and he still felt as though

Vivianne might walk through the door and make him whole again.

"I am deep and mysterious," Lisette told him, with a mock seriousness in her wide-set gray eyes. "Come upstairs with me and I'll prove it to you."

Klaus brushed her reddish hair aside and kissed her neck lingeringly. She sighed and wriggled a little, giving his mouth better access. "Not tonight, love," he murmured softly, traveling down to her collarbone. Across the room, another pair of vampires moved together in a similar way. Watching them, Klaus continued to brush Lisette's lightly freckled skin with his lips, but it only made him feel even hollower. He could go through the motions, but he couldn't be consumed by them. No matter how far he wandered down the path of debauchery, he couldn't quite get lost.

He wanted Vivianne back. That was the simple, scalding truth of the matter. He had tried to bury her and tried to mourn and tried to move on, because he knew that was how death was supposed to work. He had seen it countless times, even though no one would ever be forced to mourn the loss of *him*. His mother had been a witch, his true father had been a werewolf, and to save him from a certain death, his mother had made him a vampire. Klaus would never die.

It was useless to compare himself to other people.

Niklaus Mikaelson was not in a position to simply lie down and accept the workings of normal, faceless, mortal death. It was stupid and beneath him. If he wanted Vivianne Lescheres at his side, ruling New Orleans as his queen for eternity, it should not be an impossible demand. Not for the likes of him.

Lisette shifted again, rather enjoyably, trying to bring his full attention back to her. It was no use, though. "*Ma petite* Lisette, my heart is not in this celebration tonight, so I will make my farewell," he apologized, sliding her gently back onto her feet.

"As you wish," she said before sauntering off, glancing over her shoulder to make sure Klaus was watching her go. He was, of course—it was a simple courtesy after rejecting her advances. And the back of her was just as easy on the eyes as the front, so he didn't mind.

When she was gone he eased himself up out of his chair and slipped out through a different door. A few voices called after him as he moved through the dimly lit rooms, which were full of sharp teeth, ringing laughter, and sensuous limbs. He ignored them, having finally realized where he wanted to spend this night.

He climbed the ornate spiral staircase, lined with a red silk carpet that Rebekah had ordered from the Far East. As he passed by several bedrooms he heard his name called again, but this time in softer, throatier voices.

He resisted the impulse to look through the doors that had been carelessly—or deliberately—left open, making instead for a small staircase at the back of the house.

Klaus had asked his siblings to keep it private, and so Rebekah picked a medieval tapestry to conceal the doorframe: a unicorn, with a gold-threaded mane laid gently in the lap of a lovely virgin. Rebekah had the strangest notions sometimes. He glanced behind him and then swept the curtain aside, retreating from his guests and their revelry to the safety of his attic sanctuary.

This was the one place his sister's restless hands had not touched. The attic was much larger than it had been when they had first inherited the house, but it'd retained its original rustic look. Unpolished beams crisscrossed the high, gabled roof, and the rough floorboards creaked charmingly beneath his feet. There were a few windows set into the peaks of the gables, and during the day sunlight streamed in from all directions.

Klaus moved his easel with the sun, watching his paintings change over the course of each day. He'd sometimes climb up here at night and light a few candles, stepping back from the easel to take in the effect of all of his canvases at once. He had been working feverishly and couldn't remember ever being so productive.

It was a waste, though, because every last painting

was of *her*. Vivianne's left eye, black in a pale sea of skin. The outline of Vivianne running through a cobblestoned street in the middle of the night. The sound of Vivianne's laughter, captured so perfectly that someone who had never met her would still know what it was. Vivianne in his bed the first night, the last night, every night.

It wasn't work; it was torture. He could never paint anything else. Whatever he tried his hand at simply became another aspect of Vivianne.

His current painting was of her hair: black and sleek as a raven's wings, but with a life and movement that Klaus struggled to capture exactly. In the light of his candle it looked flat and wrong, an entire story he was somehow failing to tell. He picked up a brush and began to work, adding texture and light in some places, while leaving others as dark as gravity.

The wailing sound of the house's protection spell went off again, as it had been all night long. Everyone else was too busy partying to pay attention to it, but Klaus stopped, brush halfway to canvas, at the sight of a witch at the east window. She sat on the outer lintel, poised as if she were resting on a park bench.

Klaus knew her at once. No matter what Ysabelle Dalliencourt's old spell assumed, this was not exactly an unexpected intruder on their land. He could see traces of her mother's face in hers, in the strong, straight nose and the long planes of her cheeks. Her hair was darker, more of a ruddy brown than an auburn, but her eyes were the same fathomless brown.

He crossed the room quickly, wishing that he could cover all of his canvases as he went. Vivianne and Lily might have been cousins, but Lily had no right to see her image the way Klaus portrayed it. No matter her relation, Lily was one of *them*, a descendant of the cowards and weaklings who had let Viv slip away.

He opened the window and invited her inside nonetheless. Lily was also the first witch in over forty years to respond to Klaus's overtures, and he couldn't afford to slight her.

To raise the dead was difficult, but it was more than just that. It required dark and frightening magic that few would dare to even attempt. For decades Klaus had let it be known—quietly, without involving his siblings in something that was really none of their concern—that the price of readmission to New Orleans was Vivianne. The witches wanted their home back badly, but none had broken ranks to try their hand. Ysabelle had much to do with that, he knew, but now she was dead, and her daughter had come to bargain.

"I can grant you what you desire," Lily Leroux told him with no preamble. "But it will cost you. One item for the spell, and another for my daughter."

"As I have said—" Klaus began, but she waved the words off impatiently.

"I know what you are willing to offer," she reminded him. "Now listen to what I want."

Klaus was never eager to be on the wrong side of a bargain, but if it meant that Vivianne would be returned to him, he would listen to anything the witch had to say.

TWO

Rebekah had to admit that Klaus knew how to throw a party. She and her two siblings had lived in relative solitude for so long that now it was as if she could never get enough of their own kind, and Klaus always seemed ready to provide her with plenty of company. Lithe young vampires filled the mansion, dancing, singing, drinking, and casting alluring glances at one another . . . and at her. Always at her. She was more than a celebrity among them; she was practically a goddess.

After a few glasses of champagne, Rebekah found that being worshipped suited her just fine. There were a few—well, more than a few—young male vampires who made a sport of competing for her attention, and she encouraged them shamelessly. There was a Robert and a Roger she constantly mixed up, and Efrain, who had extraordinary blue eyes but got tongue-tied at the mere sight of her. Tonight was about celebrating, and tomorrow night probably would be, too.

Robert (she was almost sure) refilled her glass before it was empty, and she smiled languidly at him. They were like sweet, admiring puppies, sitting at her feet and lapping up every scrap of her attention. It was impossible to take any of them seriously, but perhaps something not-so-serious was exactly what she needed.

She had been in love, and she knew how that ended. But she would live for a very long time, and it was not realistic to spend the rest of eternity running away from every sort of connection. A good fling might be exactly what she needed . . . and then perhaps another one after that.

A cheerful-looking vampire with reddish-gold hair strolled into the parlor where Rebekah held court, and she noticed Klaus leaving the drawing room in the opposite direction. *Sulking again,* she guessed. He was as magnetic as ever, drawing in humans and vampires alike. They flocked to the house at his suggestion, and then he hid from them like a hermit. He was going up to that drafty attic again; she just knew it.

"I'm sorry for my brother's rudeness," she told the female vampire impulsively.

The girl's gray eyes widened in momentary surprise, as if it'd never occurred to her to be offended by Klaus's abrupt moods. Rebekah felt foolish for having even mentioned it, but then the vampire smiled easily. Her teeth were white and even, like a good string of pearls. "No need," she assured Rebekah, as casually as if they were equals. "He is who he is."

"Wise words," Rebekah agreed, draining her champagne and then staring pointedly at Roger. He hurried away to find a new bottle. "Klaus doesn't have it in him to think of others."

The only thing to which Klaus had really applied himself over the past forty-odd years was driving Rebekah and Elijah crazy. He had won ownership of that tawdry brothel he so enjoyed in a card game and promptly lost it again. The Southern Spot had spent all of a week under the new sign reading THE SLAP AND THE TICKLE before its old one had been restored. Still, Klaus spent inordinate amounts of time there, drinking and whoring as if he still were needed on hand to run the place. He had only stumbled out in the mornings to interrupt the French army's battles and feed at his pleasure, forcing Rebekah to use her powers of compulsion indiscriminately again and again. He delighted in tormenting the new French governors until they were driven out of town, almost ruining The Originals' claim to their land when the Spanish had used that opening to their own advantage.

The redheaded girl sat down companionably without waiting for an invitation. Rebekah raised an eyebrow, but she was amused, and the bold young thing didn't seem the slightest bit intimidated by her expression. "I wouldn't expect him to think of anyone but himself," she agreed easily. "I was just trying to help him out of his mood."

"And why would he be any less moody for you than for the rest of us? I don't even know you," Rebekah reminded her. She was sure she had seen the girl around before, but had probably been paying too much attention to Robert/Roger to notice. In any case, attending a few parties hardly made her a part of the Mikaelsons' inner circle.

"Oh! I'm Lisette," the vampire chirped, extending her hand as an afterthought. She offered no other explanation or defense for her presumption, and it seemed like she was totally unaware of it. The Original mystique seemed to slide right off of Lisette. After the fawning attention of Rebekah's admirers, it was like the shock of diving into a cool pool of water.

Rebekah hesitated for the briefest of disapproving moments before shaking Lisette's outstretched hand.

Part of her wanted to shake some appropriate reverence into the girl . . . but the rest of her actually enjoyed the novelty. A fling would be great, but a friend . . . How long had it been since Rebekah had had a real friend? Her nature, her position, and her family made it virtually impossible to make girlfriends, much less keep them. Rebekah Mikaelson was dangerous, intimidating, immortal, and guarded. But Lisette didn't seem to care.

"So tell me about yourself, Lisette," she commanded, then bit her tongue and softened her tone. "Please?"

"Oh, me? There's really nothing to tell," Lisette giggled, but that didn't prevent her from immediately producing a few chatty tidbits about the other partygoers.

She went on, and Rebekah basked in the normalcy of it. They might have been of an age: young women navigating society together. She listened raptly, asking questions whenever Lisette needed prompting, and Lisette obliged with an astonishing wealth of information about nearly all of the Mikaelsons' guests. Most of Rebekah's pets gave up and drifted away after a while, and even shy, smitten Efrain looked around as if he might prefer to be elsewhere.

But Rebekah didn't care. Admiration was easy enough to come by these days, but Lisette was a rarer kind of fun. They were still talking when a commotion broke out near the sweeping main staircase, and Rebekah reluctantly decided she needed to investigate. She had put far too much work into making this house comfortable to let it go to ruin, no matter how much fun everyone was having.

When she reached the front hall, though, she realized that the newest vampires weren't the problem at all. Klaus had returned from his sulk, and seemed determined to spread his misery around. A few nervous-looking vampires, in various states of undress, huddled together on the staircase, cowering as Klaus pushed past them. "If I find you've touched anything in those rooms I will slice you open from throat to ankles looking for it," he threatened the nearest one, who could only tremble by way of reply.

Had something gone missing? Something of Klaus's? Whatever it was, it must be important enough that he would search for it in the middle of a party. She could not imagine what would provoke him to act so bizarrely, except that maybe he'd simply gone too long without making a scene, and couldn't help himself.

"My dear sister!" he greeted her, his voice a mockery of brotherly warmth. Then a thought seemed to occur to him. "*You* probably have it," he told her cryptically, and climbed back up the staircase.

"I—do you think you're going to *my* room?" Rebekah shrieked, running after him. "Niklaus, what the hell has gotten into you tonight?" Skipping the party to brood in his attic sounded like a brilliant plan in comparison to this.

He didn't answer her. Instead, he threw open the door to her room and began tearing through her things. *Her* things; he couldn't even leave this one, tiny corner of the house alone.

She grabbed his arm, but he shook her hand off and upended a jewelry box onto her vanity. Pearls and topazes spilled everywhere, and soft gold gleamed against the painted wood. "It's nothing," he muttered, not even bothering to lie convincingly. "There's just a trinket I've lost, and it might have wound up here."

He opened another box, rifling through it carelessly, dropping a ruby earring onto the carpet without even noticing. "Get *out!*" she cried, shoving him with all of her strength. His body flew backward, crashing into the door with a satisfying splintering. "Whatever it is you won't find it here."

Klaus moved on to the next room, and Rebekah heard another crash from down the hall. If she didn't go after her brother, she realized, the damage would mount quickly. He hadn't even bothered to throw out the occupants of the room this time. Rebekah found him throwing clothing out of a closet while two vampires watched him from the bed, an embroidered coverlet pulled up to their chins as if the thin silk would protect them from a lunatic vampire. "Stop this madness," she ordered.

He waved her away dismissively and walked out to the top of the stairs, shouting that it was time for all of their guests to leave. Why was it up to Klaus to decide that the party was over? He had a special talent for ruining beautiful things.

Rebekah reached the bottom of the stairs just in time to see him disappearing into Elijah's study. She felt sure Elijah would thank her for keeping him out, and so she gritted her teeth and pushed through the crowd.

Klaus had already forced open a drawer of Elijah's desk, and Rebekah gasped. She had no idea where Elijah had gotten to, but the moment her brother saw what Klaus was doing, the house would not be big enough to hold the three of them.

"Don't touch that," she shouted, throwing her weight against the drawer to slam it closed. Klaus shoved her aside and broke open the lock on another drawer. Rebekah shoved him back, hard, and he tripped over one of the large candelabras that Elijah had along the walls. It swayed dangerously toward the window beside it, and Rebekah had just enough time to see a curl of smoke rise up from the fabric before Klaus sprang toward her.

The force of his attack knocked them both back out into the front hall, snarling and biting and scrabbling for purchase. Vampires scattered, and somewhere nearby Rebekah heard the sound of breaking glass. Tangy smoke drifted out of the open door of the study, and she guessed that the curtains had caught fire. Klaus destroyed *everything*.

She couldn't live like this anymore, not with Klaus the terror. He didn't appreciate anything she or Elijah did for him. He was so self-centered that he couldn't imagine they might prefer to *not* spend their lives either cleaning up his current disaster or trying to predict his next one.

As she gasped for breath from Klaus's armlock, Rebekah made up her mind: She'd find a way to destroy whatever was left of Klaus's happiness just the way he always managed to ruin hers.

THREE

$\mathcal{E}$ lijah ran an idle finger up and down Ava's bare arm, feeling perfectly at peace. It had not been easy, and the cost had been high, but he had persevered. He had held his siblings together and overcome every obstacle this city had thrown their way, and now it was time to reap the rewards.

The French had lost their grip on the region, and now Spain had seized power and established its own rule over New Orleans. But it quickly became clear that actually running the city was of no interest to King Carlos III, and the Spanish governor he'd sent over didn't find the task especially appealing, either. The French colonists were disgusted by the regime change, and Elijah had always viewed human unrest as an opportunity.

As a result of his savvy and foresight, everything of consequence in New Orleans now had to go through him. Trade, construction, legal matters . . . Elijah Mikaelson was the city's beating heart. And once he realized that the witches could no longer enforce their ban on siring new vampires, Elijah had taken particular delight in doing so. His family was the central core of his world, but there were benefits to building a community as well. He had everything he had wanted, and now he had Ava, who seemed determined to come up with all sorts of new things for him to desire.

She stretched contentedly across the four-poster bed, and dappled light from the fireplace painted curious patterns on her skin. Just as he reached for her again, he heard a crash and a scream coming from downstairs. He waited for a moment, hoping that it would fade back into the predictable sounds of a party, but the commotion only seemed to be growing louder. Vaguely, he recalled hearing some other thumps and shouts a few minutes before. Perhaps they had been more significant than he realized, but he'd been thoroughly distracted.

Ava protested as he rose from the bed, and the glint in her catlike eyes was almost enough to make him ignore the trouble. But Elijah had not risen to power by ignoring warning signs, and with an apology, he slid back into his discarded clothing and went out into the hall.

He could pick out both of his siblings' voices in the din. There was also a distinct crackling sound beneath everything else, and Elijah could smell smoke. Elijah resigned himself to dealing with whatever was happening below and abandoning Ava for the night.

His willingness to get involved in this kind of mess was precisely why he was in charge and the Spanish weren't, but sometimes it infuriated him to have to be the responsible one. He stormed down the curved staircase, the stench of smoke burning in his nostrils. It was coming from his study, and was growing dangerously out of hand. In addition to the curtains, two bookcases on either side had gone up in flames, and many of the books looked unsalvageable. He also noticed that the charred walls and books were not the only damage. His desk—a heavy piece of chestnut that did not move easily—stood askew, and some of the drawers that he knew had been locked were ajar. The fire had not simply been an unlucky accident; someone had been in this room, going through his things, when it had started.

And Elijah could guess who it was. Rebekah may have provoked him—she couldn't always help herself—but the destruction in his study was Klaus's work. There was no one else with such a talent for inconvenient chaos.

Even with Elijah's unnatural speed and strength, it took him a few minutes to put out the fire, then he thundered out of his study, to where Rebekah and Klaus were locked in a pointlessly vicious struggle. Neither of them had a silver dagger or, thankfully, a white oak stake, the only two weapons that could take down an Original vampire. All they could accomplish was annoying each other and making fools of themselves. Their wounds would heal, but the embarrassment would linger.

Elijah grabbed Klaus by the collar and threw him backward, then stepped forward to rest his foot against Rebekah's chest. He heard Klaus struggling to stand, and held out a warning hand. "Enough," he said, his voice full of authority. "The two of you were content to let the house burn around you. Over what?"

They both began to argue at once, and he held his hand up again to silence them. Then, reluctantly, he pointed to Klaus. He would rather hear Rebekah's version of events first, as it was almost certainly the more accurate one. But Klaus would never sit by and let her tell it. Giving him this small concession would help reestablish peace.

"Our sister is out of control," Klaus spat

contemptuously. "I asked for her help in finding a simple trinket, and she followed me around the house, attacking me like some kind of madwoman."

To Elijah's shock, Klaus stormed from the room without waiting to hear another word, scattering the remaining guests as he went.

"He's lost his mind," Rebekah argued, shoving Elijah's unresisting foot away and sitting up. "I don't know what he's up to, but this thing he wants is no mere trinket. He wants it too badly."

There was no doubting that she was right. Elijah couldn't imagine what Klaus was looking for, or why it had suddenly gripped him that he *must* have it right now, in the middle of the night. Klaus should have been enjoying the party, not tearing the house apart on some wild errand. Something had set him off, and Elijah reluctantly guessed that he would need to get to the bottom of this.

Together they followed the telltale sounds of Klaus's renewed search to Elijah's bedroom. A quick glance told Elijah that Ava had left. He felt a quick pang of frustration—Klaus's selfishness never stopped intruding on everyone else's lives.

"You're not welcome in this room, brother," Elijah warned him, his voice cold and menacing. "Whatever this trinket is to you, you are still a member of this family, and this sort of behavior is unacceptable."

He thought he heard Klaus chuckle under his breath as he opened Elijah's wardrobe and began hunting. Elijah understood why Rebekah had lost her patience and attacked him; there seemed to be no other way to get through to him in this state.

"If we knew what he wanted . . ." Rebekah whispered, her blue eyes flicking sideways to meet his own. She was right. If they could find it first, they would have some leverage to make Klaus . . . what, though? Apologize? Explain? Think? None of those were likely, no matter what they held hostage.

It wouldn't matter anyway. The house was full of powerful objects that they'd collected over the centuries, and Klaus could be after any of them. Their mother had been one of the most powerful witches in history, and they were the oldest and strongest vampires in existence. Useful, pretty, and priceless "trinkets" were so common in their house that they never would have missed one if they had not caught Klaus searching for it.

"Tell us what you want, brother," Elijah ordered, guessing that it was futile.

To his surprise, Klaus emerged from the wardrobe, looking almost reasonable. "I want to be left alone, *brother*," he retorted sarcastically. His voice was light, but his blue-green eyes blazed with a passion that Elijah thought bordered on madness. Perhaps Rebekah was right: Maybe their brother really was losing his wits. He had not been the same since that terrible night Vivianne Lescheres had died, but it wasn't as if they all hadn't experienced a few losses during their long lives.

"You don't have the *right* to be left alone," Elijah said. "I have put everything I have into building this haven for you—for both of you." He saw Rebekah flinch, but he didn't care. "I have spent decades building a kingdom for us, and all you have to do is sit back and enjoy. Instead, you spend your time on this nonsense. You let our house burn while you think only of what *you* want. The same will happen with this entire city if you aren't careful."

Klaus simply walked away. He didn't respond or complain or argue, just sauntered past them as if he had not heard a single word.

Elijah tried to make sense of the entire scene that had just played out. Something had shifted within his brother. They heard a door slam downstairs, then Elijah felt the hair stand up on his arms. He could hear the sound of Klaus whistling. Cheerfully.

"Good riddance," Rebekah muttered, once the sound had faded into silence. But Elijah knew that this wasn't the last they'd hear of this. Klaus was up to no good, and whatever his plan, he was just getting started.

*J*ulie Plec skillfully juggles work in film and television as both a producer and a writer. She is the co-creator and executive producer of *The Vampire Diaries* and the creator of *The Vampire Diaries* spin-off, *The Originals*, which tells the story of history's first vampire family.

Plec got her start as a television writer on the ABC Family series *Kyle XY*, which she also produced for its three-year run. She also collaborated with Greg Berlanti and Phil Klemmer on the CW drama *The Tomorrow People*, the story of a small group of people gifted with extraordinary paranormal abilities.

Her screenplay adaptation *The Tiger's Curse* is in development at Paramount, and she will produce the feature *@emma* with Darko Entertainment. Past feature production credits include *Scream 2* and *Scream 3*, Greg Berlanti's *Broken Hearts Club*, Wes Craven's *Cursed*, and *The Breed*.